POWER MOVE

AN ACCIDENTAL PREGNANCY WORKPLACE ROMANCE

LAKESHORE EMPIRE
BOOK 3

MAUDE WINTERS

We can have opinions about ketchup on a hotdog, but not on someone's identity.

I still put ketchup on a hotdog. I know I am wrong and do not care.

People like Eva and me deserve to be seen in stories. I hope this book makes others feel seen.

"Harder," I moaned.

Davey picked up speed, slapping my ass harder. Without prompting, Davey leaned forward a bit, stimulating my clit.

"I don't want to cum until you do," Davey said. "I want to cum *with* you, Eva. Can you be a good girl and cum for me again."

"Yes," I gasped, unable to fight how good this felt.

As he pounded me and rubbed my clit, I fell over the edge once more.

Pulsing around his cock, I fell forward temporarily, overcome with pleasure, my face in the pillows. He gripped my hips, then moaned, having reached his own climax. I felt him cum inside me and hold on to steady himself. We panted heavily as he pulled away. As I flipped on my back, he discovered an issue.

"Oh, fuck," he said—not in a sexy way.

"What?" I tried not to panic.

Davey held up the condom—in pieces.

"Oh, shit," I said.

"I'm so, so sorry," Davey said. "I have never... this hasn't happened to me. Uh... are you on the pill?"

"No," I answered.

I'd been trying to conceive for months using artificial insemination and sleeping with a woman, so the pill didn't cross my mind.

While I anticipated his anger, I got none. He calmly said, "Oh, well, I can get you the morning after pill. I feel awful."

"You don't have to do that," I knew the likelihood of that was less than him even texting me after tomorrow morning.

"No, I'm serious. It's not your fault the condom broke," Davey said.

"It will be fine," I said for both of our benefit. "You're right. Plan B will be just fine. Promise."

I hoped the girls wouldn't judge me for stopping by the drugstore on the way back. At least I'd made it to twenty-nine without needing emergency contraception, right?

4. FINAL THOUGHTS

Davey

I DUCKED OUT TO GRAB THE MORNING AFTER PILL—FOR THE FIRST time since college. The too-small condom fucked everything up. What had been mind-blowing sex had given into an awkward dance. While I gathered Eva didn't hold it against me, I gathered she remained nervous about what happened. Who wouldn't be? It's not like she knew me, and a broken condom could have disastrous consequences.

Out of a desire to earn trust, I ducked into the *same* drugstore early that morning and grabbed a packet of Plan B from the pharmacist. When I returned, I admired Eva's naked ass as she slept. She stirred only as I entered the shower. When I emerged, I found her sifting through the pharmacy bag. As she lifted the box from the bedside table, she stared with her brow furrowed in confusion.

"I hope that's okay?" I asked.

"It's… wow, you really are full-service," Eva laughed.

"I told you I'd do it," I said. "I feel fucking awful about it. I mean, sex was…"

"Can you put on a towel?" Eva asked.

"What? Oh, shit. Uh…" I pulled the towel all the way around me.

"No, it's just… damn you have impressive… well… all of you is even better in the morning light and it's really fucking distracting."

"Sorry," I blushed.

She stammered, flirtatious grin gone, "No, you're like a God. You must spend forever at the gym. I'm a mess. I should go."

She rushed to her pile of clothes and pulled on her underwear and bra.

"You really don't have to rush. I have a late check out."

"No, it's okay. I am sure—"

"I really feel bad, Eva, I don't want this to end all fucked up."

"No, it's not that. You have—in many ways—reminded me not *all* men are dicks. So, well done. No, it's that… you look like *you*. I look like *me*. And now that we're in beautiful daylight, I realize you must have had second thoughts."

Her words surprised me. This wasn't about the broken condom. This was her concern about her *body*? Why?

"No, I didn't. You're beautiful."

"Uh-huh."

"Eva, you're gorgeous. What are you worried about? I couldn't help myself last night."

"Uh-huh." She repeated, pulling her dress over her head and zipping it with finality.

"I mean it. I don't chase women. I don't know if you know who I am, but—"

"Yes, I'm a pity fuck who should be lucky enough to have your million-dollar dick inside me, right?"

That annoyed me. "Eva, I am pouring my heart out. I was going to ask to see you again. I like your personality. Your body is just a nice bonus."

"Yeah, I'm sure I'm your type."

"You are, actually," I said, annoyed.

She grabbed the pill box, shoved it in her purse and took a deep breath. "Thank you for this. It really was sweet. I had fun. Don't call me. Don't even *try* to call me. This would never work."

Then, she left.

What the fuck just happened?

* * *

Eva

Flight was my usual conflict response. When Davey surprisingly got me Plan B, I wasn't prepared to respond. Everything with people in my life seemed transactional. Mona and I ended our relationship fighting about who got the fucking dog—spoiler alert, her. She claimed that she'd done all she could to support my "fertility journey" even though we entered it together.

Of course, Davey pulled the "I don't chase women" card. It was *so* typical. Rich, cis-het white man sleeps with girl nowhere near hot enough for him on paper. I knew my worth. I knew I was a good lay and my body didn't quit, but men like him didn't pursue girls like me for anything other than a good time. He'd never bring me home to his stuck-up parents.

I swallowed the pill in the bathroom after returning to my room. Everyone was asleep. Before he could text, I blocked Davey's number. There was no need to hear anger about my ungratefulness.

I suffered through brunch, mainly sticking by Jace and ignoring the other bridesmaids. I didn't get a chance to speak to Ellie until we were on the train headed home.

"What happened with the guy?" Ellie asked. "You said nothing. Was it that bad? He seemed nice."

"He was nice," I said. "But you know that would never work."

"Uh, why?"

"Well, because I'm me and he's him. It was a nice fever dream while it lasted. That's all it was."

"What? He was *into* you. Did he do something weird?"

"No," I said. "He was sweet, but he tried to tell me he was attracted to me one too many times. The man had *cumgutters*. This morning, he was even *more* gorgeous than the night before. He doesn't end up with me."

"Sweetie, you're not ugly."

"I know. I said. I'm pretty, but I'm not his type. He protested too much. I don't own a watch that costs more than a decent house. I don't end up with him. I live with my fucking middle-class parents in podunk Indiana. Meanwhile, he's probably got some Christian Grey style penthouse."

"You wrote him off because he told you that you were pretty *too* much? You said he made you squirt the first time he fingered you. Do you know how many times Mike has fingered me to squirting? Never. Zero. You should have locked that shit down."

"You are locking it down with Mike right now!"

"I know. I love him. He does lots of other things better than my ex, but I miss that sometimes. There is no perfect man. Don't be the bitch who complains about a rich man wanting to spoil her!"

"I am, I guess. Look, he proved that straight men aren't hopeless. The sex was good. He wasn't selfish. Maybe I could consider dating a dude, but not *that* dude. Eat the rich."

"Eat the rich? Girl, Mona was fucking *loaded*, and you stayed with her for five years."

"Mona built her own wealth—"

"Her parents sent her to one of the best private schools in England. She was privileged and you loved her."

Still do.

"Fine, she was rich. But not like he is rich. If you saw the suite he got us… damn! I am not even sure it was real. It feels more like a dream."

"You should text him!"

"I've already blocked him."

"Eva!"

"Don't go there. It's over. We're done. I start my dream job in two weeks and need to focus. It was nice while it lasted. Who knows if he was even *really* single?"

"Eva, I saw no indication he was married. And having a job doesn't preclude you—"

"I am starting off in a totally new position well beyond anything I've ever done. And after everything with Mona I'm in my Me, Me, Me Era. Now, did you have a good party?"

"It was *the best*. Thank you for putting up with all of it. Jace and you were rockstars, as was the mystery man. It was lovely. Callie is… a wreck… but you took care of her, so I appreciate it."

"I am not on duty at the wedding," I warned. "I plan to get blitzed and not be the babysitter."

"Her boyfriend will be there to deal with her. Promise."

We soon arrived at our nearest stop—Hammond. Ellie departed with her fiancé, Mike, and her daughter, Jane. Ellie and her ex, Clay, co-parented admirably. Their marriage ended over a *legendary* cheating scandal. I hated Clay for stepping out when his kid was an infant, but Mike and Clay got along for Jane's sake. Jane ran to hug me and talked my ear off. Jane and Ellie were the best part of my transatlantic return. I missed being in their lives so often. I chatted for a bit with her and climbed into my old truck.

My parents lived between Hammond and Dyer in a little town called Krakow. Founded by Poles, the place's one street lacked so much as a four-way stop. My parents owned a hobby farm just outside town. Before I reached it, I passed dozens of McMansions. In the last ten years since I left for college in the UK, Chicagoans moved here for cheaper taxes and "better" schools—better being coded language for "whiter". The land where they'd planted these terrible architectural monstrosities previously belonged to my grandfather.

I pulled in the drive, feeling a little queasy from the meds and reticent to say more.

My mom and sister sat in the kitchen drinking iced tea as I carted my overnight bag in and threw my clothes down the laundry chute. The benefits of a hundred-year-old farmhouse were immense.

"How was it?" Mom asked.

"It was good," I said. "So much screaming and ridiculous behavior, but Jace and I survived."

Brooke, my suddenly religious sister, rolled her eyes and patted her growing baby bump. Brooke, like Ellie, was divorced. She remarried a few years ago. Her husband—a manchild named Ian—was the builder of many of the new McMansions in the area. His family—like ours—was Catholic, but much more "devout". That was a nice way of saying they were judgmental fundamentalist Catholics who thought the pope was illegitimate because he was down with AIDS prevention. I hated people like them. My sister hadn't always been this way, but now she even abhorred Jace, who spent years here as a surrogate younger sibling. Mom and Dad didn't agree but stayed out of it. Nonbinary Jace was always welcome, but my parents avoided hosting both at the same time.

"Well, as long as you got home safe and Ellie had fun." Mom smiled. "That's all that matters."

"Agreed," I said. "I'm gonna go out and ride Poco. Is Dad in the barn?"

Mom nodded. "He might join you. He's bored."

"I wouldn't mind," I said.

A ride around the woods might do everyone good. I had a few weeks before I started my new job at a downtown Chicago firm. I had such a chaotic breakup and move that I promised myself a slow ease into this. Life was better from the back of a horse, so I had to get out more.

PART II

THE NEW-ISH GIRL

5. FIRST DAY JITTERS

Eva

I ARRIVED AT MILLENNIUM STATION EARLY ENOUGH TO GRAB COFFEE and food. Taking the L north, I observed my fellow commuters. It was different than taking the Tube, but hey! There was *air conditioning!* I took a deep breath before stepping into the staff entrance of Delphine Holdings LLC. When I'd done a quick walkthrough with some introductions last week, my future bosses showed me the ropes. A security guard handed me an official badge, granting access to the leftmost elevators.

Delphine's was a Chicago retail giant—among the first to hit the market in the late 1800s. When others like Marshall Field's fell, it lived on. As such, the store's massive footprint remained. The building behind it was now the official HQ of Delphine Holdings, purchased sometime in the 1960s for a song. I didn't know this place existed until Daphne Delphine herself gave me a tour.

An assistant greeted me. "Miss Pavlak, I can take you to your office if you'd like."

"Thanks," I said. "I'm excited."

"We're happy to have you. Miss Ngyuen has taken a call but will be with you in a bit. She's very excited to meet you."

Claire Nguyen was the company's first female Chief Information Security Officer and my boss. Well, one of them. My reporting line was a little confusing. I answered to Claire and Daphne. Either way, they worked closely, and I was excited to begin. As Business Information Security Officer—known mainly as the BISO—my job was to bridge a gap between Claire's role as CISO and Daphne for the rest of the organization. I was there to translate technology speak from one side and business buzzwords from the other.

I settled into my office with a nice view of the street. It wasn't the grand Michigan Ave view that I was sure Daphne and her ilk had from their offices. I wasn't *that* big, but it was still the nicest office I ever had. It was airy, light, and a pretty watercolor decorated the big wall. I even had a nice hutch for books and photos. I admired as Daphne arrived, groaning.

"Sorry, one moment," she grimaced, pressing against the door-jamb, her face relaxing. "Sorry. That's embarrassing. I had a human treating my cervix like a drum. How are you?"

Daphne was *heavily* pregnant—due in September. She served as retail division president. She was the late CEO's daughter and my former mentor. I matched with her in my time as a soon-to-be Oxford grad. I studied law and computer science there. Because she worked in corporate law, she took me under her wing more than anyone needed. We always kept in touch. After deciding to create a position she felt I was perfect for, the offer came.

The timing was bad. I was amid fertility treatments and couldn't accept the job. When that person didn't work out, I was first on her list to call. And given I needed a job in the U.S., it was perfect. Even though I felt like a pretender, I took the biggest opportunity of my life and moved away.

"I'm good, thanks," I answered. "The office is great. The staff have been so kind. I'm excited to hit the ground running."

"Great. I have a round robin planned with the execs. I saw your lunch was blocked off. Is that a daily thing to expect? Not that I ask because I care... just so I know."

"Just today," I answered. "I had a doctor's appointment I had to reschedule."

"Oh, are you okay?" Daphne asked, downright maternal.

"I'm good. Just establishing care with a new practice now that I'm back and have health insurance," I answered.

"Nice thing, that," Daphne checked the clock behind me. "Shit, I have a meeting with Devon in HR in ten to discuss benefits. You're first up with my brother."

"Oh, really?" I asked. "The CEO?"

"Yeah," Daphne snickered. "He's a puppy dog. Just me—but taller and more handsome. Promise. Of the two of us you'd want to anger, it's him. Tears work. I am going to stop talking like your friend now."

I smiled. "It's okay. I am glad to be here."

"We are so pleased you accepted our offer. If there is anything I can do, just reach out. I want this to be a good post for you. You deserve that. I'll have them send you in when David is ready for you."

She stepped away as I sat in my comfy leather executive chair. I was doing okay. This would be a good summer.

✳ ✳ ✳

Davey

"Your nine AM is our new BISO, David," Daphne's voice rang.

"What?" I groaned.

"David, what the hell? Are you okay?"

I probably looked terrible after a night out before with a fraternity brother who was only in town for a hot minute. However, partying didn't look good on me anymore. I grimaced in anticipation of Daphne's disappointment.

"Can you re-explain what a BISO is?" I winced.

"Are you hungover?"

"You sound like Mum when you do that," I groaned.

"What? Do what?"

"The overbearing pretend-concerned thing with your voice going up at the end."

Daphne, hand on hips said, "Maybe she's right about things like this, then. One second."

She disappeared, heading across the small office lobby to her office, then back to mine. She held out a sachet.

"Electrolytes," Daphne said.

I picked them up, opening the water bottle I kept on my desk and dunked them.

"Daph, why do you have these? Last I checked you were not running marathons."

"When I vom, I need them to settle my stomach. I have a whole pack in my desk," Daphne said. "Pregnancy sucks."

"Well, I do try to avoid it," I half-heartedly joked, taking a swig.

"Drink that and be ready to meet her. She's here already."

"Again, what does the BISO actually do?"

"You'll rely on her for insight into tech. She's a translator of sorts and will join the Tuesday 10," Daphne informed. "Claire and I need her to keep the pace between technology and the rest of this circus. Unlike the last one, we think she will be able to handle human conversation."

"So can she un-fuck my second laptop that has been stuck updating for ten years?"

Daphne slapped my desk for effect. "Don't be an asshole. That's a question for end user support. Don't insult the woman with a law degree from Oxford."

"How do you people always find one another?" I groaned. "God, she must be absolutely nightmarish."

"She's a gem," Daphne said. "And she was my mentee when I was assigned a recent grad. She's smart, David. You'll like her. Promise. I told you all of this—"

"Sometimes, I tune you out."

"I couldn't tell," Daphne groaned. "Okay, I'm off to chat with

HR about benefits. Be back later. Be nice, Davey. Don't be a fuck-up."

I wanted to be nice, but only if my head allowed it. I knew this woman meant a lot to Daphne by the way she talked about her candidacy. She even wanted me to sit in on interviews, but I'd been dealing with our Canadian operations in Toronto. And while I knew tech support *was* likely an insult, I began looking for my other computer in a locked cabinet to see if I could pick her brain. I was not a tech guy. I'd sooner call any of my four sisters before I attempted to fix something myself. They were just *better* at it.

There was a knock, and I called, "Come in!"

I was too focused to turn, expecting my assistant.

"Uh… Mr. Delphine… your assistant stepped away and Daphne said I was supposed to meet you," a little voice said behind me.

"Are you the new computer person?" I asked, still digging in the cabinet.

Her voice sounded vaguely familiar, but I couldn't place it.

"Not quite, but also probably in your eyes, yes. It's more of a compliance role—"

"Please do not tell me this shit has anything to do with internal audit. I do not care about control mapping—whatever the hell that is."

I grabbed the edge of the computer, pulling it free from the cords on top of it. I needed the charger.

"I mean, my job largely deals with GRC frameworks. In fact, a first order of business for Claire and I is to choose—"

"Can you help me fix my laptop?" I asked. "It keeps getting stuck as it boots up."

"Mr. Delphine, that is probably a better question for the support desk. I've never done end user support and can assure you, I don't have the patience to troubleshoot something like an OS or driver."

"I have no idea what any of that means." I finally grasped the charger.

"The OS is your operating system. I'm assuming you mean an OS update—"

I spun around, laptop and charger in hand and stared at a beautiful face I knew. Her slight smile faded as she realized we were here—face to face—very much clothed. I'd cursed this woman three weeks ago and now she was here in the flesh as my sister's friend and direct report. I tried to keep a hold on the computer and charger as I approached my desk once more but tripped over the charger and lost my grip.

The useless machine's body separated from the battery in a spectacular crash. Eva jumped in to assist, kindly picking the battery up and helping slide it back into the case. I said nothing and tried to be useful, all while resisting the scent of her perfume or glimpsing down her blouse. The skirt she wore only emphasized every bit of her. She was *gorgeous*. Why was Eva only back in my life as an employee? Why couldn't she have just texted me?

6. MAKING ENEMIES

Eva

Listening to a CEO dress me down about tech support *seemed* typical. However, watching the millionaire—scratch that, billionaire—CEO of a massive holdings company losing his mind over me was not in the books. Finding out the man who fingered me to completion in a club bathroom was now my big boss, wasn't on my bingo card. Now I knew why I found him so familiar. He was Daphne's older brother!

Instead, Davey—David Delphine—dropped the laptop. The poorly built brick's case shattered. The bottom panel flew across the room and exposed the battery with a loud crack, releasing it. I helped Davey pick the thing up and he sat, unsettled and annoyed with me.

"Sit, please, Miss..." He looked at his briefing, realizing neither of us shared our surnames. "Miss Pav-lack?"

"Pavlak," I corrected. "It's Polish. You say it like 'pauv-lock'."

Davey nodded. "Okay. I will remember that Miss—"

"Actually," I corrected Davey, "it's Ms."

He rubbed his temples, annoyed. "Ah. Alright, *Ms.* Pav-lak. And what brings you to our fine place of business?"

Confused, I furrowed my brow. "I'm your new BISO. Daphne said—"

"Oh, shit, yes."

This man was an *epic* disaster! Why wasn't Daphne in charge? He barely held it together!

"Sorry, sorry. I'm… well, you've put me in a weird predicament."

"Me?" I gasped. "*You* came on to *me*!"

He set his jaw, looking handsome as hell. The man was gorgeous, and I hated him for it. I feasted on the visual as much as I marveled at how big of an ass he was. Daphne and Claire said *he* needed me. Yet, he acted like a hot mess dickhead.

Davey closed the door to muffle our conversation.

"I believe the feeling was mutual and all left fully satisfied."

"Speak for yourself, Davey," I growled. "You dressed me down and—"

"I told you that you were pretty! So fucking sue me, Eva!"

"You laid it on thick. And I was right. Someone like you doesn't end up dating a girl like me."

"Correct," he said. "You're not a girl. So, I'd not date a girl, right? But you aren't one."

"Don't lay into me with semantics!"

"Yes, I forgot you were an Oxford-educated attorney. If so, why did you tell me that you were doing admin work when I was complimenting your karaoke stylings? You lied, Eva!"

There was a knock. I saw a woman at the door.

"David, Leighton Donaldson is here in the lobby for your ten. Should I get her a coffee?"

"Yes, but I think this will be a short meeting," David snarled at me.

"Alright…" the woman said awkwardly. "I apologize for being out when Ms. Pavlak arrived. Ma'am can I get you a drink?"

Before I opened my mouth, Davey flatly said, "No. She will not be staying long. Please close the door as you leave. Thanks."

She followed his orders, leaving fast.

"I was honest with you," I continued our conversation.

"Then why did you oh-so-clearly lie?"

I groaned. "Because men—men like you—are intimidated by educated women in technical fields. If I told you, your eyes would have glazed over all because your little peabrain couldn't handle a woman with a better education or math skills."

Davey's nostrils flared in anger. I braced, afraid he'd yell as I talked back in the most insubordinate way. I'd forgotten myself in a fit of rage directed at a man who could fire me in an instant. What happened to the giving man I met at that bar?

"I am glad you think I am so narrow-minded that—"

"I didn't say that," I sighed, done with this conversation.

There was no winning with men like this.

"Look, obviously we must co-exist," Davey said. "And no one needs to know—"

"Yes, that's for the best," I said. "Specifically, for you. Because you wouldn't want anyone to know you bothered so much as *look* at me, right?"

It felt like a dirty little secret.

"I texted you several times to let you know I felt bad about how it ended," Davey said. "You never responded. So, don't give me this pity-party about how I was some sort of liar who didn't care."

I didn't know how to respond.

"You could have at least given me a 'no thanks', Eva."

"Yeah, well, I did. In the…" I lowered my voice, "the hotel room. But you didn't want to hear me."

* * *

Davey

Eva's harsh words led our conversation, but her face signaled they were a brave front. While I wanted to lash out for hurting me and being completely insubordinate, I knew that was a legal liability. She was a younger woman I'd not only slept with but put at risk with a broken condom. This woman—one I would now oversee—was, unfortunately, the one I'd thirsted over. This was the woman whose body I'd put to memory, even if I wished to forget her. And while I could be angry, I still wanted her. Why did she singularly make me act like a buffoon?

"Uh-huh," I sat back in my chair and looked at my broken laptop. "So, I'm guessing you can't help fix my broken PC?"

"You really are an asshole!" Eva scoffed, standing. "Let's see as little of each other as possible, okay?"

"Sounds great!" I called.

As she left my office, the sway of her hips tortured me. Why in the hell did she think I wasn't interested? What hadn't I done to show I cared? I was one of the good guys, right? She acted as though I treated her like shit from the beginning. Bewildered, I called in my ten o'clock.

As I discussed legal matters, I couldn't give a flying fuck. I cursed my sister for sending Eva to us. Maybe the woman was competent—she seemed whip-smart—but she was a thorn in my side. She was also a legal liability. So, with the head of general counsel in my office, I changed the subject.

"I have a hypothetical for you, Leighton," I said. "Just purely fiction."

"Uh-huh." Her face suggested she heard this not-hypothetical totally hypothetical at least once today already.

"So, if an officer in the company was to date an employee, what would you say was the *legal* concern."

"Is he her direct supervisor?" Leighton asked.

"Well, let's assume it is a woman who has dated a man. And she's two lines above him in the org chart."

"When did this relationship start?"

"Say it was before the company employed him."

"Did she sign off on his hiring information?"

I thought about the document I'd signed with Daphne's approval. I also had to approve that level of appointment.

"Technically, yes… for budget purposes… but she wasn't even in the interview."

"So, they signed off but didn't *know* the person?"

"What if it was like a hookup—something casual?"

Leighton rubbed her temples.

"What, it's bad?"

"David, you aren't giving me much good news here, are you?"

"I mean… he… or she… they didn't do anything wrong?"

"That's first an HR question, but I suspect they would tell *her* that she should probably end the relationship or at least make it clear she is recusing herself of any personnel or disciplinary matters with this hire—and do so to the direct supervisor *immediately*. But from a legal perspective, if there is no disparate treatment or retaliation with separation of employment or promotion, this officer should be fine."

"Good to know… in this hypothetical situation," I said, a bit relieved.

"But I strongly would urge this person—if they report to you—to notify the direct supervisor of this hire. It might be helpful to involve HR in that conversation just to CYA, too."

"Sure."

Oh, great, a meeting to confess my sins to my sister with HR in the room! That would *not* be happening, but I probably did need to come clean. Of course, my sister was a pregnant, hormonal disaster. Yes, it would be just one more Davey fuck-up for my sister to judge me about. She was the golden child, after all.

7. AN UNWELCOME SURPRISE

Eva

"WE DIDN'T FIND ANYTHING ON YOUR TESTS TO WORRY ABOUT."

I sighed relief, sitting at the gyno office in my paper gown. Ever since the chance encounter with my asshole boss, I'd been nervous he'd given me something. I told myself it was better safe than sorry.

"So, what made you run in for tests?" She asked. "Was it a concern or something else?"

"I had an incident," I explained. "It's not like me to hook-up with anyone, mind you. I just left a five-year relationship with a woman. But like… I slept with this guy. We tried to be responsible. And the condom broke. I took Plan B, though."

"This is a judgement-free zone," the doctor explained, compassionate. "No worries. Do you want to discuss contraceptive options?"

"That's not a bad idea."

"Great, let's get you a pregnancy test, confirm it's negative, and we can decide what works best."

She pulled a pee cup from the drawer, and I went to the bathroom. I knew this drill. My heart pounded—not out of fear of pregnancy—but from the many complicated and failed attempts at it. I felt sick thinking about how this road ended and how it cost me everything as I placed the cup on the tray by the lab window.

I returned, pulled on my clothes, and waited to talk about what options worked best, ashamed to admit I'd never before had such a discussion. In high school and early university, I used condoms. My parents weren't okay with the pill for a teen. And by my early-twenties, I only slept with women. I didn't *need* the pill. My periods were mostly regular, only altered by stress occasionally. I had a thirty-day cycle and knew what to expect most months.

When the doctor returned, she had a packet in her hand.

"So, the test was positive," she said.

"For which disease?" I asked. "You said—"

"Not a disease. Your test results for the STIs were negative. You're pregnant."

"Pregnant?" I gasped. "But I'm not sick. And… I took Plan B."

She sat on the stool before me once more, empathetic.

"I… I had a miscarriage earlier this year," I explained. "I had symptoms right away. And my cycle is…"

My voice trailed as I pulled out my phone. I scrolled through my calendar app and did the math. "Well, fuck. But I took Plan B."

She grimaced. "With your BMI—even at 170 pounds—this drug is less effective. I'm not going to tell you to lose weight now, since you're already pregnant, but you will want to watch your weight."

I beat down an urge to roll my eyes. I was a runner. I was active. I moved my body because it made me happy. I didn't apologize for my BMI in the "overweight" category. I'd spent my teen years torturing myself next to skinny-minnie Ellie. I didn't argue but also did not accept her judgement.

"I am sorry, Eva," she said. "But at this point, I'm going to give you information on our OB clinic. I don't handle OB patients, unfortunately. Head over and schedule an ultrasound… or ask about… abortion resources."

I nodded. "Thanks."

Why was I *thanking* her for the worst news I'd ever gotten on a lunch break?

I didn't know what to do. In my experience, this could all still end poorly. I'd never made it past twelve weeks, and I was only about five weeks along now. I stepped up to the OB window and handed in the paperwork.

"Hello," the medical assistant said.

"Hi. I need to schedule… something. But I've had a chemical pregnancy and a miscarriage already. I want you to know that in case you do something differently."

"Two losses? I'm sorry." She looked at my paperwork. "Five weeks? Do you have time for a blood draw?"

I checked my watch, knowing my next appointment wasn't for half an hour. "I could do it quickly."

"Sure. Let's do two 48-hours apart to make sure you're progressing as is protocol. I'll have the midwife send your orders. Do you want to schedule your eight-week scan?"

"Yes, please," I pulled out my phone.

We scheduled it. I went to the lab to sit through another poke. I wandered back to my office, in shock and awaiting results, and made it through the rest of my day somehow. I didn't plan to be pregnant. I did *not* want to have a baby with my asshole boss, but what if this was my last chance at motherhood? The perfect man may never come. In my early twenties, I'd have ended it without a second thought. Now, my gut told me I wasn't prepared to say goodbye yet—or ever.

* * *

Davey

"So, what did you think?" Daphne asked, eyebrows raised.

"About what?" I sighed, my headache worsened.

I wanted this day to end. On top of my normal anxiety, I now had to avoid Eva Pavlak. I saw her making tea this afternoon and doubled back around the office to avoid her. This wasn't sustainable. I didn't care what Daphne wanted. It could wait until I fled the scene.

"Our new BISO?"

"Oh, Eva… what's her name?"

"Pavlak. It's Polish."

"Yes, of course," I said, flatly. "Who isn't?"

"What is your problem today?" Daphne asked, annoyed. "You're in *such* a mood."

"I'm just tired."

"Well, try staying sober for a week—"

"Look, I don't need your fucking judgement. I don't drink all the time, Daph."

She crossed her arms. "It's neither here nor there. What do you think of Eva?"

"She's fine," I said. "Wouldn't help with my computer, though!"

"Are you fucking serious, Davey? You *asked* her?"

"Well, I tried."

"I'm embarrassed for both of us, honestly. What the fuck, brother?"

I needed to tell her. She deserved to know.

"I need to talk to you about—" I stopped as her husband, our dear mayor, Cal Markham, appeared.

Daphne turned to Cal and gave him a quick kiss.

"You ready to go?" Cal asked.

"Davey was just saying he had one last thing to wrap up."

I wasn't going to do this with Cal present. *Hell no!*

"Yeah, it can wait. Go home. Enjoy your evening," I said.

I'd tell her someday, but I wouldn't do it with her perfect husband around.

8. BETAS

Eva

My phone pinged while I returned from work. I noticed the push notification from the medical app. Heart beating in my throat, I opened it and clicked on the link. I knew what beta results should be. For someone who was five weeks along, my hCG levels looked good. If they doubled in two days, I'd know my pregnancy was viable for now. Concern grew as I didn't have symptoms—no back pain, no breast tenderness, no nausea. With previous pregnancies, I had all of these within two weeks of insemination. Since symptoms usually equaled success, I prepared myself to say nothing until my eight-week scan—nothing to anyone.

I got into the old truck to drive home, feeling silly in my nice suit with my very expensive laptop bag. Mona commissioned it from some fancy Saville Row guy when I'd gotten a director position two years ago. She was *so* proud of me. I cherished the bag and that memory. But right now, it provoked strange feelings—signaling the series of contradictions facing me.

I made it home to the smell of sloppy joes. Normally, I'd dig right into this American delicacy, but I could barely stomach being in the same room as this meal.

I made an excuse. "Uh, Daphne stuffed me full of food at lunch, you know? So, I will probably just eat leftovers, if that's okay?"

I sensed the disappointment in my mom's voice, but Mom nodded. "Whatever works, sweetie."

The first unnerving symptom sent me spinning. I changed clothes and drove around aimlessly, saying I was visiting Ellie until I pulled into the local hotdog stand. I knew hotdogs were a no-no when pregnant. So, I ordered the biggest bucket of crinkle fries I could get and a massive slushie. *This* sounded amazing. The craving convinced me I was pregnant.

Ellie stood behind me, holding Jane's hand, "Eva! Oh my god!"

"Hey," I said, embarrassed to be shoving fries in my mouth alone.

"Oh, can I have a fry?" Jane chirped.

"Yes, sure," I agreed, knowing Ellie wouldn't care.

She wasn't a granola mom. She didn't judge.

"I'm picking up food for us. Are you alone?" Ellie asked, concerned.

"I'm… having a thought," I said.

"Well, do you *want* to be alone, or can we join you? It's just us tonight. I was too lazy to cook."

"Oh, definitely, you can join me."

"Great. Let me order her a hotdog and I will get myself something. You want anything else?"

"No, I'm good."

"I'll order a kids fry, too. She will eat all of yours."

I didn't fight her. I was endlessly hungry after missing lunch.

Ellie returned with drinks, a Chicago dog, another bucket of crinkle fries, and a hot dog with ketchup on the side. The place refused to put ketchup *on* the dog. That was a party foul. Thankfully, Jane was okay with her mom squeezing it on while she continued devouring my fries.

Ellie handed Jane a tablet that she carried in her purse. Like any mother to a young child, she packed snacks and entertainment.

"So, how was your first day?"

"It was good," I said. "Eventful, but good."

"Oh, really? Meet any hot guys? Or girls... no judgement?"

"Nope." I could answer that very honestly.

All hotness points Davey originally garnered went out the window the minute he started in on me.

"What's up then? Do you not like it?"

"No. It's great. My office is lovely, the views are nice, and my bosses and direct reports are great. Also, you'd appreciate the snack and coffee sitch. And, despite all of that, there is *still* a massive, bougie cafe in the store next door."

"Girl, you better blow some of that grown up money on nice shoes or something on your lunch break."

"What? My shoes are fine!" I looked down at my Birks.

"Uh-huh. Sure. You deserve some nice things. Mona isn't here to encourage that, so I will step in. Speaking of which, I need wedding shoes. I've looked everywhere, but—"

"I get a discount. Let me buy them," I said.

"Really?"

"Yeah. I'll set us up with a personal shopper. Pick a dress for your bridal shower and the rehearsal, too."

"Oh, Eva, I couldn't."

"Yes, you can," I said. "You are my best friend for life. I'd much rather spoil you than buy more shoes."

Besides, if this pregnancy worked out, none of my clothes would fit in a couple of months, and heels would be a forever no-go. I was blessed to be early in my pregnancy where summer dresses were acceptable almost anywhere and breezy fabrics hid a growing stomach.

I wanted to forget about the pregnancy, but my mind raced.

Ellie continued her list of to-dos, but I burst out, "Can I tell you something really secret and really scary?"

"Please do not be back with Mona and leave me," Ellie groaned.

"No, definitely not!" I laughed. "No. It's not *bad* per-se, but, it's not good."

"What then?"

"I have… a situation… one that will abate in like thirty-five weeks."

"Are you on a contract at this job?"

"No."

I watched Ellie think through it.

"Oh my God. Shit! Did you get… what? How? Was it Mystery Davey?"

Not-so-mystery-Davey.

"Yeah, it was him because it couldn't be anyone else. The thing broke. I took Plan B, but my doctor gave me a lecture about being over 150-lbs and it not working as well or something."

"Oh, shit. Eva, I am so sorry… I mean if I should be sorry? I know this is complicated for you, babes."

"It is, but I want to go through with it. There was no doubt. I know I shouldn't. I will probably have to leave my job, but I can save up and take some time off and—"

"Eva, you need to tell Mystery Davey the truth."

"Are we calling him that now?"

"What else can we call him?"

I grimaced. "Literally anything *but* Mystery Davey, yeah?"

"Well, whatever we call him, he will want to be there. He'd want to know."

"I really don't think he will. I think it's best if I do this on my own. I can support a kid and raise it by myself."

"It's hard to be a single mom, Eva. Custody is hard. Figuring it out now—planning how to coparent is important."

"I never wanted to see him again—"

"Think of it from his perspective, Eva. He will have a *child* out in the world. You cannot just ignore him for eighteen years. Your kid will ask questions. He doesn't have to be in your life more than weekends—and only after the baby is old enough—but you gotta tell him."

"What if he wants nothing to do with it? I suspect he'll just tell me he'll pay to terminate it. And I don't want that," I said. "That's not where I'm at."

"Then, he can be an asshole who terminates his parental rights, and you won't put him on the birth certificate, but at least give him that chance. Jane's dad and I weren't perfect, but he is a good father. And I like having him there, okay? It took work and a lot of expensive lawyers, but you have months to figure this out. Make him pay for your medical bills and to deal with baby shit. Have you told your parents?"

"You are the only one who knows," I said. "And I need to keep it that way. I worry they will be angry with me."

"Thank God your dress is stretchy. You'll need it. You'll be what… 16 weeks? You'll definitely be showing."

"Shit, I'm sorry!"

"Don't apologize. If we need to alter it, we will. Don't worry about that. Take care of you and this baby. You're the maid of honor. We can buy you a completely different dress if we must. You're allow to stand out."

I smiled. "I am excited to stand up for you—even if I cannot get blitzed."

"It will still be epic. And when she's born, you can show her pictures of the day and say, 'Look, you were in mommy's tummy when Aunt Ellie got married.' You'll see."

I grinned, tearing. "I don't know what I'd do without you, Ellie."

* * *

I closed my door every morning to avoid sharing the sound of retching with my coworkers and sat close to the bathroom on the train. I ate dehydrated fruit because it was the only thing keeping me alive on my commute. But at nearly seven weeks pregnant, I felt awful. I'd taken to sleeping on the small couch in my office if I got a lunch break. Food sounded awful anyhow.

Then, one day, I just couldn't function. I texted Ellie on the train headed to work.

ME

The meds they gave me aren't working.

ELLIE

Call them and ask for something else.

ME

I doubt they will. They haven't seen me.

ELLIE

If they are worth anything, they will. You always
get sick.

ME

It's not this bad usually.

ELLIE

Remind yourself that it's a good sign.

It was increasingly difficult to do that. My back hurt. I
constantly fell asleep—something made worse by the useless
medication. It made me too drowsy to function so much that Mom
worried I'd picked up a drinking habit. I told her repeatedly I was
off the sauce, which confused her more. On top of *that* grief, my
back was constantly killing me, and I still did barn chores to look
productive. I kept riding on days I felt well enough. Poco hadn't let
out a buck in years and if it was good enough for Her Majesty the
Queen to ride while pregnant, it was good enough for me.

I messaged my doctor's portal and waited. By the time I made it
to the office, they replied and said they would send a script to the
pharmacy near my home. This, of course wouldn't work. So, I had
to call and tell them to transfer it.

I was exhausted and seasick. It was already getting close to
lunch when I felt rain—rain *in* my office.

"Holy shit! It's raining!" I said loudly.

But it wasn't. A pipe exploded above my head. The dribble
turned to a downright downpour by the time I grabbed my laptop
and phone to thankfully spare them. By now, I was dripping wet
and standing in the hallway, unsure what to say.

"Help!" I said. "I have… a downpour?"

Our Chief Influencer Officer, Chloe Markham, and her assistant entered from her office, staring confused. Daphne came around the corner. Everyone stared in horror as water poured.

"Call maintenance, Lucy," Daphne said. "Send them to Eva's office. Eva, I have to leave for my diabetes test in half an hour. I'll be gone for most of the afternoon, so take my office."

"The baby beetus," Chloe joked. "Good luck."

"I swear there are about five foods I can presently consume without losing it. If they take even more out of my cold, dead hands, I'll revolt."

Oh, joy! I worried she'd figure out why I was constantly using the bathroom, but I'd ducked her so far.

"Thanks. I will gladly take the offer."

"Why don't you run and get some food while they sort this out," Chloe said. "You look rattled."

The only thing that sounded good were the huge Swedish cinnamon buns in the cafe downstairs. I elected to get two and save one for later in the day along with a half-caf cup of coffee. By the time I returned, I spotted my reflection in a mirror and realized my entire blouse and bra were soaked through. With my painful always-awake nipples there, it was dangerous. I had a change of clothes in my gym bag for the chance I got to use the membership to the club next door that gave us three free day-passes a week. That rarely happened, but it was a nice thought.

So, in a running skort and workout top, I'd finish my day. Given the top was too revealing, I pulled an old hoodie on and apologized to everyone for my disastrous appearance. My assistant sent my outfit to the dry cleaners. Fortunately, in a sports bra top, my tits were the comfiest they'd been at work since this whole thing began. I breathed a sigh of relief and settled in Daphne's office with my cinnamon buns and coffee.

I ate one, then looked at the other while typing emails. All was well until a sudden urge to vomit hit. Thankfully, Daphne had her own attached bathroom—the perks of being the prez—and I rushed to vomit in peace and into a clean bowl.

"Fuck," I groaned. "Could this day *get* any worse?"

Of course, anyone who ever asked received a firm yes. And that day, I got my yes.

9. SICKNESS

Davey

"Daph, do you—"

I stopped, looking around. My sister wasn't here. Most of the office was at lunch, but Daphne never took her lunch or ate at her desk. Her husband never got a break, so she preferred to work on through it and leave right at five to hit the gym and see him. She was nothing if not predictable.

At the small table in the corner was her laptop—still open—and two massive cartons I recognized from the basement cafe. I heard her retching in the bathroom and grew concerned. I knew she had an appointment this afternoon—an important one. Was she not okay?

"Daphne?" I asked.

The sink turned on, then stopped, and a person emerged—it was not Daphne.

"Oh, fuck!" Eva startled, then settled.

"What are you doing in there?" I asked, sounding much angrier than concerned. I projected the wrong emotions already.

I put two and two together. She was vomiting. She'd just consumed two massive pastries.

"Are you… did you just… you don't have to do that to yourself, Eva. You really deserve better than living in a world where—"

"I wasn't purging! Jesus Christ!" Eva said. "I *like* my body, thanks. I just… it didn't sit well."

She looked down, then muttered, "Bloody hell!" Disappearing again, she slammed the door behind her.

"Go away, okay?" She called through the door.

"What? Why?"

"I have sick on my jumper!"

"Eva, did you lose your mind?" I chuckled. "You sound like my mother."

My mother was a Scot raised in posh boarding schools in the South of England.

"I'm sorry. I'm overwhelmed. I don't want to come out. I've got puke on me and—"

She started sobbing irrationally.

"Can I help in any way?" I asked.

"I don't think so."

I waited her out. She emerged once more in a work-inappropriate ensemble. Her cute little tennis skirt and low-cut tank top would have been fine at the gym. It violated every bit of our dress code—and probably that of many stodgy pros at the tennis club.

"I am sorry," Eva cried. "I am out of clothes."

"What is going on?" I repeated. "And where is my sister?"

"She's getting tests run. I borrowed her office."

"And you're ill. So, what, you're spreading norovirus?"

I was a germaphobe. Any of my staff knew even a sniffle necessitated a mask or work from home. Childhood asthma left me phobic of germy confines. For all I knew, Eva was a *very* sexy Typhoid Mary.

"It's not catching." Eva grabbed a tissue and blew her nose.

I needed to get her something to wear over her top. The way her breasts spilled out of her tank top was about to send me over the edge. How were her tits better *now* than weeks ago? Or was I just wistful?

"We have polos from our golf tournament still," I said. "Some people forgot to pick them up, so they're fair game. Would that help?"

She nodded, still sniffling.

I rushed out to find an intern near the supply closet. He stared at me in terror.

"Hey, can you grab a size small polo out of the golf tourney box?"

"Where is it?"

I rolled my eyes. "Let me do it."

I knew I was a sight to see as I crawled through boxes to grab one labeled "golf shiz". Who the hell oversaw organizing this place? I tossed the box down, found a shirt, and raced back to Eva. She was bent over at the waist at her computer typing an email. I tried to look away from her cleavage for fear she'd turn me to stone.

"Here you are," I looked down. "A unisex small?"

Eva pulled back. "I will make it work."

She pulled the shirt over her head and settled into it. "I look very… festive. Thanks."

She looked great wearing our logo. *Damn.*

"I'm sorry for the confusion," I apologized. "Really."

"No… it's okay," she said. "I… I need to run out to get my medication. Can I leave my stuff in Daphne's office or—"

"You *sure* you're not contagious?"

Eva grabbed her wallet and glared, saying nothing. She marched past, out the door, and ignored me. Once again, I must have said the absolute wrong thing. I noticed her hoodie balled up in the trashcan. Despite my fear of puke, I picked it up, bagged it, and took it to the small laundry unit off the executive suite that we used for linens from board meetings and other VIP events. I figured Eva didn't want to get rid of her hoodie but was mortified. So, I tossed the hoodie into the washer before scrubbing my hands with soap for the next five minutes.

10. LONGEVITY

Eva

I TOOK MY FIRST ZOFRAN PILL AND STARED AROUND MY OFFICE, praying it kicked right in and cured all my woes. My phone buzzed. It was Ellie, so I answered.

"Did you get the meds?"

"Yes. Finally!" I said. "No clue if they work. Pray for me. It's all a terrible disaster."

"I am sorry you are sick."

"No, it's worse than that. I have an open hole in my ceiling." I looked up at the 150-year-old pipes overhead. "A pipe burst and doused me with water. Then, everything was see-through, so I changed into workout clothes. But that meant this skort and a tank top which *right now* looks better than ever. So, I put Mona's old Cambridge hoodie over it, but it smelled like her, and I wanted to die."

"Oh, sweetie, I'm so sorry. I promise it will all get better soon."

"Oh, no, it got worse!"

"How?"

"The CEO showed up, assumed I was binging and purging because... you know, I'm the fatass. And I'd puked all over my

57

hoodie. So, I tossed out my hoodie and fled to the pharmacy. Now, I regret tossing it but… what can I do? And he *hates* me."

"The CEO?"

"Yes. He's Daphne's brother but all he's done since I got here is complain about me. I think I'm about to be fired for 'bad fit.'"

"That's not legal."

"Well, technically, it's the U.S. So, everything is. But once he finds out I'm pregnant and *not* covered by FMLA, he will can my ass so fast."

"He wouldn't do that. You will figure it out," Ellie said. "Are we still on for dinner later or are you not up to it?"

My heart sank. "I haven't kept anything down all day, Ellie. I doubt I can do tacos."

"Now, I *know* you're sick," Ellie said sweetly. "Why don't I bring you a slushie and some fries and we can sit out on the back deck?"

"I'd get in the pool at this point," I said. "If you don't mind. You can bring Jane."

"She's at her dad's."

I watched Davey cross the open sitting area between the offices in a huff. There was my baby daddy wandering around in the wild acting like an absolute ass. The irony of all of this was he was about to fire the mother of his child all out of pride and rage. I would be the one with no health insurance or income in a middling job market. No one would hire me.

"Well, come by. Mom and Dad are going to something at the church for my nephew. It's going to be all quiet. I love you for it," I said.

"Don't worry about it. I've got you."

Turning my attention back to our current misguided risk acceptance program, I fell back into my work. I ignored my corporate cheerleader getup, focusing instead on this. That was until Daphne stood in my doorway.

"So, they swapped out the pipe," she looked at the offending hole. "But this looks like hell. They're going to have to patch the plaster. I'm sorry."

"Maybe I should just work from home for awhile?" I hoped like hell she'd say yes.

Daphne wobbled over and dropped onto the small couch on the side of the office. "Apologies. My feet are so fucking swollen."

She put them up on the coffee table and let out a long breath.

"How did the appointment go?"

"I have GD. They wouldn't even let me do another test. They just told me my numbers were too high, so now I have no clue what to eat. But Cal, being the absolute best husband on earth, has hired a chef to make me meals."

"That's really sweet," I said.

Davey appeared. "Daphne, can I have a minute when you... have a minute?"

He looked at me, annoyed, then back at his sister.

"I'm just sitting down," Daphne said. "Checking in on Eva. I'll be with you in a bit."

He nodded, then left.

"He's in a nervous mood today!" Daphne giggled. "He passed me on the way in and said he thinks people have norovirus."

Great.

"Oh, that sucks," I said.

"Yeah, he gets a bee in his bonnet, and I have to calm him down."

Excellent. So, I'm fucked? I sensed he was about to tell Daphne to cull me. Who could blame him?

"Are you okay?" Daphne asked. "You don't look okay."

"I think this isn't right for me," I said. "I think you all are going to fire me and it's better if I just resign and—"

Daphne hoisted herself off the couch and walked to gently shut the door. She turned back, sitting across from me.

"Has Claire said something about not being happy with your work? Have I?"

"No, but—"

"Well, do you not like the job? Is there something I can fix?"

I teared, wanting to be honest.

"I'm sick. And I think it's going to be an issue."

She furrowed her brow in concern. "An issue? How sick? We don't kick people when they're down around here, Eva. Not if you ask me, anyway."

"If I tell you something… will you keep a secret?" I asked.

"Of course. If it's health information, the only one I can talk to about it is HR."

Spoken like an attorney.

"Okay. So, I am pregnant and… it's making me sick. Your brother just caught me puking and he's like… livid."

"Oh, because he thinks you came in sick with norovirus and he's a supergermaphobe. Wait? You're pregnant?"

I nodded.

"Oh, Eva, that's so exciting! You're doing this on your own?"

"It looks like it," I answered.

"Well, I think that's great."

"It does not protect me with FMLA."

"The City of Chicago guarantees labor protections for pregnant employees so, even if I wanted to fire you—which I don't—I couldn't, Eva."

I shook my head. "You won't want me. No one here—"

"Eva, who is bothering you? Is it Davey? Is he being an ass? God!"

She rose slowly and paced. I held my tongue, confused about where this would lead.

"He has such a bug up his ass about that fucking computer! I told him not to ask you to fix it but he's still angry."

Daphne turned her attention to me. "Let me fix this, okay? Don't panic. Don't quit. And take tomorrow off if you feel sick. I found that spending a day getting hydrated vastly improved my chances of staying well. Did they give you good drugs?"

"I just took my first Zofran."

"Good. It will help. It gets better. If you need to take time for appointments or even just need to vent, let me know, okay?"

* * *

Davey

"Sit your ass down!" Daphne barged into my office as I watered plants on my windowsill.

"What?" I groaned. "Why are you so hormonal?"

"Sit down. Because I'm fucking angry."

I sat with a thud. Daphne stood, hands on her hips, ready to explode and reminding me very much of Mum.

"I'm a woman who has just been told she isn't able to consume the one type of food she craves—simple carbs—and my BISO is about to once again quit. And why? She thinks my brother is an asshole who hates her!"

Eva again?

"Daphne, I do not *hate* Eva. I find her *difficult*."

"She is not your direct report. She says you yelled at her for being sick."

"You shouldn't come to work sick. I got her a replacement shirt, but really, she has broken dress code six ways from Sunday."

"She lives in Indiana, Davey! She cannot exactly run home, grab some clothes and come back! She isn't contagious."

"I tried my best, okay?"

"Yeah, you say you did, but she's an inch from leaving me. You don't get it. She's the one who can whip this program into shape. Claire scares people off. People *love* Eva. She's got dry wit and is smart as hell. You, though, you are going to be the end of me, David Robert!"

I thought Daphne was being overdramatic about Eva wanting to quit, but now I realized she was serious. Had I really unnerved Eva that much? I thought she was contagious. I'd tried to help her! Why did she hate me so much?

"Calm down, Daph. I do not hate her. I'm sorry she feels that way. I can apologize—"

"You will do *no* such thing, David. I will smooth this over.

Every time you are alone with her, things go wrong, and you end up on her bad side."

"I'm your boss. You're *her* boss."

"But this is not the way I work. I am not hierarchical and if you want me to run the business the best way possible and bring you good earnings reports—"

"I know, I know. You make me look good. You make it easy," I agreed. "Daphne, no one is faulting you, but maybe she's not a good fit. If she wants to leave—"

"She's not leaving. And you will stay away."

I held my hands up, signaling I gave in. "Are we good?"

"Stay off my porch and I won't come back in here with Mum. Got it?"

"Got it loud and clear, Daph."

She waddled out, still angry. Daphne was intense when *not* gestating a human, but when pregnant she was ten times worse. I watched her cross back to Eva's office. They talked for a bit, before she returned to her own domain. Eva crossed into the conference room, holding it together somehow. I couldn't help but smile rather than scowl. She was *so* cute in that polo. It was a ridiculous outfit, but she pulled it off.

I told Daphne I'd stay out of it, but there was no way I could. We'd gotten off on the wrong foot, but I'd win Eva back somehow.

11.PEACE OFFERING

Eva

AFTER THE BROKEN PIPE, CAME THE AC MALFUNCTION FROM HELL. Following the pipe, I had a successful meeting with a new vendor willing to cut us an amazing deal because we were big fish who might help them land bigger fish. Returning, I found the temp in my office was at least eighty-five degrees. I kept my polo on long enough for the office to thin, finishing my emails and working on my calendar for tomorrow. But, after about 5:30, I stripped my top off, tossing it aside so my tits could breathe. Pregnancy boobs could fry an egg.

I was in no hurry to get home. Ellie texted that Jane had a fever, and she had to run to help her ex get meds before their pharmacy closed. She said she'd come by later and still get me my food, but it wouldn't be until at least eight.

As I began to pack up, Davey arrived with my hoodie.

He approached my desk. "I come in peace, Eva. Promise."

I wanted to make a Star Trek reference, but refrained. He'd never get it. I stared, very confused, as he placed a bottle of scotch on the table.

"I went a little better than the Macallan 12 and I washed this. We have a laundry area off the big suite where we host things. I figured you didn't want to lose it. Oh, and Daphne made it clear you just had a 'tummy bumble' and not to worry. So, I apologize for freaking out."

I took the hoodie, praying it still smelled like Mona's perfume, and he hadn't done something stupid like use a laundry sheet. It smelled clean but faintly like her.

"I uh… thank you." I ignored the scotch. He could leave it, and it would just stay a trophy in the office until I could drink again sometime next year.

"Great. So, let's just… have a drink and… let bygones be bygones?"

Was he serious right now?

"I don't have glasses," I said.

"I do," Davey said. "I'll grab them—"

"No, I uh… I cannot drink, Davey," I said. "Sorry, Mr. Delphine. I… I shouldn't."

"You cannot drink? You quit drinking in a month?"

"More like a month and a week, but sure?"

"I saw you drink a glass of wine last week at the reception in the lobby—"

"I pretended to drink it," I said.

He shook his head. "You think I'm an idiot, don't you?"

"No one said that." My voice grew weak.

I trembled, nervous to see what he'd do next.

"Why do you lie and avoid me? I try to make nice with you and you just cast me aside. I have tried to wash vomit off your damn sweatshirt, Eva."

"That is very kind, but—"

"What did I do to you?"

"Nothing."

"Then, let's just have a drink and chat, okay?"

"I cannot."

"Why? Why the hell are you doing this?"

"Because… I'm pregnant!" My words rang louder than I would have hoped.

He did a double take. "Since when?"

"Since about seven weeks ago, I had a period and then didn't," I hoped somehow he'd do the math.

Like a typical man, he couldn't read the room.

"Well, best of luck to you, then. I'm sorry, Eva, I shouldn't have forced the issue."

"That's all you're going to say?"

"I mean, what more *can* I say? I hope you're very happy with whoever he is."

"Excuse me?" I scoffed. "You think there's some other man, so you're going to get all weird about it?"

"I don't know how it happened. Could be—"

"Davey, it's yours."

"Mine?" He pointed at himself, then burst out laughing. "That's impossible."

"Given what happened, it's well within the realm of possibility."

"How?" He stumbled, shaking his head. "There's… no way."

"I'm telling you it fucking is."

Davey pulled my door closed.

"No one is here, Davey. No one—"

"This *cannot* get out!"

I rolled my eyes. "You think this is a threat to you?"

"Well, yes!"

"That's cute." I crossed my arms, even more annoyed.

"Can you… can you not?" Davey asked.

"Not what? Like get rid—"

"No, that." He gestured wildly. "I am never going to be able to have this *very* serious conversation with you if you push your breasts up like that!"

"These are my breasts, Davey, I'm not doing shit to make *you* feel better. Nor am I planning on getting rid of it, so just… back the fuck off!"

My voice reverberated.

Davey approached the desk, planted his left pointer finger down, and with a low voice, "I'm not fucking asking for you to do anything. I am asking you to please stop parading around here in next to nothing looking so good while I'm trying to wrap my head around how I impregnated you in a hotel room on the Mag Mile. Do you know what this could do to me? To the company?"

I leaned forward. "With *no* respect due, Mr. Delphine, you are the heir to billions, a man who no doubt lives like a prince, and with no worries. I am a woman still in the beginnings of a bright career who will be painted a whore for sleeping her way to the top. Trust me, I'm trying to quit but your sister cares too much about me to accept my resignation."

"Fuuuuuuck," he groaned, pacing. "What do we do?"

I shook my head. "If I had an idea, I would have already solved the equation."

* * *

Davey

I reeled.

Pregnant? She was *pregnant*. And she said it was mine. Did I trust her? Did I have any reason *not* to? Eva was right. The condom broke. She was of child-bearing age, so it made sense. But she took the pill, right? She didn't seem like some sort of trap queen who'd tie herself down to keep me around. She was smart—smarter than me.

I grabbed a pen from her desk, needing to occupy my fingers as I thought. The urge to smoke—something I hadn't done in a fucking decade—overwhelmed me. I'd made it through my father's funeral a year and a half ago without the urge, but I couldn't stop thinking about how badly I wanted to smoke. I rolled the pen between my fingers in my left hand.

"Are you left-handed?" Eva asked.

"If I tell you yes, will you think I'm brilliant?"

"No, but it's something I'm noticing. Nervous?"

I stood again. "How did it happen? You took the pill, right?"

"I did. They are not as effective as we'd hoped. And, for the record, there are two pills. One is better for people who aren't model skinny, and the other is for mere mortals like me. You got the skinny pill."

"What?" I furrowed my brow. "I never called you fat."

"No, my gyno did," Eva said. "Because I'm too fat."

I did a double take. "She's either daft or on drugs."

"Daft? God, you're a trip," Eva said.

"Do you ever *stop* taking the piss?"

"Do you ever stop craving it?" Eva facepalmed. "I am sorry. I do not know where the fuck that came from? It's like I am short-circuiting."

"Me, too." I collapsed into the chair. "Fuck. I need a smoke. Do you feel that way?"

"I have never smoked and definitely cannot right now."

"Shit, yeah. Pregnant."

"Look, this wasn't how I imagined this going, Davey. I thought you'd be an interesting hookup. I didn't believe you when you promised me a good time. And then... it lived up to expectations. But this—" She pointed between us. "This doesn't work, Davey. You don't end up with me. You don't want it and I'm not promising it."

"Did you plan on telling me?" I asked.

She shrugged. "I figured I'd wait until I knew more. You don't get it. I've only made it this far once. And then I found out at my second scan the baby was gone. I am *fully* expecting to find the same, Davey."

"That's grim, Eva, I'm sorry."

She'd been pregnant *twice* before? The thought blew my mind. I heard my sister's voice of reason telling me not to badger her, so I didn't ask.

"I figured I'd make it to thirteen weeks and think about telling you if the pregnancy was viable, okay? But... I want you to know I'm neither getting rid of it nor asking you for anything. The way I see it, I'm raising this child by myself."

I set my jaw, winding up. "Eva, I am not going to let you do that."

"So, I should get rid of it?"

"No! Jesus, I'm not asking you to do that. I'd never fucking force you to do anything like that! If you wanted to, I'd support you. It's your fucking body."

The surprise on her face suggested mistrust. She thought I was going to tell her she had to end the pregnancy. Instead of anger, I mustered compassion to start showing her I wasn't the villain she made me out to be.

"What I meant, Eva, was I will help you. There is no world in which I procreate and don't step up. I couldn't forgive myself, and I'd hope you wouldn't forgive me either."

She cocked her head adorably. "What?"

"I want to provide for you and the baby and support you, obviously."

"Davey, that doesn't make sense—"

"It doesn't make sense for me to not be responsible for the thing I put out in this world."

"I don't need your money."

"Does our child not *deserve* it, though? I am not saying I am here to control your life."

"Good, because we are *not* together. Not in any sense."

It pained me to admit I still wished to go back and fix whatever I fucked up the month before. I needed to earn her trust and prove I had her best interest in mind. There was base attraction for days. I'd still have her if she let me, but it wasn't just that. She cast me as the evil asshole who held her future in my hands. I never saw it that way. No matter how much she annoyed—even tortured—me I wouldn't give up.

"Maybe we aren't *together*, but we can still *work* together."

"Here? Fuck my life!"

"Look, it's not ideal and I'm not saying let's run out and say what is going on—mainly as you said, for your sake."

"You're not willing to take the heat, either."

"I will be," I promised, terrified but playing tough. "We need to be a team. You deserve that. So, whatever you need, tell me, Eva."

"I don't need your money. Like I said—"

"You will. And the child deserves to be raised in a world where it has the same opportunities that Cal and Daphne's kid will have. Should it feel less-than. Maybe you don't see it, but this child is still David and Danna Delphine's grandchild."

"I don't have the slightest clue what that means. Nor do I care, Davey."

"Okay, but won't you feel bad—"

"I was raised in buttfuck by a dad who worked at a steel mill and a homemaker."

"Yes, but you attended Oxford. You are obviously educated. You're also well-connected with my sister singing your praises. Don't bury your head in the sand."

Eva sighed. "If you want to financially support this child, then we need to go to court. If you want to even be on the birth certificate, we need to formalize everything. Because, Davey, I am still an attorney, and I refuse to let you fuck me over."

"I'm literally telling you I'll do what you need me to and have no desire to fuck you over. Why do you think I am out to get you?"

"You made it clear you didn't have to chase women—that your status made you a catch. When I decided to pull back, you got aggressive."

"I put my foot in my mouth because I liked you," I said.

"Operative part being *liked*. Past tense."

"I never said that," I said quietly. "Or at least I don't see it that way. You may think I'm the villain. That's fine today, but we're forever tied. Let me do the right thing here. You'll see you can trust me. And that includes doctor appointments—"

"My best friend is my support person. She's coming to my first scan."

"Why can you not—"

"You must earn this, Davey. My trust isn't given without blood, sweat, and tears. That goes for any person I've ever believed in.

Forgive me, Davey, but I don't know you. And to-date, all you've done is send me away crying."

It hit me hard. "You're right. I am sorry. I've not made a good impression. But I do want you to know I'm trying, Eva. That I will keep trying. And I want to be there for your appointments."

"As if you have time!"

"If Cal can take off for every appointment as the fucking mayor, I will make it work."

"Why is anger your only response?" Eva asked. "You're angry even now. Whatever. I will… let you come if you can control this rage."

"I'm not angry. I'm… determined."

"Work on that," Eva said. "Because even if your indignation is righteous, it makes me react in frustration."

"I'll work on it," I sighed. "You sound like my sister."

"She is a clever woman. She might be onto something."

12. BLUBS

Eva

I ARRIVED AT THE DOCTOR'S OFFICE WITH ELLIE TO FIND DAVEY absent—typical, I thought.

"Oh, okay. See, we thought your support person was already here," the receptionist said. "He asked if he could wait on the *other* side of the wall for *privacy*."

It dawned on me that Ellie had no idea who Davey *was*, but I needed to tell her. I tried not to be offended or ashamed by his desire to hide this since he *had* tried, but it irked me that men got awards for doing the bare minimum.

"Oh, well, he's not my partner," I said. "He's the father, but... he's not my support person."

"Oh," she looked confused. "Well, we can only have one person back for the ultrasound."

Ellie squeezed my hand. "I will stay here. I'm here for you, but he should be there."

"Ellie, you're who I want. He's just—"

"He is making an effort and it's his baby."

"You came all this way—"

"And I don't regret it. I'm still here if you need me to debrief. He's the dad. You gotta let him be there, Eva."

I sighed, knowing she was right.

"I will be right here," Ellie reiterated as the nurse brought me back.

I joined Davey in an exam room where he nervously stood to greet me.

"Sit," I groaned. "They are only letting one person back. Ellie graciously ceded her place to you. I'm sorry this is embarrassing—"

"It's not," Davey said. "I didn't ask to come back here because I was embarrassed, Eva. I came back here to protect *your* privacy since I stick out like a sore thumb when in a suit."

I calmed and sat by him. "Okay, fair."

"I'm not embarrassed, but I *am* protective. So, I will follow your lead. You asked we keep this under wraps and I am."

"You're doing it, Davey. You're getting defensive."

Davey breathed deeply. "That is not my intent. Look, I just want to be here to support you. I swear to God, that is all I am trying to do."

A woman in a cheery hot pink and orange pair of floral scrubs greeted us after knocking.

"Evangeline?" she asked.

"Eva is good, thanks," I said.

"Evangeline is a beautiful name," she remarked.

"It is," Davey agreed.

I glared.

"Follow me and we'll get started. The doctor will meet with you after."

I ended up on a sonogram table slowly inserting a hypersonic dildo into my vagina. I forgot how awkward this was no matter what—but doubly so when the father of the baby you weren't with was sitting *right there*.

I looked at the wall while she zoomed around. Not finding a heartbeat would hurt less if I couldn't see the carnage. Davey furrowed his brow, confused, but said nothing. He knew better.

"Oh, look, a nice little heartbeat. We're measuring about eight weeks and one day. Does that seem correct?"

I turned back to see the familiar flicker of a fetal heartbeat on the monitor.

"It seems right," I murmured.

"That is wild," Davey whispered.

I turned, seeing him transfixed. It was awe, not concern or confusion, that hit him. I smiled. Maybe he *was* trying? Maybe Davey *could* be trusted? It was that or he was a dynamite actor.

* * *

Davey

Blub-blub, blub-blub.

The sound of our baby's heart filled the room. Yes, *our* baby. No matter what the circumstances were, Eva and I did this together. The baby's heart chugged along. I sensed Eva's relief above all. She smiled, letting out the breath I sensed she'd been holding for weeks. I knew miscarriages were hard, so I hoped we'd get good news.

The tech printed photos and sent us to meet a smiley woman named Dr. Howard.

"So, is the Zofran doing a better job?" She asked.

Eva nodded. "I think so. Not perfect, but it's good."

"And, Dad, is she eating better?"

She meant for me to respond.

"We're not together," Eva quickly jumped in. "We're just… it's a little complicated. He's supportive, but we're not like… a couple."

"Oh, alright." Dr. Howard noted something on our chart. "Totally fine. So, do you *want* him to have access to medical records or be your emergency contact? Right now, I have an Ellie Jamison on file."

"Ellie is good for my contact," Eva said. "And no. I don't think that is necessary."

73

The doctor didn't skip a beat. "Will you be attending all of these appointments, Dad?"

She'd replaced my name with *Dad*. I wondered if doctors treated Cal—Mr. Mayor—this way. Did they call him by his first name? Or did they refer to him as Mayor Markham? Why did *Eva* get a name, but I was just "dad"?

"I will be doing my best to," I agreed. "Barring an emergency, I plan to be here for Eva."

"Good, good. We love a dad who shows up. Eva, if there is ever a matter you want to discuss 1-on-1 or a procedure we need to do where you are not comfortable with Dad in the room, let me know."

"Will do," Eva agreed.

"Now, we will book you in for the scan within a month. We can do the NT test for Down's as well as a genetic screen. At twenty-nine, you're at low risk for both, but many people opt for the peace of mind."

"I'll do the scan," Eva said. "But the test probably costs a fortune here in the US, right?"

"It usually runs a couple thousand since insurance only covers it if you're over 35."

"This country is a mess," Eva groaned. "Well, then let's just—"

"Let's have the test. I'm going to pick up the tab," I offered.

"Davey, it's not a fucking bar. You can't just leave a card on file," Eva snapped.

"I am not saying that, and you absolutely can."

"You can," Dr. Howard said. "We usually request you do that and then we process the cost of delivery over the next seven months, or you can pay the balance after the anatomy scan like most people do. Talk to billing on the way out."

"This country is… odd," Eva said. "I'm sorry. I don't mean to be short. I had two pregnancies and IUI in the UK. My partner and I did it private pay, but it was through her insurance."

The doctor's eyebrows raised. Eva's colorful history finally received a surprise reaction. I stifled a giggle. Our unfortunate hookup-cum-lovechild was fine, but Eva's attempts to have a baby with a woman raised eyebrows.

"The UK. Well, why did you come back?" Dr. Howard asked.

Eva shifted uncomfortably. "We broke up. And... I took a job here."

With my company. As my sister's employee.

"Hope that is going well."

"Oh, it sure is," Eva said, flatly.

"Well, that's all I have for you. Drop by billing and reception will schedule a follow-up."

We did the compulsory bits—payment and scheduling an appointment. I sent a message to hold time on my calendar for a doctor's appointment. Then came the awkward dance of seeing Ellie and trying to extricate myself. I knew Eva had probably thrown me under the bus to Ellie, so I expected a cold reception. Instead, Ellie was nice.

"Well, we're good to go. Baby is healthy," Eva gave Ellie a look at the ultrasound photos. "She's doing well."

Now, it was a girl. I wasn't sure why, but I went with it.

"Well, that's a relief! I'm happy." Ellie hugged Eva. "Did you get an ultrasound picture, Davey?"

"I doubt he cares," Eva blushed nervously.

Why was she being so weird? Was it the fear of being seen? I also wanted to move this along before anyone saw us, but Ellie was sweet.

"Nonsense."

Ellie pushed her way back to the receptionist. "Can I have those scissors for just a sec?"

Ellie cut the film into four squares, then marched back. Eva didn't bat an eye as she took the now-separate pictures back. Women bonded differently than men.

"Here," Eva sighed, "this should tide you over."

I appraised the tiny beating heart before tucking the photo in my suit jacket. "Thanks. That means a lot, Eva. Look, I gotta run. Do you need me to cover for you or anything?"

"I'm good. Please, God, don't say anything to Daphne."

I nodded. "Okay. Well, it's nice seeing you again, Ellie. And let me know when we can chat about the rest, Eva."

Eva granted me the tiniest nod in the world, and I departed. *Baby steps, Davey.*

13. BABY STEPS

Eva

"He's really trying, Eva," Ellie said.

"No. You're trying to play on his team," I said as we travelled back to the building.

"He cares. He was *touched* when you gave him that photo."

I rolled my eyes. "I'm the one miserable right now!"

"True, but he's trying."

"I don't like it. He's paying for everything, and I can just hear it now. I'll *owe* him for covering the cost of my prenatal care even though *he* got me knocked up."

"I'd milk it for all it was worth. Does that make me awful?" Ellie giggled. "Does ice cream count as prenatal care?"

"I don't need him to pay. I make good money, and I live at home. Look, I am here. This is my building. I should leave you."

"No! Let me come up! I want to see your office!"

I grimaced. I hadn't told her who *exactly* Davey was. Nor did I want to get a million fucking questions, but here we were. She was so excited.

"C'mon! Please!"

"Fine. But I have a meeting at 10:30," I said. "And I have to lead it."

"Promise I will be out in 5."

After grabbing a visitor's badge, we took the elevator to the executive floor.

"Oh, Eva! Great!" Claire said. "Jamie said you were going to explain the new retail tech strategy to compliance. Are you prepared for the PCI stuff? I need that for later."

"It will be in your mailbox in fifteen," I answered. "I worked on it yesterday. Claire, this is Ellie Jamison, my best friend. She's just dropping by. And Ellie, this is Claire Nguyen, our CISO."

Claire extended her hand. "Oh, fun! We don't get all that many visitors up here. No worries on the PCI thing. I will just need a bit to read over it before our 1."

"I have you covered," I said.

We continued walking until Davey appeared on his way to the espresso machine. He made eye contact, panicked, then kept walking, as if he read my mind.

"What is he..."

I pulled Ellie into my office and announced, "Isn't it great?"

Ellie's jaw didn't return to its usual spot, and *not* because my office was glorious.

I closed the door.

"Who is Davey? And what are you *not* telling me?" Ellie demanded in a low tone.

"Davey is David Delphine," I winced. "Daphne's big brother. Our CEO. The *big* boss. I found that out when I arrived for my first day at work and had to deal with his bad attitude."

"He seemed perfectly nice—"

"He swears he is working on it. I told him I won't put up with his bullshit, but you can *see* why it's a mess."

"Girl, they are *rich!* Like rich, rich, rich. Like gilded age royalty rich!"

"I am well-aware. And he's insistent I need his money to raise this thing in the same fashion as Daphne's baby."

"Well, it makes sense. Jesus, Eva! You're carrying a Princess—or a Prince, basically."

I rolled my eyes. "I am eight weeks and one day pregnant with a baby that may or may not end up fabulously wealthy but will be loved as much as I can possibly love anything. Let's leave it there."

"Babes, this is *messy*. What will happen when people find out you're pregnant? Are you going to tell them? I mean, it would have to be obvious."

I lacked answers and suspected I considered it more than Davey.

"Why are you so interested in this?"

"I work in an elementary school. There are two male teachers—both are gay—and neither one is dating the other. The women are constantly going through *sad* breakups. I am a single mom about to marry her long-term boyfriend. We are *vanilla*. We are wonderful, but it's not chaotic. This is chaotic in a great way."

"Great? Great how?"

"Your boss is *hot*. Like really, really hot. He's obviously into you. And what? Can he ignore you? No!"

I sighed, about to tell her to stop when Daphne knocked on my glass door. She gave a little wave, so I opened it.

"Hi! I hope I'm not interrupting anything, but my brother and Claire said you had a visitor."

"Oh, this is my best friend, Ellie," I said. "Ellie, this is Daphne Delphine."

Daphne extended her hand. "Oh, I've heard so much about you, Ellie! It's great to meet you. What brings you into Chicago proper?"

"I was moral support for Eva."

I winced. "Eight-week scan."

"Oh, geez. Good! I'm glad you had someone to go with you. I cannot imagine the stress of doing that on my own. And did it go okay?"

"Yeah, the baby looks good."

"Great news. Well, anytime you need time, Claire and I are supportive. Let us know if you need anything. I gotta go soothe a nervous shareholder's concerns with Davey. Thankfully, he is in a

very good mood this morning. I'm a little afraid he's seeing someone, which with me about to go on leave is the *last* thing I need,
but what can you do?"

I maintained a smile. "Well, good for him."

"Yeah, sure. I'll leave you. Let's have Ellie for lunch sometime
before I turn into a pumpkin. Well, before I become a *giant* pumpkin! Nice meeting you, Ellie."

"You, too!" Ellie said cheerfully.

Ellie waited for the door to close, "Well, that's fucking
awkward. He's in a good mood, Eva."

"Good god, please stop!" I pled. "Now, get the hell out of here
and go shopping or whatever. I have shit to do and it has nothing
to do with a man."

* * *

Davey

"Daph, throw me a bone. Norm likes beautiful women. The least
you could do is come to the dinner," I realized I just called my
sister a *beautiful woman*. "I mean, you are a conventionally attractive person he will prefer to me."

"No can do," Daphne grimaced.

"Why?"

She held onto the arm of her chair. "God damn lightning
crotch."

"Excuse me?"

Was it a band? A commentary on Norm's suspected previous
infidelity? Norm Palchuck was a notorious money guy. He was
also a total pain in the ass and preferred blondes. Normally,
Daphne would have allowed it.

"Lightning crotch is when the baby kicks or jams it's head into
my cervix and causes it to feel like there is lightning down there.
That's the medical term."

80

I did *not* want to think about Daphne's cervix, but remained mature. I made a mental note to look it up.

"Look, I need someone, or he will ignore me, throw a fit, and go on a tirade. Ever since his wife died, he's not been the same. Are Chloe and Delanie around?"

"Delanie is working. Chloe is competing. They are both busy."

Delanie was our actress sister, and Chloe was Cal's hot younger sister who held onto his shares since he couldn't vote on any matter without it being a conflict of interest. She was also the resident horse girl and Chief Influencer Officer. Either one would have pleased the old bastard to no end and would have been game to be charming.

Eva passed outside, headed to the snack bar.

"I'll ask Eva," I said.

"You will *not* ask her!" Daphne exclaimed. "She shouldn't have to deal with him. She's *my* direct report."

"Please. I'm desperate."

I didn't want to take Eva, but knew she'd fit the bill. Maybe she'd even feel special for being picked to wine and dine with a board member. I would never let him get away with anything with her present and knew she'd not tolerate his bullshit anyway.

"If she wants to go, tell her everything and *then* let her decide. If you don't tell her, I will, and you'll look like an ass."

Daphne stood.

"Yes, Daph," I followed. "Promise."

"I'm off to meet with ops. See you at Mom's this weekend."

She headed out and I dashed across the way to try to find Eva. She stood at the espresso machine waiting for a shot. I knew she'd had a long day because her hair was pulled back tightly in a clip but still spilled from it. Looking at her from this angle, I could see slight changes in her body. She rested a hand on her stomach the way Daphne did. I wondered if pregnant women *trained* themselves to do it or if it just happened. Was it organic or learned through observation?

"Don't look at me like that!" She didn't even turn.

"Like what?" I chuckled.

"Like you're judging me for consuming caffeine."

"I'm not," I said. "Well, maybe this late in the day."

Eva rolled her eyes. "What do you need?"

"Norm—this guy who owns board shares—is being a stick in the mud about an acquisition. He wants us to wine and dine him, but I usually bring a woman with me because he's more receptive to reason when there are woman around."

Eva's shot poured into the small cup of hot water. "Why me?"

"Because I need someone under forty who's conventionally attractive," I admitted.

"And he's a creep?"

"No. He's a philanderer, but he can be very charming—to women. He'll go easy on me if you're there. No heavy lifting. He's no brainiac, but he'll be impressed with your education and general no-fucks-given way of being."

"You excite me," Eva said flatly.

"I will be there. Nothing will happen. He's not a bad guy—just a *personality*. Ninety percent of my job is babying other members of the board. Daphne is the one who gets to fix shit."

Eva smiled, giggled, then gagged. It was the strangest combination. In the process, she dropped her biodegradable spoon. I tossed it in the garbage as she grabbed another.

"Shit, sorry. That happens sometimes," Eva said, as if she malfunctioned.

I reached to rub her back, then pulled my hand back. *What the fuck is that, Davey?*

"What do I need to do? And when?" Eva gave over to the idea.

"It would be tomorrow night. We have a nine o'clock reservation. Norm likes to eat late."

"That's too late. I'll never get home. The last train leaves at 11:30 and the next doesn't come until 5:30."

"I can have my driver take you home after. Or you could get a hotel room. Your choice."

"I will take the driver," Eva said.

"Thank you, thank you, thank you! You are saving me, Eva."

"You'll owe me," Eva reminded. "But I'll take it."

14.NORM

Eva

IN MY QUEST TO LEARN TO LIKE DAVEY, I AGREED TO DINE WITH A VIP. I felt alright about this—it was a small request, and I dealt with partnership bullshit before. Davey promised Norm Palchuck wasn't handsy and promised to mind himself. Even now, in his fabulous Bentley, I felt okay about it. As we approached the restaurant, all bets were off. *Sushi!*

I kept my mouth shut as Davey spoke.

"We have a reservation for David Delphine. For three."

"Yes, Mr. Delphine, of course. We've been able to guarantee you the chef's table. The other half of your party is waiting at the bar."

Oh, fuck! There was nothing worse than being stuck in a kitchen! Puke was a biohazard, and the menu was pre-fixe never mind the prohibition on sushi. Thankfully, Davey read my concern.

"Oh, shit!" Davey facepalmed. "You cannot eat sushi, right?"

The host jumped in. "We have other options if that doesn't appeal."

Before I could say anything, a woman pushed past us and demanded a table as if reservations were not a thing. I took the time to sync with Davey.

I whispered, "It's the smell."

I opened my purse and pulled out a Zofran, arming myself in hopes it would work to keep my nausea at bay like cloves of garlic against a vampire.

"That really is so bad?"

I glared. "David, it is horrendous. You have no idea."

"But doesn't it get better?"

"Ask your sister that stupid fucking question!" I clapped back.

I had no energy. I took a quick couch nap in my office but flagged about eight when I was piling my hair into a somewhat presentable bun in the ladies' room.

"Do I look pregnant?" I whispered. "In this dress?"

"You look great. Only you would know," Davey answered with a slight smile.

It wasn't rude. It wasn't skeezy, but it showed interest. Why the hell didn't he get the hint that I really didn't think about him that way anymore? Were all straight men eternally hopeful pursuers of pussy? They always told us that we confused them and weren't direct. Meanwhile, I'd always gotten clear answers from women.

"Are you okay otherwise?" Davey asked as we waited on the host to finish dealing with a Karen sans-reservation.

"Davey, this is bad news."

He turned back to the hostess once the woman left in a huff. "The chef's table… will not work for us. My colleague has a dietary restriction, and I know the menu is very bespoke. She cannot have any fish."

"Sir, the other party member requested it. I just… assumed you'd prefer it. Let me speak to the chef. I am sure for you we can make some sort of accommodation."

I breathed a sigh of relief.

"I told you that I had your back," Davey said.

"Thanks."

The hostess returned. "Yes, the chef said he understands and is glad to accommodate any dietary restrictions."

Davey looked to me for confirmation. I nodded in return. The medication was keeping my nausea at bay so far.

We found Norm—a skinny, short man in his seventies—at the bar with a fruity drink. He wasn't what I expected.

"You did bring a friend, didn't you?" Norm asked. "Who is this lovely woman?"

He was *flamboyant*. I got a feeling the reason Norm wasn't handsy was he preferred women to bro-y straight dudes like Davey.

"Norm, this is our new Business Information Security Officer, Eva Pavlak. She'll be at the leadership retreat next month. Daphne couldn't make it."

"Daphne couldn't make it? What a shame. I suppose she gets a pass with the pregnancy. Terrible thing," he made a face. "Go easy on her. She's earned it."

"I try not to be too much of an ogre to the women in my life," Davey said.

I resisted the desire to roll my eyes. Davey wasn't an *ogre*, but *would* toot his own horn.

"They said we have the chef's table," Davey confirmed. "Should we head back?"

A server took us to the kitchen. It was as "elevated" as you'd expect. I'd been to a chef's table before. Mona loved shit like this. Sadly, I preferred to choose my own food. I wasn't into gastronomy. I would have gladly consumed sushi any other time in my life. In fact, after the miscarriage, I had it as my first meal as a fuck you to the universe.

"So, what does a person like yourself do?" Norm asked as we were seated.

"I work with Daphne and Claire to translate technology priorities or concerns into real talk. I'm an attorney first," I explained. "A lot of my job is boring compliance stuff."

"Contrary to what I thought, she doesn't fix computers," Davey said.

"How is your broken PC working out?" I tried not to glare.

"It is… broken. I gave up. I am still just using my iPad at home."

I rubbed my temples. *Just what we need, a mobile device used by the CEO at home to expand our threat surface.*

"Let's order you an iPad Pro," I said.

"And why?"

Because we can lock it down like Fort Knox and unfuck things.

"You deserve an upgrade, David. Don't you think?"

He shrugged. "If you say so, Eva. You're the expert."

Davey's gaze wasn't benign *or* professional. We hadn't even gotten Sake, and he already stared at me too much. I could have been flattered, but why? In this state, I expected different treatment. Did he have some weird breeding kink?

The server arrived with Sake and three glasses.

I covered mine with my hand. "Nothing for me, thanks. I'm a teetotaler."

"Really? Oh, that's a shame. But congrats on your sobriety." Norm was kind.

I plan to drink heavily once this thing is out of me. I've more than earned it.

Davey changed topics. "Eva is Daphne's former mentee. How did that all start again, Eva?"

"We were paired up by the Oxford Alumni group for American students. She was a young barrister, and I was just leaving law and cybersecurity. I had no idea how to navigate the British job market."

"And you were staying?" Norm asked.

"I was *trying* to. I was in a serious relationship with a Brit and had no intention of moving back to the States to live with my parents and find a job."

"Oh, exciting. Did your husband move back with you?" Norm made all kinds of assumptions.

"No," I said. "Ironically, I moved back when Daphne hired me and am currently living with my family. Both my parents are retired, and my mom needs some interference now that Dad is always around."

Norm chuckled. "When my wife was alive, that was how it was. So, no husband? No boyfriend?"

"No girlfriend, boyfriend, or partner of any sort," I answered.

Norm smiled. "Oh, you young people can be so free. It is good. Davey, I know I shouldn't ask—"

"No," Davey answered. "There is someone I was sort of seeing, but that is… complicated."

If he meant me, he barked up the wrong tree. If not, he was being tacky.

"Well, no doubt Lady Danna would prefer to see you end up with someone—especially as Daphne has just gotten married."

"Daphne was married before, too."

I pulled a face.

"Oh, she didn't like the first husband," Norm chuckled.

"He was an ass," I confirmed. "Cal is much better for her. Not that I have an opinion, of course."

"I agree," Davey added. "And Mum is… a challenge in this regard. I'd like to settle down someday. I am trying."

He said it, knowing I wanted to hear it. Talk was cheap, but I wanted to believe—even just a bit—he wasn't lying.

"I keep telling that to my friend Lyle," Norm said. "He always gives me hell for acting like I'm sixteen, but it keeps me young. I think the wife sometimes rolled her eyes, but she wasn't a stick in the mud, either. Find a girl like that—one that won't bore you. Oh, and if you like sleep, don't have kids. I have no regrets on that front."

Davey choked on his water. "Well, some might say children are the spice of life."

"That's certainly what your father thought," Norm said. "Six children is not for the faint of heart. Don't tell me you want six of them."

"No," Davey saw my gaze drop. "One or two is fine."

* * *

Davey

Eva started to give up around eleven but rallied for dessert. Norm found her charming. He relaxed on his concerns and ate out of her palm. Eva was clever—more than I gave her credit for. She was also beautiful, even more so done up to the nines.

"Could I interest you in drinks? My friends are at the wine bar across the way."

"I'm good," Eva said. "It was lovely to meet you, but I'm knackered."

"That's British for tired," I joked. "Same. I should head out."

"Suit yourself," Norm said. "Nice seeing you, Davey, and wonderful to meet you, dear Eva."

She gave him a little wave as he disappeared to find his second watering hole.

"Home?" I asked.

"If that is still the offer, yes. I feel bad asking your driver—"

"It is what I pay the service for," I said. "It's their job, Eva."

"Fine," she agreed.

We dipped into the waiting car in the circle drive outside.

"What's your address, Eva?" I asked.

"7213 Thistle Rd, Krakow, Indiana. This time of night, you'll be there in about 35 minutes," Eva answered. "Sorry. It feels like the country."

"Don't apologize, miss," Earl, a regular driver, said. "I've been out that way before."

She turned to me. "And you can drop him first, obviously."

"Nah, I'm down for a tiny road trip—"

"Davey, I live a million miles away. It will be late."

"I don't have anywhere to be tomorrow. I'd rather make sure you get home safe and… I wouldn't mind the drive."

She rolled her eyes but didn't protest. As Earl made his way south, Eva gazed at the lake to our left while I stared at her. She let out a long sigh and began disassembling her hair, as if trying hard to relax.

"Do I really make you *that* uncomfortable?" I asked.

"No." Eva turned. "You don't. But my hair is pulling and everything sort of hurts."

"Everything?"

"My back is killing me. My tits hurt. My feet are swollen. It's hellish, Davey. I am not complaining to garner sympathy, just for perspective."

"It is okay to complain to garner sympathy," I said.

She shook her head. "Don't go there."

"Go where?"

"Trying to sucker me in with puppy dog eyes. I'm resistant and it won't work. It only works if you're under the age of ten." She kicked off her shoes. "Sorry, but my feet are screaming. I feel bad doing this. But Jesus Christ this carpet pile. This car is amazing."

"It was my dad's," I said. "To the CEO, go the spoils. Or, at least the things that try to make up for being that guy."

"Why do you whine about it and still do it?" Eva asked.

"I was his third choice," I admitted. "That doesn't leave this car."

Earl raised the partition.

"I knew he wanted Cal before me. Cal was Dad's favorite person. And he raised Cal up in the business—grooming him for this. When Cal decided to run for mayor, that flew by the wayside. I later found out Dad wanted to offer *Daphne* the top spot, but she never would have accepted."

"She was still married to fuckface?"

I snickered at her diction. "Yes."

"So, that's the chip on your shoulder?"

I shrugged. "While I was dyslexic and hated school, Daphne was always top of her class. Cal was good at everything. And boy, didn't my father always prefer him!"

"But he's like ten years older than you!" Eva laughed.

"Yes, but it didn't matter. As I got older, the more pushed out I felt. I loved my dad. I wanted his approval, but he didn't see me. He doted on the girls. Derrick was the clown. I'm not that funny."

"I was the brain of the family," Eva said. "But I always felt like they loved us both pretty equally."

"And *your* dad?"

"He worked all the time, but when home, he would give us everything he could. When I said I wanted to go to Oxford freshman year, he bought me a sweatshirt and promised if I would put in the work to get in, he would find a way. I ended up getting a scholarship and they paid for my plane ticket and flat share. I love my parents. They did everything they could to make sure I had opportunities they never did."

I smiled. "That sounds incredible."

"They are good. But because of my sister's wrath, I try to dress in baggy clothes, so no one guesses. I feel terrible hiding it. At work, we have reasons. At home, I just want to be honest. I never relax."

"I'd never know if I didn't know you like that," I said. "But I could see your mom picking up on it. And I get that. I suspect Daphne will give me shit and my mother will want to die inside, but they will get over it. If your parents love you, they will figure it out."

"My sister won't." Eva looked out the window as we continued south. "We used to be close, but we haven't since she married Ian. He's totally corrupted her. He's abused her and she cannot see it. In some ways, I can't blame her."

"How so?"

"He gives her an allowance—a very strict one—but they live in a house that cost a million dollars to build. His parents had money and paid for his school and startup costs, but he will tell you he's a self-made millionaire who owns the finest luxury home company."

She said it with stank which made me chuckle.

"So, he's as self-made as me?"

"Pretty much. Anyway, he does nothing with my nephew. He burdens Brooke with making everything perfect. He polices her like she's a child and has turned her into this fundie who judges everything."

"He sounds like an asshole."

"He is. But he's not unlike so many other men I know, so… par for the course."

I read her pained expression, seeing vulnerability. "Hey, I get why maybe you are reticent to trust me now, but… I only want to be involved. I'm not going to keep you on a leash."

She returned to tough Eva. "Well, you never could."

As soon as her walls came down, they went back up. I changed the subject.

"So, is she mean about you being… you know… gay?"

"I'm not gay!" Eva laughed. "I'm pan. I fall in love with people. I lust after *people*. While I may tend to be more homoromantic, I swing both ways. Originally, my sister was supportive. She liked Mona—Ian didn't—but she didn't want to be rude to her. So, she put up with it. But this? This is different. This is me refusing to marry the dude who knocked me up unapologetically and choosing to raise a kid on my own. That won't fly without commentary."

"But, Eva, you won't raise this baby on your own. And, if you wanted—"

"Please, God, do not say to get married! Stop!"

"I wasn't saying that," I laughed. "I wanted to say if you wanted me there to tell them, I will suffer through it. I can take the heat and the rage. Promise."

"I don't," Eva said. "It's too confusing for them. And I'd like to keep who the father is secret for a bit, because I don't want your personal wealth changing how they respond."

"Really?"

"Yes, really," Eva answered. "I dunno. I don't want the takeaway to be that I'm with a dude whose family is basically American royalty and now my kid is somehow born into it. Davey, it's fucking weird for me."

"Why? Why isn't that good?"

"Because I don't know! I don't want to feel weird. I worry about everyone comparing *our* kid to Daphne's kid—which is impossible.

We aren't the same. I feel like my parents will do the same with ours and because she's illegitimate, they will love Brooke's kids more."

The idea our kid wouldn't be good enough wounded me.

I squeezed her hand. "I can promise you that—to us—that kid will be everything. And anyone who belittles our kid will hear about it from me."

"You say that with conviction," Eva said.

"Because it is true. Eva, this baby will be loved."

"I want to believe you. I just worry it's a shiny object and we're going to end up in court screaming at one another like every other straight couple."

I set my jaw and resisted anger because I hated these doubts. "Eva, I don't know how I can prove it other than by taking the time to show you."

"It's not affecting you."

"It is, though. I look at the picture of our child every morning as I get ready for work. Somedays, I hate work with a burning passion just like anyone does, but I show up because it matters to our family." I squeezed her hand tighter. "And you are part of it now."

Eva shook her head and pulled her hand back, shrinking away from me.

"Eva, say something," I pleaded.

"I have my concerns. I will try to set them aside and give you— and your family—the benefit of the doubt."

"Thanks."

She turned back, face and voice softer. "I am trying. But the parents? It frightens me."

"I know, but we can only put it off so long," I said. "After all, you're going to see too much of my family at the retreat in two weeks."

"What a disaster," Eva said.

It was. I also realized it gave me an opportunity to show her my family wasn't a load of classist assholes who would hate her. She trusted Daphne. She'd trust me eventually. The challenge would be resisting touching her. Because, right now, all I wanted to do was pull her tired body into my arms and hold her close. I wanted to see her happy and safe. If she was secure, so would be our baby.

* * *

Eva

"Is that a horse pasture?" Davey pointed down my parents' drive.

"Yes. We've still got a few. Bubba is a rescue. Maggie is my dad's mare. Poco is my old man," I said. "I used to show quarter horse circuit, but Poco is now in his thirties and only goes out on the trails."

"He's in his thirties and *rideable*?"

"Totally," I said.

"Dora—my youngest sister—still rides competitively. Daphne and Delanie rode, too, but neither like Dora does. Cal's sister, Chloe, is a real world-beater. She is known as a horse influencer. You should have warned me, Eva."

"Why?" I laughed.

"Because I avoid horse girls," Davey joked. "It's a disease."

I smiled slyly. "And you wanted to come all the way out here?"

"I wanted to bring you home safely."

The car slowed. The driver lowered the partition

"Just give us a second," Davey said.

"I'm here," I murmured, feeling half asleep.

"Well, if you… if you want to talk about anything at all. Just text me. Or if you *need* anything—"

"You're going to flee to Indiana? C'mon!"

"Sure."

I patted his knee. "I don't think I need saving, Davey. But thank you."

He squeezed my hand. "I'm just saying… as you said… I owe you, baby."

Baby?

My face showed it all.

"I… I'm sorry." Davey pulled his hand away and looked down. "Shit, I… we were bonding, and I fucking ruined it."

I suddenly believed him. His reaction was genuine—I *flustered* him. I made David Delphine *nervous*. He trusted me.

I grabbed his hand. "It's okay. It's been a long day."

His eyes met mine in the low light, sending an impulse which confused me. I wanted to *kiss* him. I hated it. Why, oh why, did I want to kiss this man? His eyes were soft, and his hand was gentle in mine. He was vulnerable and already missing me.

Say something idiotic so I can hate you again, Davey!

But he didn't.

"I'll… text you," I dropped his hand.

The driver rushed to open my door. Davey watched me step inside the house. I watched their headlights fade, creeping upstairs. It was the weirdest night—my billionaire boss with a Bentley dropped me off at my childhood home after we wined and dined another very rich man. My boss was my baby daddy. Shit was weird right now.

I crawled into bed with as many pillows as I could take from the linen closet without my mother finding out. I couldn't rest yet. My mind filtered back to Davey's genuine concern about my reaction to calling him baby.

I picked up my phone.

ME

Do you want to try to get together and start talking about arrangements for this kid?

It was bold and I worried he'd react poorly.

BOSS MAN

Yes. When and where? Are we still incognito?

ME

Yes.

> Chesterton has an artisan market tomorrow. Do you want to meet at the Bluebird Cafe for brunch? It's about all I can keep down.

BOSS MAN

> Honest talk. Did you go puke in the bathroom after dinner and before dessert?

I snickered.

ME

> Also, yes.

> I'm sorry. I know it's gross, but nothing suits.

BOSS MAN

> Then you shall have your breakfast. Whatever works.

I smiled.

ME

> Does 11 work?

BOSS MAN

> Sure.

15. BRUNCH

Eva

A VINTAGE MASERATI APPEARED IN FRONT OF MY CHOICE OF DINER. People stared.

"A fucking Maserati. Too predictable," I said to myself.

For the first time, I saw the man I'd only seen before in trousers or a full suit sporting nothing but a t-shirt, a Cubs hat, and khaki shorts. He looked *normal*—a mere mortal. As he entered the diner, I gave him a small wave, and he slid into the booth across from me. We didn't hug like old friends or kiss like lovers. We were neither. Despite the awkward dance, we focused on coparenting.

"Your car is… attracting followers."

"It's a 1971 Ghibli Spyder. It should," Davey said, like I should know what that meant. "I inherited it. It was my dad's. First, my grandfather's, then my dad's, now mine."

"It's nice," I said. "And totally impractical given our discussion today."

He grimaced. "Well, that's not my daily driver."

"So, the Bentley?"

"That's my car when I'm not driving. I have a G-Wagon. You can put car seats in a G-Wagon, Eva."

"Fine," I said. "That is true. "How do you—one man—have three cars?"

"Lots of people have a car for nice days and a car for work," Davey shrugged.

Lots of *rich* people.

"What do you drive? Are you investing in a mom mobile?" Davey looked over the menu.

A server with blue hair and anime tattoos appeared. "Can I get you coffee or anything?"

Davey looked over. "I'm ready to order if you are, Eva."

"I'll have an order of french toast with double the whipped butter and syrup on the side," I said. "And you already brought my coffee, so I'm good."

"I'll have a mug of coffee and breakfast platter 5. I'll have eggs and the hashbrowns not the home fries."

The woman nodded and took our menus.

"So, what is your ride?" Davey pressed.

"I drive a 1997 Ford F-250. It is beat up, both mirrors are scraped to hell, there are no cupholders, and it sounds like a plane taking off."

"You're kidding."

"Definitely not. I'll show it to you if you want. It even has a bench seat."

"How old are you versus that thing?"

"It's a little wild," I admitted. "But it's our other vehicle. We haul hay with it and pull a horse trailer. It's the car that taught me how to drive. But really, I just needed something until I had money to buy a car outright. Or enough of a paycheck to get less-shady financing."

"What?" Davey cocked his head.

"I have very little money from before my split," I said. "Not enough to buy a reasonable car. And I have no credit in this country—only in the UK. It counts for essentially nothing."

"Shit. Well, we should remedy that."

I shook my head. "David, I don't want to do that. This is why we're meeting. I will buy a car when I can get a good deal—"

"I'll just buy you a car. It's for our kid. You deserve to have a safe car. If that truck got in an accident—"

"What if your car got in an accident?" I asked. "Don't police my body."

He backed off.

"Okay, so here's what I want," I got back to business. "I don't want to exclude you as you demonstrate sincere intent. I also need you to understand that babies are dependent mostly on their mothers. They need us for food and general welfare for the first few months."

Davey nodded. "Yeah. The baby will need to feed every couple hours at first—at least once every 3-4 hours. And then it just depends. So, it's not like you will be going far for awhile."

I cocked my head. "What are you, Encyclopedia Britannica?"

He blushed. "I read some stuff."

It was endearing beyond measure.

"So, I don't think overnight custody exchanges are going to be a thing in the first year of life. That's just being realistic. If it changes or we want to try some things, we can do that. I don't even know if you want to be responsible for any of this. I don't want to speak for you."

"Why?" Davey asked as the server brought coffee. "I'm the baby's parent. I should want to parent. That's not my concern."

"What is?"

"Bonding? It's *my* baby, too. I will ultimately defer to you because your body has kept it alive and will continue to. I know that Cal has taken a rather hands-off approach on these matters, as Daphne is the one growing a human. I still want to bond, Eva."

I shrugged. "I don't know what my situation is, and I am not sure how comfortable my parents will be with you dropping in."

"Oh, you're planning on staying… here?"

"Well, my parents are both retired. They can help me. You'll be busy working. The commute doesn't make sense."

His face fell.

"Don't start with the puppy dog eyes, Davey," I sighed.

"Eva, I want to be there. I am taking leave."

"CEOs don't take leave."

"Well, my dad fucking did!" Davey's frustration bubbled.

I took a deep breath, not wanting to fight. His indignation came from a good place.

"You said your dad was involved—"

"My dad took leave even if he was also available. Don't ask me how it will work, but we will figure it out. Daphne will be back by then. I can jump in for the big things, but that first month should be all about you recovering and the baby growing. I want to bond. Even if I must sleep on a motherfucking couch, I will do it. I just want to be there."

He thought this through.

"You say this like it is instinct."

"I'm the dad, so it is."

I shrugged.

"Why are you so resistant to believing me?"

"I don't know you," I said.

"And?"

"I want to believe you. I want to also believe that you don't feel the need to buy me or my child off. I don't need your money."

Davey groaned. "That's not why I offer. Think about it this way, Eva. You work a full-time, demanding-ass job. Don't you want help?"

"You work all the time."

"So? We hire a nanny."

"A nanny that works where?" I asked.

"Eva, you need to either hire a nanny or put the child in a center. I don't want our newborn in a center. The germs alone—"

"Why are you such a germaphobe?" I asked.

"I had awful childhood asthma and hospitals terrify me."

"Kids go to the doctor a lot," I said.

"I am a grown man. I can handle it," Davey protested. "I want this to work, Eva. I am willing to do what you need, but there need to be some basic assumptions."

"Go on."

"You need a place of your own, a car of your own, and we need to hire a nanny," Davey said. "I don't have to pay for the first two unless you want me to, but I think that is the point of child support, right?"

"Yes."

"Given I don't think you're a particularly spendy sort, I want you to tell me what it costs, and I will cover it."

"I don't want to be a kept woman. I've worked my ass off—"

"Well, I'm the one who got you pregnant. I have means. I want our child raised in a nice, safe home and I want his mother to be well-taken-care-of even if we're not together."

"Oh my God, the savior complex on you!"

"It's not that. I mean, maybe a little. I'm me. I'm going to provide for you because I can and it's the right thing to do, but it's also because happy mothers have happy babies and well-adjusted kids. We both want that, don't we?"

The rant was never-ending.

"You can think I'm a classist prick, but money makes life easier. Has no one ever taken care of you before? This is not a gift. It is support for our child."

Our food arrived. I sat, thoughts milling. Why was I so bothered by his desire to spend money? Mona spoiled me. I never told her *not* to. I lived in our nice house in a beautiful neighborhood. I ate at good restaurants. I wore the clothes she bought happily. So, why now was it different?

"It's because you're a man, I guess. I don't… it always feels like a transaction. It gives me the ick. You're a prince. I'm a peasant. The imbalance of power isn't just about class, either. You are my *boss*, Davey."

"I know, I know. But I don't think about it like that."

"That's because you're the king of the hill. You don't fucking *have* to, David. I do. And when this news comes out, we both will."

* * *

Davey

After breakfast, we milled through stalls at the farmer's market, trying to relate, I couldn't help but feel alone. Eva had no place to live, no car, no childcare plans, and she wouldn't compromise. Last night, I gave her vulnerability, and she trusted me. Now, she dug her heels in. As I was about to ask what it was she needed, she rubbed her temples and stopped. An admission came that changed the tenor of our conversation.

"Look, I don't want to agree to much right now. I'm frightened it's a bad omen. And while you probably would see it ending prematurely as a blessing in disguise... I don't."

"I don't feel that way. I'm invested," I said. "It would be worse for you, I'm sure. But for me, it would hurt, too. You're afraid to hear the worst?"

She nodded as tears welled. "Two weeks. Two more weeks to know if this can continue."

"Is this when you got the news last time?" I asked.

Eva's voice grew small, "Yes."

Unexpectedly, she hugged me. I wrapped her in my arms. She cried—losing herself in public. I thought by planning, I was being a grownup and proving she could trust me. Instead, I pushed buttons. Every attempt threw salt in her wounds.

I rubbed her back. "I am sorry. I pushed."

"You didn't know," Eva murmured.

"I know now. You can tell me anything about what happened if it helps."

"All you should know was that at the scan—alone—I found out the pregnancy was unviable. There was no heartbeat. I scheduled surgery to end the pregnancy without my ex's support. And when I told her, she said it was for the best. She told me she didn't love me anymore."

I pulled back. "Eva, baby, that is… cruel. No one deserves that. I will be there. If you want Ellie there, too, I understand it."

"Ellie cannot make it. She has got to be back home for a teacher's meeting. She told me last week."

"I will be there if it kills me."

"Thanks."

I cupped her face. "I don't want you to feel like you're burdening me. We're doing this together. I have no idea what you need from me most of the time, but don't feel bad for asking. If I cannot do it, I will tell you, but have I told you no yet?"

"No."

"Then trust me."

Her intense eyes focused on mine, as if finally hearing my words—all of them. And for a moment, I felt the urge to kiss her. I was still so drawn to her—even when she infuriated me.

"Okay. Can we just agree things will need to work different in the future but put off the big things until we know more? And just survive the retreat?"

"Sure," I agreed.

As if by reflex, I kissed the top of her head.

Eva pulled back, her eyes meeting mine. She took me in once more—inquisitive, unsure, probing—before pulling me into a kiss.

Unable to resist, I ran my hands through her soft, honey-blonde hair and soaked her up. It felt as good as it had the first time.

She upended the moment with trepidation. "I'm sorry. I shouldn't have."

"You can always impose," I said.

She turned to rush away. "No. It's complicated. I should… go."

I trotted after, catching up. "At least let me get you back to your car—"

"I'm good."

"Eva, talk to me. Don't run!"

We rounded a corner. Eva speed walked.

She stopped before a blue pickup. "Here I am."

"Eva, tell me that didn't feel like anything," I said.

"I… I just… I cannot do that."

She hopped in the truck and slammed the door. I watched her drive off, confused. How did we go from an argument to a fabulous kiss to more arguing? Why did she always flee?

PART III

PARTNERS

16. BUFFALO SHORES

Eva

I drove my mom's CR-V north to Buffalo Shores, Michigan for the company retreat. We'd have a weekend of wine, fine cuisine, and strategy all set against the backdrops of the family's lake compound, farmhouse, vineyard, and fruit orchard. I couldn't drive my beater up there. It was too bleak. I was about to hobnob with the rich and Chicago-famous. I needed to impress the board, not look like a hick.

The board invited everyone to drinks and apps at the Harbor Country Suites and Spa—a fancy hotel with lake views. Daphne decided to attend, despite her late-pregnancy fatigue. I was just grateful to have a friend. Daphne circulated me through conversations with a dozen people, including her fabulous sister-in-law, Chloe Markham.

Chloe was different. Ensconced in expensive resort collection goodies, she didn't have the same easy Old Money aesthetic the Delphines did when "casually" dressed. She was chic, outspoken, and possessed *all* the tea.

"You're staying with us across the street," Chloe said. "Well, up the road, but pretty much."

"What do you mean?" I asked.

"Daphne put you at the house. We're split here and there. It's a block up the way."

"Their house?" I asked.

"Yeah. It's massive. Look, this place is trippy. It's like The Hamptons. The house immediately across the street is owned by a prince."

"What?"

"Yeah. The Queen's brother and his husband. No joke."

I gaped.

"Buckle up, baby. These people... they aren't like anyone else. Even Cal isn't like them. He married in, but it's not the same. I got you."

I smiled, realizing what she meant. We were outsiders looking in.

"Don't scare her off, Chlo." Davey approached. "She's new."

"I like her. I'm doing the opposite. I'm spilling tea about this place."

"What do you think of the area?" Davey asked.

"It's beautiful. We used to come up here to play at the beach as kids, but... it hits differently in these digs."

"Oh, shit. There's my idiot brother! One sec," Chloe raced off.

"She's... a lot," Davey said. "She's Lanie's best friend and might as well be one of us."

Not in her point of view.

"You're staying with us," Davey said. "At the house. Not here."

I raised an eyebrow.

"Look, it wasn't my idea, Eva. I worried it would make you uncomfortable, but my sister was insistent. She's being all protective."

"She knows about me—not the whole story," I said. "So maybe that's what it is?"

"That explains her urge to shame me for asking you to do anything," Davey chuckled.

It was sort of adorable.

"Did my mother introduce herself yet?" Davey asked.

"No. I have stayed as far away from that as possible."

"You'll be fine."

That's not what Chloe said.

"I am going to get through this, and that is all, David," I said.

"You'll be fine. Norm has sung all your praises."

"That's sweet of him."

"Maybe he has a crush?" Davey joked. "Either way, he thinks you are smart."

"That man is closeted," I said. "I hate to break it to you, but his friend… he's not a friend."

"What?" Davey's astoundment surprised me.

"Who is?" Chloe returned with Davey and Daphne's sister Delanie.

"She thinks Norm is…" Davey lowered his voice, "gay."

"Well, he's good friends with Prince George," Delanie said. "And goes to all their parties in Chicago, so I'd guess your girl is right."

Your girl. I wanted to remind him that in youth speak that didn't mean I was *literally* his girl.

"How the fuck do you know that, Lanie?" Davey asked.

"I just spent months shooting with that prince's daughter in New York," Lanie answered. "She's an actress. You know her?"

"Leah Roughy?" I answered. "You know Leah? She's like a gay icon on her own."

"What?" Davey asked.

"Leah is bi," I explained. "And anytime she is in London, she throws a party. The woman is fab. I've only been to one."

"Oh, do tell! How?" Chloe asked.

"My ex was a friend. She had a mutual ex with Leah. She works in entertainment law and IP protection."

"Wait… are you? Can I ask that?" Lanie asked.

"Jesus, Lanie, she's my employee! It's considered discrimination."

"Legally, no. But we're not in a hiring situation, and I'd say this is a casual conversation. I'm pan and it's not a secret."

"You get increasingly interesting. You take care of computers? What is that about?" Delanie asked.

"I promise you I'm pretty boring on paper," I said. "Now, my obsession with privacy law is unhealthy and will put you to sleep. I'm *so* fun at parties."

"Norm would say you are," Davey said. "Even if you did explain how we were on the forefront of privacy while also data brokering responsibly."

My mouth dropped. "You listened to me?"

"I was sitting right there, Eva. Lanie, she's an attorney. She doesn't fix computers."

"Alright, everyone!" Daphne shouted. "David, do you mind?"

"Nah, you're doing a great job!" He joked.

She glared his way. "For those of you staying at ours, grab your luggage and toss it into the car. We can walk up that way and you can leave your cars here. There's not enough room for everyone at ours. You know who you are."

I followed, ready to toss my carryon into the waiting luggage car. It made things easier.

"I'll help you," Davey offered.

"Don't be weird," I whispered.

"Me offering to help you is *not* weird. And if I don't, my sisters will give me so much shit."

"Fine," I agreed, walking out to my mom's car in the adjoining parking lot.

"New car?" Davey asked.

"No," I answered. "My mom's because I didn't think you'd appreciate my broke pickup at your retreat."

"It adds *flavor*," he joked, pulling my bag from the lift gate.

I threw a Longchamp containing my makeup over my shoulder and followed.

He did a double-take at my expensive luggage.

"It was a gift," I answered.

"I am silently judging you for fighting me about paying for brunch."

"Judge me all you want, Davey, but this is just how I am."

Davey tossed my bags into the waiting car and sped to catch Daphne and his mother. I gathered if we lingered, people would suspect something was up. I hung back with Chloe.

"He has a crush on you. Watch out," Chloe said.

I coughed, horrified. "What?"

"Davey. He has a crush. I can tell. He gets all aggro and prince on a white horse. I'm not saying he's a red flag, but... he's a man-child and he's not... without his issues. None of them are. His mother is a pain in the ass. I am warning you woman-to-woman."

"Good to know." I broke into a sweat.

The Delphine's compound gave little indication about the house hidden behind its grand stone fence. Once the gates opened, a gorgeous country house emerged, set just above the dunes. Lake views abounded. It was big as could be and somehow effortlessly elegant in a way only billionaires could make it. Danna Delphine had good taste.

"Come with me," Daphne beckoned. "I put you just around the corner from me. If you need *anything*, just let me know. I want you to make yourself at home."

"This is too much, really," I said. "The hotel would have been totally fine."

"Well, I would have worried too much. You're new and it's a lot. The party animals are over there, and you'd have to explain dozens of times why you weren't drinking. I wanted to make it easier."

"I appreciate that."

My room looked over the boardwalk and shoreline. The breeze felt wonderful. The bathroom had a big soaker tub. It was better than any hotel. I was living a life of luxury. Mona's parents had a wonderfully decorated grand house in the Lake District, but it paled in comparison.

Lovely or not, I was staying in my baby daddy's family's place—the family who had no idea we even slept together, let alone that I was pregnant with his love child. We kissed, didn't talk about it, and now I wanted to run for the hills but couldn't.

* * *

Davey

During sunset, we hosted dinner for everyone on the patio. A chef worked in the kitchen while I observed the table setting. Where had Mum put Eva? I was seated at one end of the table—though not the head—and Mum at the other. She'd placed Claire and our CFO around me. I went down to the other end to find Eva was right there—right by Mum. I flew around to the other side, praying she'd be near Lanie or Chloe. No such luck. She put her across from our Chief Marketing Officer. All he'd do was flirt all night and back Mum up because he was a kissass.

"David Jr.!" Mum spoke as if she knew I was onto her.

"Mum, please," I groaned.

"You better not be moving those seating cards around, Davey!"

"I would never do that, Mum," I said. *Though I would if you'd disappear.*

"I very carefully curated the table for balanced discussions. You said she got on with Norm, so I put him on this end. And she doesn't know the marketing boy—"

I kneaded my temples. "He's our CMO, Mum."

"Well, he is young and handsome, and she could do worse. Do you know that she drives a *Honda*?"

If you only knew, mother.

"Are we judging people on the cars they drive now?"

"She has a very well-paid position at a prestige company. She's an up-and-comer. The people who want to succeed take pride in their appearances."

I investigated the living room, where Daphne and Eva appeared deep in conversation. In her jade-colored dress, Eva couldn't be more beautiful. I didn't know what my mother was talking about.

"She's a pretty girl," Mum insisted. "She should have a car to match, is all."

"I agree," I said, "but I think it makes more sense to put me in the middle. We'll put the least senior people on the outside."

"What?"

"Put Daphne down there. Let her have it."

"Why?"

"She's gestating a human."

"But, darling, you're in charge."

"I would like it to feel more egalitarian."

I pushed my way over to the place cards and moved my card catty-corner from Eva.

"That's good enough," I said. "Better."

"I had six children and had no special treatment," Mum protested.

"Yes, mother, you had six children, but Dad treated you like a queen when you were pregnant—don't deny it."

"Cal worships the ground she walks on."

"And that's great. But she's been busting ass while relegated to vegetables and I'd like to pump her up. The poor woman is always hungry," I said.

"I blame the amount of donuts Cal let her eat for the first few months. That's how babies come out with problems."

I rolled my eyes. "Gestational diabetes is more genetic than anything."

"We didn't have that in my day!"

"They didn't screen for it back then," I protested.

I crossed back into the living room, leaving my mother to fuss with napkins. Eva poured another pop from the self-serve bar.

"Is your mother measuring place settings?" Eva asked.

I looked over my shoulder. "Yes."

"Yeesh."

"Look, I switched our seating arrangements."

"Why the fuck would you do that?" Eva's eyes narrowed, but her tone remained forcefully sweet.

"Because Mum is in a mood and wants to hook you up with

Mr. Marketing," I sighed. "And she'll keep trying and trying, and it will wear on you."

"Oh," she calmed.

"I thought you were being an ass."

"No. I am protecting you as I agreed I would. Is your room okay? Are *you* alright?"

"You can back off, Mom," she groaned. "I'm fine. It is… intense… but I will survive."

I turned, looking over the patio, trying to keep things neutral, my thoughts anything but.

"You look lovely," I said, unable to hold back. "The color is beautiful on you."

"You really—"

I turned, my eyes laser-focused on hers. "I mean it. You deserve to hear it. I won't apologize."

"You don't think it's inappropriate—"

"I think that train left the station about three months ago," I said.

17. A SHIP NOT A BOAT

Eva

"Eva, you attended Oxford?" Danna Delphine—known to all not in the family as *Lady* Danna—asked.

"Yes, ma'am," I answered. "I was in Mansfield College."

Her reaction to this answer would determine how I felt about her.

"Oh. You were… studious," Danna said. "I was in Magdalen."

Of *course* she was.

"I met my husband there. He was a postgraduate," Danna continued. "David and I were happy when Daphne chose Magdalen and received a placement. It was a good opportunity for her. Did your parents attend Oxford?"

"No," I said.

"Where did they attend? Something more local? Business at Indiana?"

"They didn't attend university."

I knew she felt superior, based on the glance she exchanged with Davey.

"Well, I suppose that is a credit to brilliant people finding their way no matter the challenging circumstances," Danna said.

I felt an inch tall.

"Mum, that's rude," Davey said. "Just because her parents didn't go to college doesn't mean they are indigent. And so, what if they were? Why would you say it?"

If eyes could hiss, Danna Delphine's would have.

"I found out recently Eva is a horse girl. I told her to talk to Chloe and Dora," Davey changed the conversation adeptly. I couldn't help but smile in return.

"Oh, did you show?"

"I have a horse I showed in the all-around growing up," I answered. "He's an old man now, but we got a few hi-points in our days in showmanship and western riding."

"Oh, quarter horses," Danna was flat.

This was *not* going well.

"Lady Danna, is this wine from your vineyards?" Chase, the CFO asked. "It is just impeccable."

The wine was fine. I had *one* sip after Chloe goaded me for ages. I did not contribute. I kept quiet for the rest of the dinner, only paying attention to my food. When dinner wrapped, the hotel people ditched us to drink. I soon found myself in my room alone. It was too soon to sleep. I pulled on a t-shirt, some shorts, my Birks, and headed to the beach for a nighttime walk. After making it down, I realized I had company.

"Great minds, huh?" Davey chuckled from where he sat in the sand.

"I needed a break from feeling so useless," I said.

"Ignore my Mum," Davey said. "I'm sorry. She... she cannot relate to anyone normal."

"Yes, I am sorry I am a mere mortal."

"Sit. I promise I don't bite." Davey patted the sand.

"If I sit, I might not get back up. My back and hips are fucked— and for once, there is no fun reason for it."

"I'll hoist you," Davey offered

I plopped onto the cool sand indelicately, resting my eyes on the horizon. A few boats remained, their lights bobbing. The waves were calm, breeze cool, and the evening perfect.

"I love this place," Davey said.

"It's incredible," I admitted. "I'd want to just work from home and never leave."

"You're not much for city life, then?"

"Oh, I love the city, too. I love London still. But, as I get older, I appreciate the quiet more. And now that I never have it, I want it even more."

I leaned back, bracing myself with my hands.

Davey looked over, then at my stomach.

"It's bad, yeah?" I laughed.

"It's good," Davey said. "I mean, it's progress, but... it's hard to hide in this shirt."

"Next week. Just let there be good news."

"Agreed."

It was awkward. A tension hung.

"I—" We both said.

"Sorry," I said. "I missed that."

"I wanted to ask you if I could just touch your stomach. If it's weird, I... don't have to. I'm just genuinely curious. Is it soft or firm? It looks firm, but... who knows?"

His interest surprised me. "Yeah, sure."

Davey put his hand on my stomach gently. "It's firm. Wild."

"That's mostly my stomach muscles," I said. "It's nothing impressive yet."

"The baby is the size of a plum," Davey said. "That's impressive enough to me. I cannot grow a damn thing."

"You researched it?"

"Yeah. I bought actual books," Davey answered. "Stupid, probably but—"

"No, you tried. I appreciate it."

I was glad he sought knowledge rather than me answering every question.

"You're not comfortable here," Davey murmured. "Eva, I would like you to be—"

"Why would I be? I do not belong here. Your mother made that much clear. And… I don't want to torture either of us with this game… it would never work."

Davey looked at me, hand still on my stomach.

"Tell me that you didn't enjoy it, Eva."

"What?"

"The kiss," he said. "Tell me you aren't thinking about it now."

"I… I…"

"You can't, Eva. Because we both enjoyed it."

"It wouldn't work. I'm getting big as a house. We work together. The whole thing is a fucking disaster! Why? Why can't you glom onto some hot, tall woman?"

"You are so caught up on not being attractive, but damn, Eva! You're gorgeous. You may be *built*, but you're beautiful."

"You don't prefer statuesque women?"

"I think maybe *you* do, but you are absolutely my type. I prefer shorty, curvy women with a big ass. You not only have a fabulous ass, but your tits are also amazing."

I flushed, something that lost in the moonlight.

"Did I get it right?"

"I like tall people—you want what you cannot have. You got that right."

"When I saw you across that bar with that creep bothering you, I fell *hard*. I don't get like this. You frustrate me to no end. You love to argue—I hate it. You also melt me when you finally unlatch the gate and let me in. Fucking you is addictive. I'd do it dozens more times—"

"Not like this," I said. "Davey, I'm—"

"Gorgeous?"

"Pregnant," I said, annoyed.

"So?"

I cocked my head. "You really don't care?"

"There is something remarkably sexy about it. I mean, I was the one who got you pregnant. Should I be embarrassed?"

I shook my head.

"Can I kiss you?"

He hit every note perfectly. His check-in put me at ease. The way he told me I was beautiful made me swoon. I lost myself to the base urge, ending up pinned to the sand as we kissed. It wasn't hungry like before. It was sweet and gentle. Davey looked at me.

"This isn't a power move, Eva. There isn't an agenda beyond me wanting you to give me a chance and for us to have a healthy relationship—whatever that looks like—for the sake of this kid. But, Eva, I cannot help but want more. I'm sorry."

The urge for more overcame me as I pressed his hand down my torso to my shorts. "Show me."

"What?" Davey said, confused.

"Get me off. I am... so desperate. Show me what you mean."

"If this is a test, I will ace it," Davey said.

"A new thing for you?" I teased as he slid his hand inside my running shorts and found my clit.

"Not the *first* time," he dipped one finger inside to pull out some of my wetness.

It was *so* good. I realized I might have reached the horny part of pregnancy where Ellie said reserves were low. Last night, I'd awoken on the verge of climax, and my drawer of vibrators were uncharged from six weeks of no use. Davey thrust two fingers inside, then three. I moaned too loudly.

"Shh," Davey said. "You don't want to let the house know."

"N...no," I breathed shakily.

"Your pussy is so wet." Davey kissed me. "And desperate. You're dirty, Eva."

"I'm... so horny," I pleaded. "Don't stop."

"Cum for me, baby," Davey whispered.

My body lit up with a crash of the waves. As if fireworks fired overhead, I came with my hand clasped over my mouth. I couldn't trust myself now. It just felt so good. Davey gave me another mind-blowing orgasm with nothing but his hand, leaving me breathless. I looked back at Davey, still weightless with pleasure, and noticed once more his boyish, satisfied grin—the same he'd had when he made me cum before.

"That's not enough." Davey's fingers slowly slipped from my pussy. "That's the problem."

"What?"

"I want more. Every time you cum, I want more, Eva."

"You cannot have more—not out here. I… I don't want to risk any of this."

"You think this is the first time people have ever hooked up at this retreat?"

"In your parents' house?" I asked.

"Eva, you make me desperate."

"We cannot fuck out here like this. And… if I go—"

"Come with me."

* * *

Davey

"Where are you dragging me?" Eva gasped.

"It's not far."

Every time I watched Eva's face as she climaxed, the more of her I craved. She gave over and her walls fell. I needed her, having gotten creative in hopes I'd break my weeks-long celibacy streak.

"Why are we on a pier?" Eva asked.

"We have a yacht," I answered.

Eva rolled her eyes, "Of *course* you do."

I ignored her judgement, finding our slip and climbing aboard. I looked around for the panel that controlled the cabin lock. The passcode was Dora's birthday.

"The *Lady Danna*. Original," Eva said.

I snickered. "Dad was nothing if not completely in love with my mother. Hence naming the ship after her."

"Yes, it's a *ship* not a *boat*."

"Correct." I opened the door and returned, holding my hand out to help her.

Eva looked around, shaking her head. "This thing… is… wild. Okay, where are we going?"

I led her below deck, flicking on the low galley lights and tracking back to the main stateroom. We hadn't taken the yacht out since my last visit a month before to park it here for fall.

"Does this work for you?" I asked.

"There is a bed. So, yes. I cannot believe I'm doing this."

I couldn't either. It was ridiculous. We were sneaking around— as if she wasn't already pregnant with my child. Once the news broke, it wouldn't matter. We'd be *those* people and able to fuck openly with no shame.

Eva settled on the bed and began to wiggle from her shorts. By now, I'd tossed mine aside, wasting no time. With finality, I tugged them off and whipped them across the room. I spread her legs, intending to eat her out.

"No, I… it's weird, right. You're… right there."

I popped back up. "Eva, I'm going to go down on you. I *have* to be right there."

"It's weird, should you?"

I didn't understand her concern. If this was about the obvious pregnancy, I didn't care.

"You're hot. I want to taste you. Let me get you off, Eva."

"I want you inside of me," Eva pleaded. "Now."

I wanted to taste her but gave up. If she wanted me inside, denying her was ungrateful.

"Are you good… have you slept with anyone else since me?" Eva asked as I crawled up, pressing my hard cock against her entrance.

"No," I answered.

"Really?" She rolled her hips, allowing me to settle at her center.

"Finding out I impregnated the incredibly hot woman I hooked up with three weeks before blinded me to anyone else," I said.

"You don't have to lie."

"I'm not lying."

I kissed her, wetness rolling across the head of my cock. Breath ragged, Eva wrapped her legs around me tightly, pulling my hungry cock into her pussy.

"Oh, fuck," I said. "You feel amazing."

"Better than last time?"

"Every time I enter you, it gets sweeter," I said as I thrust, basking in how the feeling hit.

She gasped. I ground into her again, eliciting a beautiful moan from her pretty pink lips.

"Fuck me," Eva pled. "You're so good. Your cock is…"

Her voice faded as she lost her sense of reason.

"Yeah? Is that what you want, baby?"

Eva bit her lip and nodded. As her hands went up my shirt and dug into my back, I watched her unwinding with obsessive excitement. She was *so* beautiful when she came and so appreciative.

"Cum for me, baby," I said. "Cum hard for me."

"Harder," Eva panted.

Obeying, I thrust harder and faster. Her head fell back as she moaned, then screamed, "Oh, yes, fuck me, Davey!"

It took a moment to conjure a "good girl" as she pulsed around my cock. Now that I was freely inside, no longer tortured by a too-small condom, I felt every moment of her orgasm—a whole body experience.

As I continued to fuck her, basking in the way her tits bounced beneath her shirt, I knew I wouldn't last.

"Fuck, Eva, I'm gonna cum," I moaned.

"Cum for me," she gasped.

As she said it, I exploded, pinning her to the bed. When I pulled back to take her in, a cheeky grin crossed her face.

"You good?" Eva asked.

"Yes," I panted. "So good."

I felt like fucking her might never get old.

18. AN OOPS

Eva

AFTER SEPARATELY RETURNING UNDER COVER OF DARKNESS, I FELL asleep with any pillows I could find. Pregnancy continued to kick my ass. I thought sleep might make me feel less uncomfortable or horny, but neither came true. I woke up thinking how much I wished I'd be dumb enough to run down to Davey's room and wake him. I didn't know how one person could grind my gears so much. Davey *terrified* me because when he signaled his desperation to have me, I folded like a house of cards. The sexual chemistry remained. Now, coupled with a growing bit of trust, I wanted more.

I climbed from bed and pulled on another flowy dress for day number two—corporate strategy session number one—to find my entire body changed overnight. What felt normal yesterday seemed gone forever. My stomach *exploded*. I gathered my dress below my stomach and nearly fell. Why now? I had two days left of this. I was three days shy of 13 weeks. *Thirteen weeks.* I needed to make it to the wedding and wear the same dress. I still needed to fool others at work for *weeks*.

I considered the *angles* of standing or sitting as I moved downstairs. I grabbed breakfast and sat at a patio table. As I drank my coffee and ate a beautiful pain au chocolate, I watched two boats sail from the harbor.

I was surprised after spotting Davey running up to the house via the dune that sheltered it. He trotted upstairs, staring directly at me as he did, stopping to catch his breath by the patio door. I tried *not* to look at him. I'd never remarked on Davey's thighs prior to this moment—for better or worse—but they were *impressive*. He dabbed his brow with his t-shirt revealing abs that made me weak.

"You doing okay?" Davey panted. "You look… off."

"I'm fine," I answered. "You are… barefoot."

"I like running barefoot for a couple miles in the morning when I'm up here."

Weirdo.

"You're not eating inside with everyone, Eva?" He wiped his brow—more abs.

"I've been enjoying the boats on the horizon," I said. "I'll go in by the time we start. I'm just enjoying the weather."

"Oh, okay. We're good?"

I rolled my eyes. "We're good. Very good."

Why did I say it like that?

"Great," Davey's sneaky smile crossed his face.

"I should smack you," I snickered.

"That wouldn't teach me any lessons, Eva."

Oof! I could only think about what it felt like to ride his face and how I should have just let him eat me out last night rather than get all self-conscious.

"I gotta go shower," Davey thumbed his chin. "And shave."

"You could shave… or nah?" I shrugged. "Be lazy?"

"Ah, you *do* have a preference about facial hair," Davey's voice slowly trailed as his eyes fixed on something.

I turned to the point he stared at. Lady Danna circulated in the living room.

"I should go," Davey said. "Later, okay?"

"Okay," I agreed.

As Davey entered the house, Chloe emerged, carrying a massive coffee mug.

"Watch out," she said, "because the party people have arrived."

I snickered. "For a bunch of old people, they go hard."

"I hope I'm that interesting in my seventies."

I laughed.

"Oh, there is the darling Eva Pavlak!" Norm announced, finding his way out as if on cue.

"Norm. How are you?" I asked.

"Good," Norm said. "While you all strategize, I'm going on a wine tour with the other less-important people."

"Don't do anything I wouldn't do, Norm," Chloe said.

"You're the fun Markham," Norm declared.

"Tell Cal that," she said. "Although, he will be even *less* fun soon. Daphne was having contractions last night. Who knows if we'll have a baby soon."

"That's mildly terrifying," Norm shivered.

I reacted internally, crossing all my fingers and toes that no one looked at my stomach as I stood to fetch my second allowable cup of coffee and thought the Delphines might be doubly blessed in short time. I held my empty coffee mug over my stomach like a sitcom actress might if hiding a pregnancy.

As I passed through the French doors opening into the living room, our CFO strode out like he was on fire, knocking into me. My coffee and plate flew, as did I, tripping and falling flat onto my stomach with a thud on the marble floor. I tried to stop myself with my wrist and failed. It smarted and pain surged. Nervously, I rolled over, spying his panicked face. His fear was nothing in comparison to the worry within me. My wrist ached but that wasn't the real reason for concern. If a simple fall had cost me my chance at motherhood, I'd be heartbroken.

Daphne rushed over, ducking down slowly. "Oh my God! Are you okay, Eva?"

"Daph, get up before I have to hoist you," Lanie pleaded. "Good God, woman, I am sure Eva is fine."

I sat up awkwardly. I realized my stomach muscles didn't work like they used to, and I was reliant on my left wrist only as my right was fucked.

"You fell awkwardly," Daphne said. "We should get you to the doctor."

"Nonsense, Daphne. She's not made of glass!" Danna's stiff-upper-lip-ness showed..

"This is not a 'rub dirt on it' situation, mother!" Daphne said. "Come on. Lanie, help me up!"

"Cal! Come hoist your wife!" Lanie shouted. "She's again decided to get herself stuck down on the ground."

"For fuck's sake, Daphne!" Cal grumbled. "Why do you keep getting in these predicaments?"

"Eva fell." Daphne took Cal's hand.

Bob Lawrence, our CFO, stared in disbelief. "Oh, Eva, I feel terrible. I was focused on something else. Are you okay?"

"It was an accident," I said. "My right hand is really screwed up."

"Oh, God!" Bob panicked, holding his hand to assist me to my feet.

"You should see a doctor," Daphne said. "I'll take you."

"We have a strategy session," I protested.

"Your *wrist* is more important than that." Daphne knew my worries.

"I suppose," I said.

I needed to go but not by myself. Unfortunately, I'd have to get creative because Davey was off-limits.

"Can someone let David know that I'm going to go to the hospital? So, he doesn't think I blew this off? I swear I don't hate strategic planning *that* much," I joked.

"No one would think that," Claire assured.

"I'll tell him," Daphne said, already gone.

* * *

Davey

"Davey! Davey! David!"

I opened my bedroom door a crack to find my sister, face white as a sheet.

"What? Are you in labor?" I asked.

"No! Eva needs to go to the hospital," Daphne said.

Now, *I* panicked. "What!?"

"Bob bumped her, and she fell on the tile floor. She needs to go to the hospital."

"Shit! The baby!" I immediately wanted to die.

Why did you do that, David?

"You know?"

"About the baby? Yes," I furrowed my brow. "Yes, of course."

"Why would she tell you? Did you shame her out of this?"

I couldn't answer her. I deflected.

"I need to put on pants, Daph. Give me a second."

I slammed the door, rushing through halfway presentable dress. What did I say? I needed to go to the hospital with her, right? If I volunteered—as CEO—it would be obvious something else was going on. My sister was already suspicious. She didn't buy Eva confiding in me.

"David, you are not supposed to say anything. Did HR tell you something? Oh my God! I'm going to go get Sandy and—"

I opened the door, buttoning my shirt. "No. HR didn't tell me anything. Has she left yet? Can I go with her?"

"What?"

"I cannot get into this right now, Daphne," I sighed. "Handle the strategy session."

"David, it is *your* company."

"Right now, it's *your* strategic plan. I'll explain later," I finished buttoning my shirt.

I rolled my sleeves, ignoring all as I rushed past Daphne to find Eva speaking with Mum and Lanie about hospitals.

"I would say go to Harbor Country," Mum said. "It's a small hospital, but they will fix up your wrist well enough."

Daphne caught up, still hopping mad, but compassionate as ever.

"No. She should go to Michigan City," Daphne said. "They have a better hospital—a *full-service* hospital."

I had no idea what that meant, but I figured Daphne did.

"Why does that matter?"

"I don't know. I'm maybe paranoid, but my OB told me that if something happened, I needed to go there if I couldn't make it to Chicago in time."

It made sense.

"She's not delivering a baby, Daphne!"

Not yet.

"It's better imaging equipment and such," Daphne said.

"Mum, I agree," Lanie said. "Makes more sense."

"I can go with," Daphne offered.

I shook my head. "No. I'll take her. You all should stay and map out strategy. I'm… I will make sure she's okay."

"That's ridiculous!" Mum threw her hands up.

"I'm going," I said, unwilling to argue.

I watched relief wash across Eva's face.

"Eva, I'll drive you down there," I grabbed my keys off the sideboard by the front door. "C'mon. Daphne will manage the strategy session."

Daphne set her jaw, annoyed. I could just hear her saying, "You better have a good reason for this, David, Jr."

Eva said little, following me to my car in a trance. She climbed in.

"Top up or down?" I asked.

She glared. I knew the answer was *up*. What sort of question was that anyway? She probably felt like she was off to sudden doom and here I was worrying about my convertible.

"It's… I just want to make it easier on you. I am sure it is—"

"No, David. Don't talk to me right now," Eva said. "We're fucked. Everything about this is fucked. And if we lose this baby—"

"We won't," I said. "This is going to work out, baby."

"Davey, what if we just went through hell—what if we just threw ourselves under the bus—for nothing."

"It's not. It's... we'll be fine." If I said it enough, it would be true.

19.DOUBLE OOPS

Eva

I ARRIVED AT THE HOSPITAL ER ENTRANCE ALONE AND CONFUSED. We were 40 minutes from my front door, but a world away mentally. While Davey parked his ridiculous car as far out as he could to protect its precious paint job from door dings—the horror—I walked to the reception desk. A surly man in green scrubs greeted me. *Oh, joy!*

"Hi," I said. "I've got a potentially broken wrist—"

He cut me off and handed me a clipboard. "It's going to take half a day probably. We have a line."

I turned to see a packed ER.

"Sorry," I said. "I didn't finish. I'm 12 weeks and 4 days pregnant and just had a spill. I landed on my stomach. I need to see someone."

"Oh…" His concern replaced antipathy. "I will have to call L&D and see if they want you up there first. Just wait a minute."

I stood there nervously as Davey appeared, breathless. "Is everything okay?"

"I'm waiting. The intake guy had to call up to the maternity ward. They may want me up there, I guess?"

"Oh," Davey said. "This is that serious?"

"It is," I said, annoyed.

"I'm sorry. I'm panicked, Eva. I'm… not myself. All I want is for you and the baby to be okay."

I squeezed his hand with my good hand. "I know. I'm also panicking. I'm not in a great place."

He rubbed my back. "It's okay. I'm… I'm so sorry."

Comforted, I rested my head on his shoulder.

The nurse returned. "L&D will check you out first. They'll transfer you to imaging afterwards."

He gave us directions and pointed.

"I hope you got that," I said. "Because I'm zoning out."

"I got it," Davey confirmed, leading me to an elevator. "Fifth floor. Turn left at the first hallway."

We said nothing on the way. When we arrived, my voice didn't come. Thankfully, Davey was calmer. For the first time since I met him, he wasn't losing it in a high-pressure situation.

"Hi. This is Eva. She's due February 6th. She had a fall after one of our coworkers ran into her. She fell hard, and needs checked out."

I nodded.

A perky redhead smiled. "Oh, that's right. Almost thirteen weeks. I think you're probably okay, but we're going to check. Come with me and we'll get you an ultrasound."

"Thanks," I squeaked.

Davey stopped. "Do you want me in there? Am I allowed to be in your room?"

"Are you the dad?" The nurse asked.

"Yes. But we're not… together. Not really. I'm just here for support."

"Of course. You can be here as her support person. No worries."

She helped me with a gown. Davey tucked me in with a blanket she left on the bed—burrito-ing me. Then, citing germs, he nervously wiped down every surface with antibacterial wipes he found in a cabinet. His germaphobia was not borne out of selfishness, but concern. God, why was he earning so many points? Did men magically change after a round of good sex? Then, continuing to win, Davey took down all my information on the intake form since I had a busted right hand.

"This is why you gotta be left-handed," Davey joked.

Soon an even *more* attractive blonde arrived, and they wheeled me off to the ultrasound room. The nurse left me in the hallway. I watched Davey watch her leave, unable to avoid a snicker.

"What?" He asked.

"You're watching her walk away."

Davey blushed.

"I'm *not* judging. It's like the nurses on that ward were all pulled off a Hollywood medical drama set. I was only paranoid she *was* the ultrasound tech, and I was about to have the fun of her giving me the most awkward ultrasound on the face of the earth."

"So, we share a type?" Davey asked.

"We've established she's not tall enough, but I wouldn't say she's ugly. Look, I don't fault you for looking, just please refrain from hitting on people in front of me. I'd ask for a *bit* of common decency. I'd grant you the same, but I'm guessing she's straight."

"How do you know?"

"Vibes. I don't know. Tread carefully."

"I won't hit on women in front of you, Eva," Davey agreed. "I'm trying to be a reformed bad boy, not a dick to you. Besides, after last night, you are heads and tails above the competition."

That warmed my heart more than I wanted to admit.

"Evangeline Pav-lack?" A woman called.

"Here," I answered, not even correcting her.

"Alright, we're going to do your scan before we send you over to imaging for an x-ray on that hand of yours."

"Great," I said.

"Can she have an x-ray while pregnant?" Davey nervously asked.

"Yes. It is safe. We will cover her up well. Promise. An OB is monitoring all of this. She's in good hands."

It was a Catholic hospital, so I was concerned if that was true or not, but it was the best I could do. Driving back to Chicago felt like a chore, but I sensed Davey wouldn't have resisted if asked. He was wildly protective.

"Should I take my panties off?" I asked.

"Let's try to get a picture externally first," the tech said.

I breathed deeply. Last time, we'd started this way, only to switch to the dildo wand of doom so I could learn everything was over. My world once came crashing down in a room like this. As my heart beat out of my chest, the tech squirted ultrasound gel on my growing stomach. I looked away, catching Davey's gaze. He held my good hand tight and lovingly tucked hair behind my ear. My curls from earlier fell in the humidity on the way here.

"Well, here's a nice little heartbeat," the tech said. "Good for the gestation."

I turned back to the screen as she took photos. Sure enough, I saw a baby looking very much like a baby with a proper beating heart. Last time I made it here, a stunted fetus with no activity looked back at me. Tears welled in my eyes as relief set in. As I breathed again, the tech began scrolling. I realized something was amiss from her confused face.

"I'm just going to go get someone quick," she said. "No need to panic."

Of *course* I was fucking panicking!

"It's going to be fine," Davey reiterated.

The tech returned with someone else a few excruciating minutes later.

"So, I see worried faces," the man said. "Deep breaths. I'm Dr. Wallace and Alyssa identified something but there is no need to panic."

"See. Deep breaths," Davey said.

"They won't tell us until they know beyond any doubt there is a reason to panic," I said, now crying sad tears.

"There is the second sac." The doctor pointed. "You are correct."

"Second?" I gasped. "Second sac?"

"It was hiding. But the placenta... that's the concern."

"Looking here..." The doctor swirled the ultrasound wand on my stomach. "That's the giveaway. It's Mo-Di."

"In English?" Davey asked. "What are you saying?"

"Sorry," The doctor said. "These are Monochorionic-Diamniotic twins. That means they share a placenta but separate sacs. That is preferable to sharing both. Alyssa couldn't confirm the separation, but she has now."

"I'm sorry, but... what the fuck? Are you saying it's twins?" I asked.

"It's twins. Identical twins," Alyssa said. "Congrats!"

* * *

Davey

Identical twins. That wasn't on the list of expectations I had for struggling through a leadership retreat with the employee I'd impregnated and fucked on the family yacht last night for fun. *Two* babies? What business did I have with one baby—let alone two. Eva sobbed. I couldn't confirm based on her face whether these were happy or sad tears.

"So, let's get you to x-ray," the tech said. "Dad, I can print some pictures. You cannot go back with her, but you can wait in the hall."

"Sure," I murmured.

As the medical team x-rayed the hand of my crying not-girlfriend, I sat silent. Fear filled me, but I had hope as I reviewed the pictures of our two babies. They possessed her delicate nose and my more prominent chin. Two babies. How was it possible I could already know what they looked like and missed a whole second human on the first scan? All the doctor said was "it often happens with a shared placenta". That didn't satisfy me.

As the hot nurse rolled Eva back in from X-ray she lit up.

Maybe it was just the hot nurse? Shared ogling with a sexual partner was a new experience.

"So, you had a surprise?" The nurse asked in a sing-song way. "How was that?"

"It was definitely surprising," I admitted.

"A two-fer," Eva noted.

The nurse tucked Eva back into her room and I took a seat once more. Down the hall, I heard a woman screaming in pain. Unnerved, I said nothing.

"You're… okay, right?" Eva asked.

"I mean, what can I do?"

"It will be okay," Eva said. "But you win. We're hiring a nanny."

"Small miracles," I muttered as my phone rang.

"It's Daphne," I said.

"Answer it," Eva confirmed.

"Yes?" I picked up.

"I sent everyone to the winery and made some excuse about moving the thing," Daphne said.

"That's smart."

"So, how is Eva?"

"She's fine."

"And the baby?"

"Also fine. We're waiting to hear about her arm."

"You want to confess something to me right now or wait?" Daphne asked.

"I will speak with you when I return. I appreciate you handling this. Is Mum enraged?"

"To say she is enraged would be an understatement but ignore her. It's me and the board you should fear, David Robert."

I winced. "I will take my lumps. Promise."

I turned back to the only person I cared about. Eva's gaze shifted to her stomach. She rubbed her belly lovingly. This woman *wanted* this. And in a way, I did, too. The stunning admission that it was two and not one was a lot, but everything within me wanted to protect all three.

"Don't make me kill you."

"I'd like to be here for at least a few more months," I sighed. "Don't go into labor over this."

"For real. How will you plug the well without me covering your ass?"

"I will grow up," I answered. "That's all I can promise you."

20. TAKING LUMPS

Davey

"I NEED ANSWERS AND EXPLANATIONS," DAPHNE SAID. "AND I NEED them from you, asshole."

We sat in my father's old office, piecing together a strategy to deal with this.

"Do you want me to begin at the start and explain the nitty-gritty or—"

"I want to know how you impregnated my employee, yes. What the fuck, Davey? The timeline *does not* work. And you were such an asshole to her—"

"Fine, you asked for it," I said. "I met Eva at a bar. She was overseeing her best friend's bachelorette party. I sort of ran into her, found her cute, and… we hooked up."

"So, you just willy-nilly think it's cool to have unprotected sex? That's so stupid, Davey!"

I did *not* need a lesson from my baby sister on wrapping it up right now.

"Daph, the condom broke. I went out and bought her Plan B. It didn't work. Then, she decided to block my number. She sorta freaked out. It upset me. That's why I was an ass."

"So, she's a conquest?"

137

I balled my fists. "Can you stop it with the fucking accusations, Daph? No. She's not. I care a lot about her. I am obsessed with her, in fact. She's gorgeous. I find her addictive. Is that what you want to hear? That I'm completely wrapped up in a woman I have no business with—one who probably doesn't want me? That we've been hiding it because she's terrified of you firing her?"

"I should fire *you*. I have the votes and everyone is here!"

"Fine, try it," I sighed. "Daphne, I'm so tired. So fucking tired."

"You're tired? I'm cleaning up your fucking mess right now while about to pop! I'm worried about your ability to manage the company—"

"I can manage the company," I assured. "I did it before you. I'll do it for a few months without you, damn it! And you should be relieved. I wanted to IPO. This will kill those chances the minute my philandering gets out."

"You wanted to IPO? You wanted to take Dad's company *public*?"

I winced. "I told you I was being honest."

"No. I won't permit it. That's a hornet's nest. Why would you want that?"

"I'd rather take my chances with shareholders—"

"Why?"

"Daphne, I hate this job. Honestly, you're better at it," I said. "I fought you tooth and nail for it. I wanted to be good at it, but even Dad knew better."

Face sympathetic, Daphne sat on the desk's edge, defeated.

"What? You don't want to be CEO now? You wanted my head on a spit a year ago, sister."

"I... I like to win a fair fight. And anyway, that's not what I need right now. I need to be able to sleep—"

"I can hold the well. You've done a great job. This acquisition with the sustainable building firm will wrap up in a couple of weeks. But I don't know what I want to do. Everything is up in the air, Daphne."

"Yes. We're both having babies. Are you planning to parent or just cut a check?"

I paced. I wanted to scream at my sister but knew doing so only made me look like a monster. I remembered Eva's words about my only emotion being anger and took a deep breath.

"Daphne, I plan to parent these babies—to be a good father like Dad was to us. Don't throw that at me. It hurts. I have been there with Eva for every appointment. She fought me at first, but she's coming around."

"But you aren't together?"

"Not right now—not really."

I wish.

"Are you still sleeping with her?"

"Consistently?"

"Oh, good God, Davey! I cannot even with this!" Daphne threw her hands up. "What the hell are we going to do?"

"She doesn't report directly to me. There are no *policies*. As well as we are clear about this, legal will look the other way. HR will, too. We just cannot fire her. But given that I'm going to be paying child support to the tune of who even knows, I think it would be hard to say I was treating her poorly."

"But if people—people like Claire—see favoritism, you could also be in trouble."

"That is why I am not supervising her," I said. "What else can I do? Resign?"

In a way, that would be a relief. Suddenly, I wanted nothing to do with it all.

"Not right now. That's everything I don't need. No, you will take your lumps, tell everyone how much you love this woman you didn't know I was going to hire, and move on. You will be a father to that baby. You will take time off to help her. And you will support her. After all of that, we can talk about the next steps."

"Fine," I sighed. "And Mum?"

"You're left to swing in the wind there. Protect Eva. Mum is on a warpath. I told Delanie to stand by her and fight Mum if necessary. She's not happy."

"Eva is a wonderful woman," I said. "She should be grateful."

"Trust me, I'm glad you knocked up someone with a brain if you knocked anyone up, but Davey, this wasn't what Mum wanted. It was bad enough me getting pregnant while engaged. She shit a brick. This is *far* worse. She *works* for you. She's not even remotely from our social circle. It's bad."

"She's more than I deserve. Everyone can fuck off if they don't want to accept her—that includes Mum," I roared. "And you... of all people... to throw Eva under the bus? How dare you!"

Daphne stepped forward, pregnant rage palpable. "I am never going to complain about Eva, okay? I think she's *definitely* too good for you, brother. However, it *looks* bad. And you know nothing about her family. If you think Mum is conservative, good fucking luck!"

I didn't know what that meant. Eva was out as bi, right? She was also close to her parents. That felt like an empty threat. It would be fine. Everyone would get on board.

"The line is that you're in love with her. That you fell for her before she came on. The baby is an oops, but we don't have to say that—they'll understand it. You two are taking it in stride. You'll plan to leave when I return to the office."

"Daph, it's *babies*," I said. "We're having twins. Which means, she's actually due in the new year."

Daphne's mouth dropped. "Tw-twins?"

"Yeah They missed them on the first ultrasound. But that's what we just found out today. And while Eva is wild about it, I'm... I'm still wrapping my head around somehow being a father to *two* babies instantly. Her pregnancy has gotten infinitely more complicated. We cannot just hide this. The press will find out. She's going to be *huge* soon."

"Oh, I'm sorry! I hope her body doesn't disgust you too much, brother! Never say that—"

It didn't. I found her sexy as hell.

"It's not that. Jesus! Why does everyone assume I mean the worst!? I'm speaking in practicalities, Daphne. She's gorgeous. To me, she's fucking perfect. That's not it. This is for fear of reputation—of the company. I'll take the hit personally. But we cannot slow ease into this the way I thought we could."

"Well, you've got a room full of people who want an explanation. I will not speak over you. I won't be your adversary, Davey. We need to project strength."

"I'm quite aware," I said. "But I must speak to Eva first. Because if I proclaim my love for her in front of our entire leadership team, it's going to freak her the fuck out."

"Fine," Daphne said. "She's in the drawing room. You are treading on the thinnest of ice, brother."

Don't I know it!

* * *

Eva

I got nosey during my exile to the drawing room. With an arm in a sling, I spied something in the corner on a mahogany writing desk I doubt anyone used. A series of family photos in heavy silver frames sat on it. My mother would have been envious of how nice they looked. I filed silver frames away as a Christmas present idea, praying I still had a job in December. I observed these normal family photos—starkly contrasting to the dining room's massive family portrait. There, the family presented as the royals might—if royals casually gathered on the shore of their private beach for a portrait. An elegant oval frame held a photo of a beautiful woman in an off-the-shoulder dress looking out a window. I figured that was Lady Danna in her prime. If so, it made sense why Lanie and Dora, her mini-mes, had such presence. Another photo showed Daphne and Cal on their wedding day.

Finally, a larger rectangular frame held a photo of Davey's father on the phone in his office—a place I recognized—

surrounded by his brood. Teen Davey and Daphne camped out on the floor—Daphne on a laptop and Davey leaning over, pointing at something. Dahlia read on the couch. The brother I'd yet to meet, Derrick, played on a gaming system nearby. Delanie played with a car at the foot of the desk near Daphne. In David's lap sat a fat, chubby baby eating something. It had to be little Dora.

"Eva?"

Fear shot down my spine as Lady Danna approached.

"Yes?"

She gently plucked the frame from my hands.

She smiled and cooed, "Oh, this one. It's one of my favorites. Daphne has another one like it up at home. I took it when they were all there."

"Your husband had all of them in his office at once?" I asked. "Was that... a normal thing?"

"We were hit with a bad storm," Danna explained. "The kids were all out of school. I'd not slept in days since the baby was up about five times in the night. Well, David let me sleep. He didn't wake me, just packed them all off to work. He bundled them up and Davey and Daphne helped herd the little ones. Davey pulled Dora and Delanie in a sled there per what I was told. David kept them all morning until the staff told me what he'd done. I was concerned. By then, the roads were passable enough. So, I went to collect them."

I smiled. "That is sweet. He didn't mind?"

"Our lives were chaos, darling. Six children is madness. And Lanie was supposed to be our last baby, but... fate had other plans. David never complained—not once—when they had nowhere to go. They'd wind up there after school. Davey and Daphne were common sights in that building. Their school wasn't far off. The man had the patience of a saint. The joke was he closed more deals with a baby on his knee than any other man in the business."

"That's so adorable. Everyone says the sweetest things about him."

"He wasn't perfect, but he was ours—all ours. He'd do anything to protect us. It has been difficult on all the kids. They lost their biggest champion. And Davey..." Danna shook her head. "Well, he's struggled the most. He lacks direction. Daphne struggled through a divorce, but she is so ambitious. Davey is... cocky, but projects because he's insecure. The others didn't rely as much on their father. They never wanted to work for the business."

I snickered at that assessment. "I'm sorry, but you just confirmed something for me."

Danna set the picture down, turning back. "Why my son?"

Once more, words failed. "I... I..."

"You do not have to tell me. I realized something was going on the day before yesterday. Davey was... preoccupied with you. He got defensive at dinner. He doesn't do that unless he's invested."

"It's complicated," I said.

"Everything with you young people is complicated! There is very little in common between you two."

"Well, perhaps, Lady Danna, it's better to ask your son why he has come onto *me*?"

I recognized that face from when Daphne would put someone in their place.

She set her jaw. "Darling, you take offense, but you shouldn't. You're ambitious and clever. He likes pretty girls, yes, but you're not his average date. You're *too* bright."

"Davey isn't my type, either," I said. "When I met him, I had no idea who he was. Daphne and I are friends, but I never met any of the rest of you. We just met at a bar and... that's how it started. I didn't intend to throw myself at him or anything. Dating the boss isn't my thing."

"What *is* your type?"

I grimaced. She was the overly involved mother who would doubt a woman who didn't find her precious son attractive.

"What? It cannot be that embarrassing!"

I opened my mouth but stopped as the door opened. I was saved by Davey's arrival.

"Mother, I need to speak to Eva."

"Well, I must speak with you," Danna said.

"No. Not until I speak with Eva and leadership. Then, you can let me have it," Davey said.

They exchanged the steeliest of glances before she reluctantly disappeared, closing the door. Davey approached, rubbing my shoulders.

"Eva, I am sorry if she said something—"

"We were talking about happy old memories," I said. "It's okay. She wasn't rude."

Davey kissed my forehead. "I'm sorry. For all of this, let me just apologize."

"What is happening?"

"I am about to beg for mercy in front of everyone," Davey said. "And I wanted to explain to you what will happen. It *will* affect you."

"Okay, so how?"

"I have to make up a story about how much I'm in love with you. It needs to look much more innocent than it began."

"Oh," I said. "Well, I'm sorry you have to pretend to like me."

"Eva, I don't have to pretend to like you. I do. I like you a lot. I *adore* you." Davey pulled my chin towards his gaze. "It won't be hard to make it believable, but, I don't want to freak you out. I will smooth everything over on your behalf. I am taking all of this on the chin. Don't panic. Focus on you."

"This is a disaster. Claire is—"

"If Claire says boo, I will fire her," Davey said. "But she won't. She likes you more than she likes me."

I snickered.

"Are you okay with the ruse?"

I shrugged. "It probably would make the medicine go down better. Whatever we must do."

* * *

Davey

"So, given the events of today, I must explain my situation," Davey said. "This matter that will be… uncomfortable. All I ask is that you consider that it involves someone else in this room."

How did anyone say with credibility that they knocked up their sister's direct report but didn't know who she was? On top of that, I had to lie that I was in love with her all while I felt her internal cringe from across the room.

"Miss Pavlak was rushed off this morning for her wrist but also out of an abundance of caution for her well-being," I explained. "And I've had some questions about why *I* went with her and rescheduled the strategy session. Well, I am going to answer all of that."

"Obviously, you two are in a relationship," Norm said. "I knew that from when you brought her to dinner."

"Wait, how?" I asked.

"You left with her," Norm said.

"I… I brought her home. I can assure you that was all very innocent."

Norm crossed his arms.

"Are you in a relationship with my direct report, David?" Claire demanded with a frightening glare.

"Yes, but it wasn't my intent to date your direct report. See, a funny thing happened."

"Funny?" Our head general counsel wanted to kill me.

"He didn't know who I was. I didn't know he was Daphne's brother." Eva valiantly bailed me out. "He was a guy I met while out with friends. It was all very Shakespearean and innocent like he said."

Innocent. Was a broken condom and a resulting couple of kids innocent? Was making a strange woman cum on your hand in a men's room quaint?

Under her expectant gaze, I cleared my throat. "So, when she appeared on day one, neither of us was sure how to act."

"Is that why you've been so cold to her?" Claire asked.

No, I've just been an asshole, and she barely tolerates me.

"Yes," I said. "I actually love Eva, so that is difficult."

The words rolled off my tongue effortlessly. This conversation pained me, but the words didn't. I tested the waters.

"We figured we'd just ignore it. And given that I've been *very* clear with Daphne about Eva reporting to Daphne and you, Claire, I have stayed out of it. I intend to do the same. We will remain professional."

Eva nodded.

"So, why did you feel the need to tell us?" Norm wondered. "Bosses date their employees all the time, Davey."

"Yes, well, there's more," I moved uneasily on the balls of my feet. "Eva is pregnant. And while that is a bit of a *surprise*, it's... well, it's happening so, when she fell—"

"Oh my God," Bob said. "Eva, I am even more aggrieved. Are you sure you're okay?"

Eva smiled. "Everything is good—minus the sprain."

I wanted to rush through the rest, crawl into a hole, and die. "I know there will be some logistics to clear up. I will take leave shortly after Daphne returns. We will work everything out in the coming months."

"There will be continuity," Daphne insisted. "I will step up to fill the role of CEO in the interim."

"Correct," I agreed.

She said it with such pride, even *my* heart swelled.

Claire did the math. "Eva, you're *sixteen* weeks pregnant or thereabouts?"

"I'm almost thirteen," Eva said. "We weren't planning on telling anyone."

"But why so soon?"

"I'm having twins," Eva answered. "Which is why, returning from the hospital, we needed a moment. They didn't see the second baby until they were checking me for any issues. Thankfully, both are fine. But they are going to deliver me by thirty-six weeks."

"Three babies in a few months," Norm said. "The office will be busy. Your father would approve."

I smiled. It was bittersweet because I knew there was nothing more Dad would have wanted than to be surrounded by a bevy of rambunctious grandkids. My only regret in that moment was that Dad would never meet our children—he'd never know them. It wasn't how they came to be. It wasn't the complication. It was how much I missed him. In truth, he would have loved Eva. She'd have charmed him with her dry sense of humor but would never meet him. Grief hit.

Daphne saw it, probably felt it, too. "It's hard. Sometimes, I feel like he's still around. And while life is wild, we're a family company—we're not a public company. So, in situations like this—unexpected, wonderful ones—we pull together, right?"

"Right," I agreed. "You cannot keep a Delphine down."

21.DECLARATIONS

Eva

Feet leaden, I processed into my parents' kitchen to the smell of lasagna, which would be a treat under any other circumstance. Though bruised and battered, it was time to come clean.

Mom was making a salad.

She turned as I entered, her face pulling in concern. "Eva! My God! What happened?"

"Another exec bumped me," I said. "I went down and sprained my wrist. It'll take a while to heal, but I'll be back to normal soon."

"Bert!" Mom called towards the living room. "Come help Eva!"

Dad popped his head out. "Well, shit, Eva!"

"I sprained my wrist. I cannot really carry my bags and handle that door."

I also wasn't allowed to lift something so heavy anymore. I had *restrictions.*

"Sure, sure. I will help the walking wounded."

"Sit, sit," Mom said. "You need to rest."

I sat at the kitchen table as she took out the lasagna. Dad hauled in my luggage, bringing it upstairs.

"Do you have to see a doctor?" Mom asked.

"I went to the hospital. They referred me to an ortho person in the city. I've got a couple appointments lined up. I'm off tomorrow. I have an appointment with a specialist. I promise it will heal."

"A specialist!?"

Dad came back down.

"Bert! She's gotta see a specialist!"

"Well, kid, what did you do?"

"It was an accident. I got taken out by a colleague. He feels terrible."

"Go sit. I will bring the food in." Mom shooed us into the dining room.

With a heaping hunk of lasagna on my plate, I knew it was time to come clean.

"So, I need to go to the doctor tomorrow, but it's not for my wrist."

Mom and Dad stared at me dead on.

"I'm pregnant," I said. "And I'm thirteen weeks. So, we're doing an ultrasound tomorrow."

"What?" Dad said.

"It was... an accident of sorts—a happy accident."

"How?" Mom asked. "How did you get pregnant... by accident?"

"The typical way," Dad said. "I'm assuming?"

"But she doesn't... you know... with men."

"Mom!" I laughed. "Oh my God, yes. I do. It's been awhile, but... there was a guy. Something happened despite our best efforts, and now I'm pregnant. We're committed to co-parenting."

"I am... I'm going to need a minute," Mom said.

"Does he at least have a job? Can he support you?" Dad asked.

"I can support myself, but he does have a job. And a house. And several cars," I said. "It will be okay."

"Several cars?" Dad asked.

"Well, he's kind of rich. Long story. I.. I don't—"

"Who is this man?" Mom asked.

"It doesn't matter."

"Well, are you dating him?" Mom demanded.

"Not... quite," I winced. "Look, it's complicated. We're not together—not in a permanent sense—but we're trying to make it work. The point is that he loves the babies, not that we're obsessed with one another. Maybe that would happen? I dunno."

"Babies?" Mom and Dad asked in unison.

"It's twins. Mo-Di twins, which basically just means they share a placenta but are otherwise separate. They are identical. Tomorrow, we'll ensure everything is perfect and find out the sex if we decide we still want to. He paid for the fancy test."

No response came, just open-mouth silence.

"Uh, so yeah. I hope you will accept that. I'm a grown-up and I want to have these babies. I think we'll be okay. There's a lot of questions I don't have answers to, but they won't let me go past early January—and I hope you will love these babies just as you will Brooke's kids."

Dad squeezed my hand. "I cannot imagine a world in which we don't love your children, Eva. It's just... a shock. Why didn't you tell us?"

"I worried you'd be angry. And after his mother verbally abused him for an hour for it a couple days ago, you can understand my concern."

I realized I'd given it away.

"His mother? Wait... is this one of the Delphine's?" Mom asked.

"It's David," I answered. "Davey is what we all call him, but... yes."

"You're having your boss's baby?" Dad laughed heartily. "Eva, that is nuts! Kiddo, you weren't the one I expected that from."

"We met before I worked there. I didn't know who he was—beyond Davey." I shrugged. "He wanted to date me. I ran away. I wasn't—and still probably am not—ready for something major, but here we are. He's been sweet even when I haven't been."

"He better be so you don't sue him for millions," Dad said.

"Dad, it's not like that. When I told him, he completely stepped up. I didn't even want him to, but he did."

"When is he going to come over and speak to us face-to-face?" Mom asked.

"He wanted to come. I didn't want his identity to complicate things."

"And where will you live?"

I winced. "I'm not sure. We have a lot to discuss, but it will work out. He wants to buy me a car, and we had an argument about that yesterday. I want to sort that out first."

"Why are you arguing about a car? He wants to *buy* you a car and you're complaining with him?" Mom laughed. "It's the *least* he could do. His family is worth billions. Let him do it."

I groaned. "I hate that. I can buy my own car. The truck is—"

"Not safety rated. You're carrying two babies. We need to get a car for you. I agree with him there. Until then, I'm driving you to the station and back," Dad said. "Because I don't trust that thing. It doesn't even have airbags."

Davey would have lost his shit if he knew that. And, for once, I agreed the men in my life were probably right.

"I will tell him," I said. "But Dad, he's the one buying—"

"I'm coming, too," Dad said. "It will be good to meet the man who suddenly shook your entire life up."

"And ruined your reputation," Mom sighed. "Eva, is this really the right thing?"

"Mom, you're a *good* Catholic."

"I'm also a realist. Although, at least it appears he is *trying*. No wonder his mother is angry. This is her second child to conceive children out of wedlock."

I snickered. "Oh, he heard *all* about that. To my surprise, she was much nicer to me *after* she found out I was pregnant with her grandchildren than she was with her son."

"Better that way," Mom glared at Dad. "Better than having your mother-in-law become distraught at the news of any of your pregnancies."

"My mother wasn't happy to hear about either of you," Dad

snickered. "I always had to protect your mom. Hopefully Richie Rich takes that approach to protecting you, too."

"I think he will," I agreed. "Whether I like it or not."

* * *

It felt good to finally hop in the pool on a hot, humid August evening without a care in the world. I didn't have to cover anything. I felt free as I lounged in a bikini, my stomach on full display. Every day, it grew slightly—further fucking up my back. As I floated on a pool float, Ellie's head popped up the steps.

"I brought sparkling alcohol-free wine," Ellie said.

I laughed. "Don't tell me you drank the water."

"Hell no. We're done," Ellie said. "Mike is perfectly happy the way we are, and I think that's beautiful. Speaking of beautiful—"

She poured two glasses. "You are *glowing*, Eva. And that belly! What a difference a week makes!"

"I exploded. I am so relieved I could finally say something," I sighed. "Not without issues. And I am sure Brooke will shit a brick. I've asked Mom and Dad not to tell her. I want to wait a few more weeks until after her baby 'sprinkle' or she'll lose it."

Ellie waded over, handing me a cup with one hand. "So, how did it go? I mean, after you fell?"

"My left hand is the only one that works. I'm sore and my back hurts. Tomorrow, I get to see what I'm having. It's a hot mess."

"But the baby is fine?"

I sipped and took a beat. "Well, don't freak out but it's actually twins. The ultrasound blindsided us."

"Twins?"

"Identical twins."

"The man's swimmers work!"

"Oh, stop!" I said. "It was my eager ovulation that did the work. Honestly, I cannot believe it. For months, I struggled to conceive, but a one-night stand and a broken condom finally made my dreams come true."

152

She snickered. "Eva, that's terrible. Give him more credit. It's been more than a one-night stand. He's stood by you."

"I am not giving him credit for doing the bare minimum," I said. "However, he's going above and beyond to support me. Also, there was a thing on a boat."

"A thing on a boat?"

"We sort of lost control and shagged on his family's yacht."

"Evangeline!" Ellie screeched, smacking my bad arm.

"Fuck! Ouch!" I said as my wrist vibrated in pain.

"Oh, shit, I'm so sorry, sweetie. Well, fuck! So, when is the wedding?"

"Never," I said. "How are the final things coming along? Are we still on for shoes on Wednesday?"

"I will be there with bells on," Ellie answered. "But you?"

"I will be. Of course, tomorrow night, Dad is insistent we go car shopping. The minute I texted Davey about it, he agreed. The men are conspiring against me. Although, at this point, I would say Dad just wants to vet him."

"There's nothing to worry about. He's gorgeous, rich, and falls all over himself around you."

"He does not!"

"He does. He's always running into things or dropping something. That's *because* of you—not a coincidence, babes."

I shook my head. "He wants to buy me a car."

"Yeah, so? I looked up the house he lives in. It's a 26-million-dollar penthouse."

My mouth dropped.

"Let him blow 100 grand on a car. He's not hurting for money," Ellie said.

"But that makes me a gold digger."

"You're suffering through a twins pregnancy while bopping around in a broken-down farm truck."

"It runs great!"

"It's a beater."

"Dad won't let me drive it anyway. It's no longer safe. The men are *so* annoying."

"*The men?* Someone's gotta keep you on a leash, sweetie. Oh, speaking of that, are you bringing him?"

"Who?"

"Davey."

"To what? The appointment? Yes. He's coming."

Ellie shook her head. "The wedding."

"No. I don't have a plus one."

"Technically, you do per your RSVP. Because you told me Mona was coming back when Mona was with you."

"Ah," I sighed. "No."

"Eva, please! Bring him! It would be fun."

"Why do you want this to be a thing?" I groaned.

"Because he likes you. Because you're cute together!"

"We really aren't. We're not a couple."

"Uh-huh. That's why daddy rushed you off to the ER the minute he heard you'd fallen, right? That's why he's always around these days?"

I rolled my eyes. "I love you, but that's not what this is."

"Bring him."

"I will think about it."

"You've got five days. I need a final head count."

22.JUST SHOPPING

Davey

"What cars do you want to look at?" I asked Eva while waiting to meet the genetic counselor.

I tried to take her mind off the stress of our genetic report.

"I just want something safe and simple," Eva said. "Lower budget."

I rolled my eyes. "Eva, I am not assuming you want a Bugatti, but I'm not buying you a Ford Fiesta, either. What about a Mercedes?"

She snickered. "Me... what? Driving your hand-me-down G-Wagon."

"Nah. I'd not give you a secondhand car. The truck—"

"It's gone. Dad drove me this morning. He's worried without the airbags. That said, there's no way I'm riding in that tiny car of yours for the same reason."

"Oh." The thought of safety never occurred to me, but made sense.

"What about we meet in the middle?" Eva asked. "Like a Volvo. It's a nice, solid car. It's upmarket, but it's not a Ford Fiesta."

"Are you sure? Parts cost a fortune."

Eva rolled her eyes. "They make electric hybrids and the safest cars on the market. It's either that or Rivian."

"You want an electric?" I gasped, shocked.

"Yeah. Or a plug-in hybrid. Why not?"

"Hello, hello!" A cheerful man with a wide grin entered, and our attention turned to the more important of the two tasks—the genetic screening.

"So, the first thing I wanted to ask is before I hand you these results, would you like the sex-blind results or the ones with the babies' sexes? I always want to confirm."

"Oh, as we said," I answered, "we want to see the sex of the babies."

"Technically, your wife is the patient."

"I'm *not* his wife," Eva clarified. "But we're on the same page. Please show us the sex of the babies."

"Great," the counsellor said. "The second thing, I didn't find anything elevated in these results that would be cause for concern, but I do want to be here to answer any questions you have."

"That's good," Eva said as he handed her a piece of paper.

"It's wonderful, but not surprising. You're young and healthy."

She read through the results, mouth dropping. We were having not one, but two boys.

"Two boys. Two boys!" She gasped, then teared.

I didn't care either way, but she clearly did. I couldn't tell if this was bad, good, or overwhelming. Treading carefully, I squeezed her good hand, minding that the right remained in a sling. The poor woman looked pitiful.

"But, as I said, based on this and the scan, the babies are developing well. We don't see elevated risks. Now, do you have a meeting with your specialist upstairs? If so, I will take you up."

Eva nodded, crying. We were transferred to a maternal fetal medicine specialist—an MFM—because of the pregnancy complications with Mo-Di twins. Upstairs, a man in his fifties who looked like he hit the gym six hours a day greeted us enthusiastically. Eva was still a sobbing mess.

"Is there a concern you want to start with?" The doctor asked. "You seem... upset."

"I'm... overwhelmed. We're having two boys. I wanted girls!" She sobbed. "But I'm okay. I will... feel better about it. I'm just sad and excited and... hormonal."

I rubbed her back, having compassion for the woman I'd done dirty with two boys.

"Of course. It's a big day." The doctor's tone felt dismissive and condescending. "So far, you're healthy. Your blood pressure is good. Your OB said you are measuring well, and the babies are of similar size and date. That's what we want to see. We will regularly check your placenta and fluid levels. That is key. Now, regarding weight gain..."

He flipped through the chart on his computer. "You shouldn't gain more than 20 pounds... given your weight. A normal woman, I'd say fifty. But you came in here overweight."

"She's already lost fifteen pounds," I protested. "She's struggled with food. It's getting better, but... why would you say that?"

"Your wife is overweight. Plain and simple. It is a risk—"

"Excuse me, but does that seem kind *or* helpful?" I asked, sounding like my baby sister stopping an argument.

Eva patted my arm. "Stop. It's not worth it."

I felt the vein in my neck brush against the collar of my oxford shirt. "Sir, this woman is in great shape. Eva takes care of herself when her body allows. I don't think it is helpful to suggest she fucking starve herself while growing multiple babies. Do you?"

"We would like to keep tabs on her weight. Overweight people—"

"She is a person. A beautiful, smart, talented woman. And while you may claim you're doing your job, you're just being a judgy asshole."

"That is your *opinion*. Science—"

"Stop," Eva held up her hand. "I don't want to talk about it. Let's just move on."

I seethed, glaring at the doctor.

He continued, "We have a birth class for multiples starting in two months. I'd like you to consider it. Most parents find it helpful. We have special discussions about baby care and breast-feeding."

Eva nodded, a shell of her former self.

He handed me an information packet, sent us to scheduling, and we said nothing until the elevator. Eva collapsed into a puddle of tears.

"Eva, I'm sorry he said those things."

"They *all* do," Eva said. "And I'm a 'small-fat' you know. People don't even really consider me 'fat' until it's convenient. I'm used to all this rhetoric—his touting bad, biased science. But fighting him does no good, Davey. Trust me. It's every doctor."

"Well, when he does it around me, I *will* say something," I said. "You are a living human being. You're the mother of my children. He doesn't get to talk to you like that. Okay?"

She squeezed my hand. "Okay. I'm sorry for crying about the boys. I don't want you to think I won't love them. I will."

I turned to her, with all the love in the world. "Of course you will. You'll love them because they're ours. And they will be loved —by everyone, I suspect."

"We need to do so much," Eva murmured.

"Like buy a car? Yeah. We do." I chuckled. "It's fine. We'll do it tonight. One big thing off the list. The other stuff will happen. It will come together."

Eva sighed as we left the elevator. "It's good news, though. This is a relief."

"It is. Oh, I almost forgot. Mum is having a party for her birthday this weekend. She wants to invite you."

"Me?" Eva laughed. "Really?"

"Yeah. She wants you to come. She's trying. I am as surprised as you. You don't have to, but... it would be good."

"For you or me?"

For me most of all.

"Look, I'll go if you come with me to Ellie's wedding. I'm

getting nothing but pressure from her to bring a date. I don't want to, but… it could be fun."

"I would love to!" I jumped at the chance.

"What?" Eva said, surprised.

"Well, hot bridesmaids are sort of my thing," I joked.

"Davey! Remember the talk we had about flirting. I'm the fucking Maid of Honor!"

"Oh, well, then hot Maids of Honor," I said.

She stopped dead and glared. "Are you fucking hitting on me, David?"

"Is it working?"

Eva set her jaw and shook her head. I fought the urge to pull her close and kiss the angry look off her lips. She was so adorably infuriating. The more pregnant she looked, the cuter she became. I now knew the difference between anger and Standard-Issue Grumpy Eva.

"Maybe. Depends on what you're going to do with your mouth after." Eva walked towards me.

"Oh, if you'd let me do that *last* time, I would have gotten you off more," I said.

"I wasn't comfortable with it. But if you're still hitting on me after talking about lactation consultants, I can trust you're not going to get all weird."

"The test was lactation consultants, Eva?"

"It's whatever occurs to me. You said you would work. Thankfully, I give out awards generously for effort." Eva tossed her hair over her shoulder. "You've been a good boy. So, maybe there is hope for you after all."

"Just to clarify, is this a date?"

"I think we can call these dates, but to be certain, I wouldn't say we were *dating*."

I'd settle for that.

* * *

Eva

"You *really* want an electric car?" Davey asked as we waited for a salesman at the Volvo dealership.

We'd kicked off work early to come south—at Davey's suggestion. Dad was on his way—driving in rush hour.

"Yes," I said. "Aren't you all about sustainability these days?"

"I am about ROI," Davey answered. "That is different than driving a toaster."

I rolled my eyes. "I want one."

"Do you even have a charger?"

"I will get one. We have one at the garage near work. You give privileges to those who drive electrics," I said. "And if I am going to drive in some days, I'd take advantage of it."

"Do we?"

"You really should talk to HR," I sighed.

"That is what Daphne is for."

"Daphne is not your everything woman."

"As president and leader of the HQ, she is. When I was President, I dealt with that. When I became CEO, I stopped."

A man approached, either recognizing Davey or knowing what a rich man looked like.

"Can I help you two?" He asked

"We're looking for an EX30," I said.

"Oh, come right this way," he beckoned, going into the car's features.

Davey poked his head in. "Eva, this thing is tiny."

"It's cute. It's efficient," I said.

"It's not big enough."

"Your car is the size of a pin," I said.

"And it's not a minivan replacement, Eva."

"There ya are!" Dad walked to hug me.

"I'm here," I agreed.

Davey came around the car for the world's most *awkward* introduction. I silently hoped our salesman wouldn't run away screaming and suspected that Davey had "cash offer" written all over. If he wasn't born yesterday, he knew this was a slam dunk.

"Dad, this is David. David, this is my dad, Robert."

"Hello, Mr. Pavlak," Davey said. "It's nice to finally meet you."

Dad looked Davey over, sizing him up. I waited with bated breath to see how this played out.

Dad extended his hand. "Well, it is good to meet you, although you'll have to give me a minute. I'm… still very confused."

"It is odd, yes," Davey blushed, shaking his hand. "But we agree on one thing—that Eva needs a proper car. Can you please talk her out of electric?"

"Eva, please," Dad groaned.

"In London, we owned an electric car. I want another," I confirmed.

"At the very least, can you tell her this car is too damn small, Bert?"

Dad burst into laughter. "Sweetheart, where will you put two car seats?"

The sales guy said, "Are they forward-facing? Rear-facing? This can be a great car for people with one rear-facing in the middle and a sibling forward-facing next to it."

"Two rear-facing," Davey said. "Twins."

"Oh, you're…" The salesman pointed at me and did a double-take. "Well, congratulations."

I choked a tiny, "Thanks."

"Okay, well, I'd recommend the EX90 with six seats—the captain's chairs are great with two car seats."

We followed him around the corner to a *much* larger vehicle.

"See, this is nice," Davey declared.

"Davey, it's like twice the size. It's giving soccer mom."

"Well, they might play soccer," Davey said. "I did."

"Not the point."

"Eva, just take it for a spin."

"It can't hurt to drive it." Dad shrugged. "It looks very safe."

I gave in. We took it for a spin, and I grudgingly admitted it was more fun to drive than a beat-up old truck. Within a couple hours of my negotiations, Davey handed off his credit card and walked through the sale's final steps. He'd pay for it. I'd insure it and pay the obscene taxes.

"He's just going to drop 90k on a credit card," Dad whispered.

"It's bizarre. Don't try rationalizing it. After five days with them, I still don't understand how it works, Dad. It's something you or I will never understand."

"Well, at least he's doing the right thing."

"Dad, it's not his responsibility alone. I am the mom. I can contribute, too."

As we stood before the new car, keys in hand, I said, "This was nice of you. Thanks. And it's late, so I should let you go."

"In my family," Davey said. "A new car necessitates dinner out. So, I think we should find a place, go grab dinner, and celebrate the new car. What do you think, sir?"

"I think that's great," Dad said. "What do we think sounds good?"

"I don't even know," I said.

"Cheesecake Palace," Dad said. "Her favorite place since childhood. There's something for everyone. That's where we'll go."

And that is how I ended up taking my billionaire boss to Cheesecake Palace for the evening.

23.MEET THE PARENTS

Davey

THE CHEESECAKE PALACE HAD SOMETHING FOR EVERYONE. YOU could get lost in a massive booth, eat whatever you wanted in peace, and enjoy cheesecake on your way out. While I quickly warmed to the idea, Mum would have lost her mind at the mere suggestion of a restaurant without a white tablecloth and none of my past girlfriends would have embraced its casual ambiance.

I gathered this, too, was a test. Bert seemed genuine but determined to put me through the wringer to determine if I was a condescending, pampered asshole. If you asked Eva, I am sure she'd say I could be. Tonight, though, I was on my best behavior. I'd not met the parents in a dozen years—no one ever stuck around long enough to introduce me, or I actively avoided it. I turned over a new leaf among the many pages of The Cheesecake Palace's menu.

Conversation focused on the car, work, and other minor things over dinner. I eased into the tougher subjects. And, while we waited to order cheesecake to-go as Eva swore she couldn't bear the uncomfortable booth anymore, the topics deepened.

"So, Eva says you met at a bar," Bert said.

"Dad," Eva groaned, annoyed.

"It is a fair thing to talk about. You're in a relationship—"

"We are seeing one another. It's not being in a relationship."

I ignored her retort and reminded myself about recent baby steps. She let me buy the damn car. She agreed to take me to a wedding as a date and to visit my Mum's house for a family thing. Whatever she wanted to call it, we were together.

"We met at a bar. She won't admit I saved her from an asshole hitting on her, but I did. It was her spirit I found incredible. Unfortunately—or luckily for us—my sister hired her. I didn't know who she was."

Bert raised his eyebrow in doubt. "Incredible? But you say you aren't dating her?"

"Ask your daughter about that one," I said.

Eva folded her arms. "I'm not discussing this with you, Dad. Oh, my God, my back is just… miserable."

"You should tell the doctor," I said. "It's not good."

"Well, I would but I know he'll just blame it on me being fat and move along."

"I'd never let that fly," I promised. "You know I would come for him. It's not okay. You're miserable. I can tell."

"He's right. You should tell him. Why would he blame it on you being fat? That's ridiculous!" Bert said.

"That is what I said. I reacted poorly, but I refuse to accept that is 'normal' or 'acceptable'."

"Welp, you're not a woman dealing with shitty physicians," Eva said.

The server returned. Eva ordered not one but *two* slices of triple chocolate cheesecake. And, given she'd barely touched her food, it would make up the bulk of what she ate today. She took it on the chin—just like the back pain—but I wasn't about to give in.

"Have you gotten one of those pillows?" I asked.

"What?"

"The one that takes up the whole bed."

"I have no idea what you're talking about!" Eva laughed.

"Well, my sister has one. Cal claims he no longer gets any bed real estate, but she said it really helps her back. You should get one."

"That sounds silly, Davey," Eva said.

I knew she'd never buy something for herself, but the wheels turned as the bill arrived. I swooped in to pay it, but Eva's quick reflexes stole it first.

"No. You bought a car. I will pay this tab."

"Eva, I swear—"

"Nope. I am not listening to your bullshit, David," she said.

Bert shot me a look of sheer exhaustion, signaling the women in his life ran the show.

"Are you headed back?" Bert asked.

"To Chicago? Yeah. I live on the Near North Side."

"You came all the way down here just for this?" Bert elbowed his daughter. "That was nice of him."

"Yes, Dad. It was nice of him."

"Why don't we go back and see your mom?" Bert asked.

"All of us?" Eva panicked.

"Yes. I mean, he came all this way. And she'll tan my hide if I don't invite him back."

"It's getting late—"

"Well, he can stay the night if he needs to. It's up to you, David."

"I'd love to meet Mrs. Pavlak," I said.

My cheerful response wasn't genuine. I sensed Eva's mom was rather demanding and probably would be the bigger boulder I'd need to move to get "in" with the family.

"I've got to grab something," I said. "And I'll be over. Just text me the address."

Eva flashed a confused look. "Sure."

I dropped everything, racing into the mall linked to the restaurant once Eva left the parking lot. It was 15 minutes to close, and I was a man on a mission. There *had* to be a baby store. Indeed, Babies 'n Bumps awaited. I headed in, flustered. Two girls preparing for close looked at me, confused.

"I need a pregnancy pillow," I said, breathless.

"Okay. We have one," the older one said.

"Great, thanks. It's… not for me. It's for my partner."

They grabbed a massive carry bag with a huge snake-like pillow inside and rang it up. As with all things baby-related, the cost was that of highway robbery—nearly $100 for a goddamn pillow. No wonder Eva wouldn't go for it. She refused to spend money on herself.

They handed me the bag, and I was off in a flash—headed towards the address Eva sent. Despite her constant insistence she lived in the middle of nowhere, I pulled into the drive I remembered within 15 minutes. The crush of gravel reminded me of our Michigan farm. The farmhouse was even more charming in this light.

Climbing out, I grabbed my cheesecake, pillow, and rang the bell. A minute later, a blonde woman who looked much like Eva answered.

"God, Eva, your boyfriend is here! Where are you?" She held the door. "I'm sorry. She just disappeared. Come in, please."

"Hi," I said. "I'm David. Thanks for inviting me."

"I didn't," she said, cooly. "Bert did."

"There you are!" Bert said. "This is my wife, Emma. Emma, this is David Delphine."

"Yep. I guessed that," Emma said flatly.

She did *not* offer a hand or shake mine. *Oof!*

Bert asked, "Want a beer? Eva got some good stuff a week ago as a bit of a surprise."

"I'm not drinking. I've got to drive back—"

"It's late. You should stay."

Eva's mother glared, "Yeah, you're better off staying and driving in. Evangeline Mary, where are you?"

"I'm here. Calm down!" Eva descended the front stairs. "Hold your horses. I sweated through my work clothes and changed."

Dressed down, I found Eva irresistible. She was even cuter in shorts and a tank top. I felt the same way I had that night on the beach—unable to look away. It felt special to see her with her walls down—as no one else did.

"What are you holding?" Eva asked.

"I swooped back to grab that pillow since I knew you'd never do it," I chuckled.

Bert snickered.

Eva sighed, annoyed, "Thank you."

"What pillow?"

"It's for her back," Bert said. "She's miserable but won't do anything. He's trying to help."

"It is the least I could do, Eva."

"Well, if we don't get to our cheesecake, I'm going to murder someone," Eva rubbed her back. "Can we just sit down on the couch and eat?"

The idea of eating on a couch in a parents' living room confused me. Mum would have lost her mind. However, their farmhouse's living room was more family room than drawing room and afforded a casual setting for sucking down cheesecake.

"It's been years since I've had any of this," I admitted.

"God, I've been eating this and ice cream nonstop since I got back. Britain lacks this. I could eat an entire Eli's cheesecake at lunch I think. I shouldn't, but I think I could," Eva laughed.

"You should eat what your body wants. You're not eating," I said. "You need—"

"So, I can gain weight, and he can shame me more?"

"I gained forty pounds with your sister and nearly fifty with you. You're having twins. He's right that you need to eat. The doctor can pound sand," Emma said.

I nodded in agreement.

"What did the doctor say?" Emma asked. "Today?"

"Well, the babies are doing really well," Eva said. "We got some more pictures."

She flailed, trying to stand. "They're in my purse."

"In the entry?" I asked. "I can get them."

I stood, found her purse, and brought the photos to her mother.

"Oh my. Look at these faces," Emma cooed.

Bert leaned over from his chair to see. "They're looking like babies. I swear the technology is getting so much better than when you were kids. Just like Brooke's kids."

"And the tests were good?" Emma asked.

"They were perfect," Eva said. "We're having two very healthy boys."

My mouth dropped. "I didn't realize we were telling everyone the gender."

"It's the sex," Eva corrected. "And I wasn't planning on a stupid gender reveal. It's gauche."

"I agree," I said. "I just… didn't know we *could*."

"Well, we can tell your mom this weekend," Eva said. "Since you're dragging me along to that party."

"It's Mum's birthday," I said. "I am not sure how it would go."

"Announcing the sex of our babies to her would be a problem? I mean, we don't have to make a big deal out of it—"

"She wouldn't like that," I said.

Eva suddenly looked sad.

"I would love to," I said. "But she wouldn't like it. It's got nothing to do with you or the twins. It's just Mum being Mum. Trust me."

* * *

Eva

"I cannot imagine a world in which I would complain. I'm so happy for two more boys," Mom said.

"I wasn't too over-the-moon about it," I admitted. "I wanted a girl—two if we had twins. But… it wasn't meant to be. I am getting over it. We'll love them all the same."

"What is your concern, sweetie?" Mom asked.

"Raising boys to be good men is more of a challenge," I said. "Toxic masculinity and all of that."

Mom rolled her eyes. *Predictable.*

"I think you raise them like any children," Dad said. "Just raise them to be kind and have empathy. Raise them to care about other people. That's all you can do."

I shrugged. My relationship with men remained complicated, even if Davey tried to give his entire gender a glow-up. The pillow may have been stupid, but it showed he cared. I'd never been treated so well by a man apart from my father.

"I agree," Davey said. "Although, Dad always said trying to raise us was harder than with the girls. And given that all of them are *much* more mature, I'm not sure there's a way around it. Daphne is the most grown of all of us."

"Daphne seems like a nice woman," Mom said.

"She is," I agreed. "And she's about to go on leave, so Davey is panicking."

"I'm not. But I am relying on you to keep me abreast of literally all of technology. I cannot even fix a computer, but you're—"

"My job is to translate and filter it," I said. "And I will do that. Of course, now we have the added complication of—"

"It will be fine," Davey said. "I'm giving myself a hard time. I am sure it will work. We do the best we can."

Dad changed the subject. "Well, the car is nice. It's electric."

"I'm getting a plug for the barn. I can charge it by the over-hang," I said.

"It seemed very fancy," Mom agreed. "But that's silly. Put the plug and charger in the garage. Maybe we'll get a new-fangled car. We're not *that* old-school and redneck, Eva."

"I didn't want to impose—"

"Well, you aren't. And anyway, you aren't planning on staying here, are you?" Dad asked.

"Oh… I we haven't talked about that," I sighed. "Way to make it awkward."

"That isn't true, Eva," Davey outed me. "I've tried—"

"To make me move up there."

"Well, I think it would be better if I could be closer and could actually help you."

"I agreed to the nanny."

"Eva, that's not the same thing."

"You should move up there," Mom said. "I hate to have to see you go, sweetheart, but… he's right. You will want him nearby for help. And they will want to see their father. It's a little silly to have him drive down here. Besides, Dad and I raised our children. We'll be glad to take them on weekends sometimes, but having two babies in the house isn't for us."

I felt rejected. "Okay, well I didn't realize I was getting evicted—"

"Sweetie, you aren't," Dad said. "We just figured you'd want to move up there after you got a steady paycheck. This isn't exactly the center of the universe. It's exciting up there."

I expected a superior look from Davey. Instead, his face showed sympathy.

"We'll make it work," Davey reiterated.

Mom slapped her knees, initiating a Midwestern Goodbye if I ever saw one. "It's late. I should get you some towels and make sure the guest room is ready, David."

"Oh, uh… you don't need to go to any trouble," Davey said. "Really, Mrs. Pavlak—"

"You aren't sleeping in her room," Mom said. "And I won't make you drive. Stay up. Talk to Eva. But, mind yourselves."

Mom left. Dad soon said goodnight and disappeared.

"They realize I'm almost forty, right?" Davey winced. "And that… you're pregnant with my children?"

"My mother is still very religious and traditional," I said. "So, she's going to make you earn it. And, Davey, we're not having sex tonight. You knew that."

"Did I?"

I rolled my eyes. "Do I look up to it? I'm not."

"Oh… okay. I'm not upset just… I don't know. This is peak awkwardness."

"I know," I laughed. "Fuck, it's so weird."

"It is worth it, though," Davey said. "I will keep trying. Your parents care about you, Eva. I'm sorry that sort of blindsided you."

"I'm fine."

Davey moved next to me. "No, you're not. I think I hurt your feelings about Mum not wanting a distraction. And I think your parents mean well, but it's a complicated time."

Davey wrapped his arm around the couch. "You don't have to be tough-as-nails always. You know? I don't know who hurt you, Eva, but I do want to be the one who proves not every man in your life has to be a grave disappointment."

"It's not just the man who hurt me," I said, feeling vulnerable. "It's years of thinking it was something it wasn't. Maybe in your mind, I should just move in? In fact, Ellie teases me about it all the damn time."

"Why?"

"I moved in with Mona—my ex—about five minutes after we got together. We were a walking stereotype for a lesbian couple. But that is *so* different than this."

"Yeah, I supposed my house is probably a little wild, but Eva, I'm older and have had time—"

"Davey, I don't mean it like that. You know nothing about her—or what we did or didn't do. No. Her place was immaculate. She lived in a posh neighborhood. She spoiled me with nice things. She was older than you. I felt safe—perhaps, too safe. In the end, she s love as something that can change. She was done. The baby stuff killed my sex drive, and we grew apart."

"If this is what it looks like when your sex drive is dead, I think she was asking a lot," Davey chuckled.

"It was different. One, I never got to the horny part of pregnancy before. Two, it was an endless cycle of drugs that fucked with my body and my head. And it made her not want to touch me because I was always irritable. She's not like you."

"What am I like?"

"Persistent," I said. "Annoyingly persistent. And *far* too secure when you have no right to be. Sometimes, I wish I was more like you."

"I will take that as a compliment," Davey said.

"Look, I like you. I even must admit I have *fun* with you. I find you absolutely grating at times, but I honestly adore that you care so much for me despite all the weirdness. I don't get why, but..."

My voice trailed and my eyes dropped as Davey played with the hair in my ponytail. His distraction suddenly hit me as sweet.

"I... do want to try," I finished.

"You are utterly infuriating but so engrossing, Eva."

"Is that a compliment?"

"I haven't chased a woman in *years*. Instead, I found women who threw themselves at me—low investment flings that made me feel good for a bit. The stakes were low, so I didn't have to try. With you, I must do the awkward things, but... I don't regret it."

"Why, though?"

"You are so different. You're smarter than I am. You're beautiful. I don't have to babysit you even if I don't always understand what you are talking about. If I must have children with someone, I would much rather they be smart, demanding, and ambitious as opposed to lazy, overly attached, and dumb as a brick. Who would I argue with if not you?"

"Literally everyone since you love to argue," I giggled.

"So do you, Eva."

I stared deep into his eyes for a minute, trusting him as I hadn't before. "Do you honestly care what happened?"

"With the person who hurt you?"

"It was people, but yeah," I said.

Davey nodded.

"A person I loved—or at least I thought I did—forced himself on me. At the time, I don't think I'd call it anything, but... it was not consensual."

I watched Davey's face turn sympathetic.

"Don't say anything, please. The last thing I want is your pity. But… it meant that for years, I feared men. Shouting makes me fly off the handle. Men who are rough with me, trigger the hell out of me—unless I initiate it. Until we slept together, I was absolutely convinced I'd never have penetrative sex with a man again."

"Really? Then why me? It was a hookup—"

"You wanted to prove yourself to me. You got me off like a fucking god. And you wanted me to tell you what I wanted. It had been *years* since anyone asked me what I wanted—fuck, even what I needed! Also, the idea of torturing a rich guy who could get me off appealed. Sorry, but, I sort of fantasized about it."

"I never want you to feel scared. And hey, objectify me any which way! I don't mind."

I giggled and shook my head. "I know. You always check in on me. And… that is what I need. It is taking me time to come to terms with the fact that you get aggro because you care. It's not some sort of fucked up power move. It's because you care and anger is your only emotion sometimes."

"I am working on it. Since Dad died, it has gotten worse. I feel like everything is slipping through my fingers, Eva. I suck at all of it. I don't want to suck at parenthood. I don't want to suck at having a relationship with you—whatever that looks like. The stakes couldn't be higher. Dad would have my ass if he was here and I didn't step up."

"So, you just want to do this because—"

"I want to do this because I fucking love you, Eva," Davey admitted.

As he said it, I froze. He did, too. He regretted it.

"I am sorry. That was… I didn't know—"

"It's okay. You don't love me. You couldn't."

Davey started slow, words coming to him as they filtered through his brain. "I… I did though. I do love you, Eva. And I'm sorry about that."

"I don't love you," I said.

"That's fine." Davey looked down.

I grabbed his chin, pulling his eyes to mine. "Stop. I... I am so bad at this. I'm really scared to try with anyone, but Davey, I care about you. I do. I see how you care for me and the twins. Okay? It's not that I could *never* love you or that I'm not attracted to you. It's the opposite. Those things make me want to run because I see you and I want this."

"You think you could love me?"

"Maybe... I sort of hope so... someday. But I cannot promise I'll ever say those words. So, if that is a dealbreaker, we really should stop any romantic—"

The words didn't make it out. Davey kissed me, pulling me close. He breathed me in, our tongues tangling. To my surprise, I didn't fear it. I couldn't tell him I loved him because I didn't, but his vulnerability and acceptance that I needed time was what I longed for.

Davey pulled away, his forehead resting on mine. "I don't want that. I can wait. But, I don't want to do more out of respect for your parents. So, let's part ways before I become even more obsessed with you and do something stupid."

I laughed. "Okay. I'll show you upstairs."

I turned off all the lights. Davey followed me upstairs, carrying the ridiculous pillow. His heart was so full. Davey couldn't hide the way he felt and *was* the sort of man who would teach our boys to be vulnerable.

"Here's your room." I handed him towels and tried to race away before crying overwhelmed me.

"Thanks. Are you okay?"

"I feel like I learned a lot about you tonight," I said. "I'm emotional. I'm glad, though. It feels like we're getting somewhere."

"It does," Davey agreed.

"Sleep well," I said.

Davey kissed my forehead. "Goodnight. I love you."

On that note, I left. I unfurled the snake-like pillow and tucked it into bed. I laughed as I found myself curling up, my hips properly supported for the first time in months. I could finally retire my stash of too-soft pillows. Davey was onto something. I'd never admit he was right, but I did adore his stubbornness right about now. In the end, I had the best night of sleep in nearly a year.

24.THE DELPHINES

Eva

I STOOD BEFORE A MASSIVE SKYSCRAPER, STARING AT THE ADDRESS. I looked back at my phone. Yes, this was the place. I stepped up, my overnight bag on my shoulder, and spoke to the doorman rushing to greet me.

"Hi, I'm here to see David," I said. "I'm supposed to go up."

"Ah, are you Miss Pavlak?" He asked, expression cheerful.

"Yes," I answered. "Do I need to do something or—"

"No, no," the man wrestled the bag from my shoulder. "He said to expect you."

"I can carry that—"

"Absolutely not," the man insisted. "I will carry it and escort you up."

"I'm confused. I thought this was the wrong place. Because it's connected to the hotel," I explained as we stepped on an elevator.

"The penthouses have a private entrance, miss. This is the right side—side B."

My ears popped as we climbed. *How far up was this place?*

"This is the tallest hotel in the city," the man said. "The penthouse suites are on the last ten floors."

"Ah," I said. "It is… up there."

The elevator stopped at what I supposed was the top floor.

"And we're here," he declared as the elevator doors opened.

The scene here was one of panoramic windows to the front and left. A living room sat to one side and a wall the other. I wasn't sure what was over there. Davey came around the corner to greet me, dressed only in a robe.

"Oh, thanks, Vince. Sorry. It's chaos up here."

"Not a problem, sir," he boarded the elevator.

I stared in disbelief until Davey pulled me into a kiss. How did anyone live like this?

"So, this is it. You made it. Apologies because I'm not ready, but you look lovely," Davey said.

"Thanks," I blushed.

"I'm going to go change quick but look around and make yourself at home. I'll put your bag in my room?"

"Sure," I agreed.

He wound up a set of stairs behind the wall. A kitchen and small informal dining room sat to the left. Around the corner were the stairs and two small but well-appointed bedrooms. The rearmost room was an office chock full of beautifully preserved sports memorabilia, toy trains, and the biggest monitor I'd ever seen. I practically drooled at the sight even if everything else was disharmonious.

Every surface was pristine from the white and blue walls—colors alternating flawlessly in complementary gradients—to the beautiful marble floors. On the second floor, I came across the formal dining with views of the Hancock building and Lake Michigan like I'd never seen. The formal reception room opened onto a roof deck. Down the other hall, I assumed I'd find Davey's room. I proceeded through a massive door into a hallway. A beautiful dark marble-clad bathroom was the first I saw. The way the bathtub angled, you could see more gorgeous views of the Hancock. A shower big enough for 10 people took up one wall. I walked past, finding his bedroom to the left—huge and with beautiful lake views.

I found him in nothing but underwear in a room that served his closet. The assortment of suits and ties astounded me.

"You're like James Bond," I laughed. "Jesus Christ, this is too much."

"It's a disaster."

"Davey, if this is a disaster, we can never live together. You'll fucking kill me," I said.

"I have a housekeeper," Davey explained. "She's here mostly when I'm not. I credit her with organizing everything."

A housekeeper for one person? It baffled me.

"What, does that bother you? I promise she is very fastidious. I don't like things being untidy."

"We're about to have infants."

"Well, I like to know surfaces are clean."

I snickered.

"What?" Davey scoffed, running his hands through his hair defiantly.

"You… there are two very different versions of you, David."

"How so?"

"There is the Davey who got me off in a grungy men's room and keeps a bunch of trains littering one corner of his office and the man who still thinks he can bubble wrap the world from germs and two tiny humans. What is up with that?"

"First of all, my goal is to bubble wrap them since they have a genetic predisposition to asthma, and I don't want them to suffer that. Second, I like things neat. Third, I love your pussy and wasn't thinking about the room. Fourth, you leave my trains alone. I enjoy them. I am *passionate* about them. Don't go there."

"Are you… serious?"

"Yes. My father and I always built those trains growing up. And, it might surprise you to know that I am actually a devoted trainspotter when I travel."

"A what?"

"Look it up." Davey pulled on pants, shaking his head. "I had a bit of an issue with that acquisition in London. I'm due to go back in a week. I'll be back in time for the wedding, no doubt, but legal is playing hardball."

"Ah," I said. "And there is no Daphne to smooth things over?"

"Exactly."

"You've got this," I said. "It will be fine."

"You're sweet." Davey buckled his belt.

I leaned on the doorway, not even caring if I stared at his bare torso. The man only got hotter when he was a supposed disaster. His flustered look made him touchable. He wasn't The Boss like this—just a man trying to win me over.

"Actually," Davey sensed I was ogling him, "you aren't sweet, Eva."

He sidled over, grabbing my hips.

"I'm not?"

"No," Davey said, "You're sexy as hell and I cannot have you right now, but damn I want you. We're running late."

"We don't have to be there for another thirty minutes. It's like a ten-minute drive. How long does it take you to put on a shirt, David?"

"Fifteen minutes early is on time with Mum. On time is late, baby."

He kissed me slowly, then backed off.

"Do you genuinely want to fuck me right now?" I asked.

"As much as ever, yeah," Davey said. "I have no idea what you've done to yourself. It's not the dress alone. But, damn! You're very fuckable right now."

I bit my lip.

"Don't do that," Davey said. "No. That's not helpful."

"Take your pants off," I said.

"Eva, I—"

"Take your pants off!" I repeated, kicking off my shoes.

"Eva," Davey groaned. "We cannot—"

I doubled down, taking my panties off and holding them up for effect. "Do what I say or fear my wrath for the rest of the evening. I'm much more pleasant when satisfied."

"Oh fuck," Davey tossed his pants and boxers. "I love it when you get demanding."

"I know."

Davey pressed me against the wall with his naked body. I felt his cock against my stomach and initially pulled back. Was this weird? Davey pulled me back in. He ran his hand up my dress, finding my wet clit.

"Oh, God," I moaned.

"Yeah, you like that?"

I nodded.

"Where do you want me to fuck you?"

I thought for a minute. "In the dining room—on the table."

"Bad girl," Davey growled. "But, I'll bite."

Panties in hand, we raced to the dining room where he had to help me on the table. He pulled me by the legs to the edge and slipped his hard cock inside. I gasped, throwing my head back as he pumped into me. Davey leaned me back, pressing my body down with an almost gentle hunger. I moaned louder, my nails digging into the table. Davey played with my clit, throwing me over the edge. Waves of pleasure rolled over me as I arched my back, staring just past him at the skyline. Now, *this* was a fantasy.

Davey moved my legs up to his shoulders, pumping harder until he came, falling forward to kiss me. My legs were pinned in a way that should have been impossible, but I felt sufficiently lithe in the moment. Slowly, he dropped my legs to the side, sliding out of my wet center.

"That was… fucking good," Davey said. "Fuck."

I snickered. "Yeah?"

"We definitely have to run, though, Eva."

I followed him to the closet where I reassembled myself as best I could. As Davey dressed, I tried to sort my hair in the bathroom mirror.

"Eva, can you grab the gift from my office downstairs?" Davey called. "I'm almost ready. I'll meet you down there."

"Sure," I agreed.

I wound back down, picking up a gift bag from Tiffany. Whatever was in it was heavy. The tag on the bag read, "To: Mum, From: Davey, Eva, and The Twins." Somehow, that warmed my heart most of all. I wondered if he did it on purpose. But, as he arrived in the foyer, looking hot as ever, I realized he wasn't looking for props, just help getting out the door.

"Great. Thanks," Davey said as we climbed on the elevator.

He pressed the button for the basement. I assumed that's where the car met us.

"What's the gift?" I asked.

"Mum loves silver picture frames," Davey said. "Dad always got them for her. I figured I'd continue the tradition."

"That's really sweet," I said.

"I'm a Mummy's boy. You can fucking say it." Davey laughed.

"A Mummy's boy who likes trains," I snickered.

"Don't start. They are a wonderful, green form of transport—"

"I'm not judging apart from the fact that your crown jewel is a sustainable building firm we bought out and now you are worried about trains? Davey, honestly, it is incongruous."

He pulled me closer by the hips. "I like classic cars and trains. Electrics don't have to be toasters. And, anyhow, yours isn't. You taught me something. I can be that and sappy about family. That won't change."

His gaze lingered on me in a sweet way. Yes, he was still thinking about fucking me on his table. He also dropped back into that precious vulnerable state I adored.

The elevator doors opened, shaking us awake.

"It's okay. I wish America had more trains. Also, I'd rather see you be good to your mother and sisters than be an asshole, David." I squeezed his hand tight in mine while leading the way. "It's nice that you care so much."

"I think we have that in common," Davey said. "Our families mean a lot to us."

"That may be all."

"Nah," Davey said. "We've got a company and two babies that also tie us together. That is not nothing."

"Also, our shared desire to have the Cubs shatter our dreams annually."

"This is the year. I swear," Davey chuckled, turning and meeting my gaze. "I love you, Eva. I really, really do."

* * *

Davey

"She really cleans up well," Mum said. "She's glowing."

Mum's eyes watched as Eva crossed the room, greeting Lanie as she came downstairs.

"She's wonderful," I said. "And the babies are doing great."

"Perfect."

"I am not pleased. I'm still very angry with you," Mum said. "But I refuse to take that out on your children. I would suggest you do the right thing and marry her—"

"I'm not doing that right now. That is not a conversation even on the table," I said. "I do not want to rush things."

"You'd have children with her, but not *marry* her?"

"Mum, I never said that. Today, I'm not talking about this. If I proposed, she'd say no. She's too smart for that. She'd want an earnest proposal, not an invitation to be my bride at a shotgun wedding."

"Well, the priest—"

"We're not discussing this," I said. "And no priest would marry us right now. Don't be ridiculous."

"I am sure we could—"

"No," I said sternly as Eva's gaze turned to me.

I smiled and beckoned her. I said a silent prayer that Mum left her alone.

"Eva, you look beautiful," Mum said warmly. "David says the babies are doing well."

"They're great," Eva agreed. "Measuring well. Everything is going according to plan."

"You don't have pictures?" Mum asked.

Eva looked to me.

"They're at home," I said.

"Why on earth would you have another scan and not bring me pictures?" Mum smacked my arm. "David, that's cruel."

"What?" I asked, confused.

"Did you not think I would want to see them?"

Eva pulled out her phone, scrolling through the pictures of the scan. She even played the video of both heartbeats. Mum fawned over it in a way I never expected. Who *was* this woman? She was supposedly angry with me about everything but now cooed at an ultrasound picture.

"So, are you finding out if they are boys or girls?" Mum asked.

Eva glared at me.

"What?" Mum asked.

"We know. David said that would be a distraction, so we didn't want to tell you." Eva sold me out.

I cleared my throat. "I thought you'd hate that idea. We had the genetic tests that came back."

"Of course I care! I'd like to call them the boys or the girls, obviously! Come on!"

"We're having boys," I answered.

Mum gave me a big hug unexpectedly, "Oh, so we'll have one girl and two boys. Good. That's incentive enough for someone to try for a girl to even out the ranks!"

"Mum, we don't need this to be about competitive conception," I sighed.

"Well, any excuse to move this show along. Do your parents know, Eva?"

She nodded. "They're happy with the news. Davey actually met them this week."

Astonished, Mum said, "Really?"

"Don't seem *so* surprised, Mother," I sighed. "I'm not completely uncultured and uncouth."

"I never know. If someone did what you did to one of the girls, your father would have lost his mind," Mum said.

"Well, Lady Danna, I'm not sixteen, and he's nearly forty, so… I think we're good. Their main concern is that he is reliable and shows up. So far, he's doing well," Eva said.

I rubbed her back. "They are nice people. I did have to sleep in the guest room, though. That was a first for at least the last twenty years."

"Mom is… very Catholic at times."

Mum exchanged a glance with me.

Eva read that as a negative. "Oh, sorry, you're… are you not? It's okay. I'm not religious. My parents—"

"No, darling," Mum said. "That is nothing I worry about. I am practicing even if my children are making it nearly impossible to stay in the good graces of the diocese. We were raised in the Church, no matter what the English would tell you."

As long as the checks keep coming, they will keep you around. My mother's Scottish exceptionalism knew no bounds, and the guilt came in waves.

"Mum, it will be fine. Buy them some more kegs for a fish fry and no one will care," I sighed.

"There are not enough kegs in the world some days," she grumbled before changing the subject. "Will you be coming up to Michigan in two weeks?"

"We are attending a wedding," I said. "Her best friend's wedding."

"I'm the Maid of Honor and Davey offered to go."

"That's nice," Mum said, surprised. "Well, we will miss you, but I understand. Behave yourself, David."

"I plan to," I said.

Eva smiled at me, softer than ever before. What was this magic? And why, oh why, did she make me so fucking happy?

25. LOVE ME LESS

Eva

I RETURNED HOME FROM A NIGHT OF CONVERSATION, AFFIRMING SEX, and cuddling, to find my sister and brother-in-law at my parents place. My sister was only days from her due date, and it occurred to me she was in the dark. I'd not spoken to her in about a month. She'd been so busy with baby prep and the baby sprinkle she was hosting next weekend that she had no time for me. I'd sworn my parents to secrecy, but as I paraded back into the house in a pair of shorts and t-shirt stolen from Davey, it appeared obvious.

I slumped into a chair by my nephew. He smiled and threw his arms around my body.

"Auntie Eva!" Miles declared, launching himself into my lap.

The real estate in my lap grew smaller by the day. It was so bad I had to buy a new maid-of-honor dress while shoe-shopping with Ellie this week. I'd given up trying to fit in the tight, pretty dress she'd chosen, electing for something a bit more forgiving.

"How are you?" I asked, brightly. "It's been ages."

"I got a dino!" Miles declared.

"Oh, how nice! Did you go to the Field Museum to see the dinos?"

"This morning," Brooke said. "Alone."

She was exhausted. Ian deserted her.

"Well, you should have called," I said. "I would have come. I was in the city last night. I just got home."

"Yes, just what I needed—you on a walk of shame," Brooke rolled her eyes as Miles butted into my chest, squeezing me tighter.

"Buddy, that hurts," I grimaced, ignoring her. "Can you love me a little less?"

"Be nice," Mom said to Brooke. "Your sister was offering to help."

"I'm always glad to come to the museum."

"Uh-huh. So, what is going on with this guy?" Brooke snapped.

I straightened in my chair. "I'm seeing him. He lives in Chicago. I went to his mom's party last night."

"Oh, so it's serious?" Ian asked. "Wait, this is a *man* you're seeing?"

He snickered in an immature way that made me want to smack him.

"Yes."

"And he's an actual *man*?"

"What do you mean?" I played dumb, waiting for him to tumble into a transphobic hole.

"He has the right plumbing."

I rolled my eyes and bluffed. "Does it matter? I like him."

"It's just I wasn't sure you'd know what to do with a real live man," Ian joked.

No one jumped in to defend me. I deflected, bluffing, "The plumbing... as you say... doesn't have to correlate with his manliness. But really, do you want to see a picture of it, Ian?"

I pulled out my phone as if Davey had ever sent me dick pics. He'd never do that. He knew better.

Disgusted, he said, "Of *course* not!"

I shrugged. "It's a shame, really. Or, maybe for your sake it's better? Comparison is the thief of joy."

"Eva!" Brooke declared, shocked that I would give back to her manchild better than I got.

"Are you going to come to the sprinkle with him?" Brooke demanded.

"No," I answered. "I assume he would find that a fate worse than death."

"Eva, be nice," Dad groaned.

"Look, no man wants to go to a baby sprinkle," I said.

"She's right," Ian backed me up.

"It's not a testament to not liking you. It's that he's gotta go to London and, I assume, would rather set himself on fire in a parking lot."

"What is happening in London?" Mom asked.

"Can't say. I signed an NDA."

"He made you sign an NDA?" Brooke gasped. "What is he? A murderer?"

"It's company business. I cannot talk about it, Brooke."

"Wait… are you… with your *boss*?" Brooke demanded.

"My bosses are both women."

"He's her boss's boss," Dad said. "She doesn't report to him."

"Who?" Ian asked.

"David Delphine," Dad answered. "The son of that billionaire who died. His sister is married to the mayor."

"I don't buy it. This is all so fake," Brooke said. "A billionaire? With you? No way. There is exactly *no* way!"

"Brooke, please," Mom whined. "Do not be rude to your sister."

"No, what is the proof? I think all of this is some big lie."

"He was here just this week. He's a nice boy," Dad said.

"Nope. This is a charade," Brooke crossed her arms across her boobs, resting them on her pregnant belly. "He'd never waste his time with you. Men like him don't marry fun-sucks. Men like him marry women who can manage parties and start families."

Tears welled. I shook with rage.

"I don't think what Davey wants is for me to bring him his slippers when he gets home from work. Unlike Ian, he's not a manchild incapable of purchasing a birthday present or sticking to a commitment to show up for a family thing. He does all of that."

"Pound sand, Eva!" Brooke said. "Give me my child! Give him to me right now!"

She stood with Ian's help all while he glared, then came around, holding her hands out.

"I cannot bend over," Brooke said. "Hand him to me or so help me!"

"He's forty pounds," I said. "I cannot lift him."

"Oh, are the princess's arms broken?" Brooke rolled her eyes.

"Yeah, my wrist is still hurt, and I need to be careful with it," I said.

"Oh please!"

"Brookie, she's pregnant," Dad said. "With twins. She shouldn't be lifting anything."

The room stopped, gauging Brooke's reaction. Ian came in, ripping Miles away. As he left my lap, he sobbed. Confusion crossed his tiny face. I couldn't help but cry, seeing him do the same. My mind raced as I stared down, waiting for Brooke to lay into me.

"I don't want you at the sprinkle," Brooke said. "You'll be an embarrassing distraction, and my friends will just make fun of you. It's better for you to stay home."

"Brooke, that isn't kind," Mom said.

"No. She's a whore who is bent on taking away *my* sunshine by being pregnant! Good lord! You must be so ashamed, Mom! She's always looking for attention. It's why she dated women—never men. It's why she got knocked up repeatedly before in some desperate attempt to prove she could trick science. But it failed because everything like that never works. Now, she's trapped some rich guy to prove something. The idea of Eva as a mother is a joke."

The room fell silent. I sobbed, wanting a hug or someone to defend me. Instead, no one spoke in favor of me, Davey, or the twins. No one defended my character or how hard I'd loved Brooke through the worst times or held my tongue with every disagreement. No one said shit. I just kept crying. Brooke continued to rant. Miles sobbed. I couldn't breathe, so I ran.

"Eva!" Mom called. "Eva, come back here! Let's talk!"

I couldn't talk. I climbed the stairs, threw my big suitcase on the bed, and began to pile work clothes inside before realizing none fit. Breaking into tears, I fell forward onto the bed, gasping. This hurt worst of all. I knew this conversation would hit someday —I just didn't realize it would hit when I was so raw.

"Eva, sweetie, it's going to be okay,!" Dad rushed in.

"No, it's not," I batted his hands away as he tried to comfort me. "No. Brooke will win the war. This just proves it."

"What war?"

"Her war of superiority and relegation. My children will not be loved. She will make sure they always feel like second-class citizens."

"Why would you say that, honey?"

"Because down there, no one defended me. No one called her out for her homophobia, her transphobia, or even for calling me a fucking whore. She said me being a mother was a joke. And you and Mom just fucking *sat there*, Dad."

"We don't want conflict."

"Well, I don't either. Not at a dinner table where adults are saying hateful shit to one another! Dad, Miles is distraught. I love that little boy. And God help him if he's gay, because she won't! He's going to grow up hating himself in that case. It's not okay. And I won't just sit here."

"What could we do?"

"Throw her out," I said.

My dad stared at me, more confused and desperate than I'd ever seen him—worse than on the day I'd come out. At least then, he jumped in to hug me and tell me he loved me even if he didn't really get it yet. Now, he was seized by inaction.

"Exactly. So, this cannot be my home anymore." I threw a stack of yoga pants in my bag. "I have to go. I'm not safe here."

"Please don't do this, Eva. Sweetie, we love you—"

"Not enough to do the right thing, though."

"That's not fair. We cannot just disown her—"

"I'm not asking for that. I'm asking for you to set her on her ass for calling me a whore or dancing on the fact that I miscarried two babies before I got pregnant with these. Do you realize how hard it is to hear these things from your own family?"

Dad shook his head. "I don't know what to do, Eva. You're strong. You can—"

"But I cannot. And I don't have to. I've gotta choose me and my babies right now," I tossed in a load of t-shirts, underwear, and sports bras. "I just can't do this. Please leave me. I need to pack. I'll be gone soon. Promise."

* * *

Davey

The doorman rang me around eight. I tried to go over something legal sent, bashing my head against a desk. I wanted so badly to call Daphne for help, but I knew it would come back to haunt me if I bothered her in the last weeks of pregnancy. I thought about what I'd want for Eva. The answer drove me to leave her alone.

"Mr. Delphine, Miss Pavlak is parked in guest parking and would like to speak to you," he said.

"Oh, sure. Send her up."

I wasn't expecting Eva. She'd left a few hours ago. This was odd.

A few minutes later, Eva arrived in the foyer with a suitcase. Her face was puffy from crying. She was a shell of the beautiful woman I'd put in a car earlier. What happened? I wasn't angry she was here, just confused.

"I cannot carry my bag. I am sorry," Eva said. "I don't even know what I packed and it's heavy. I had to have help to get it out. I think your front desk guy hates me."

"He doesn't. He's probably just worried about you. I'll… I'll sort the bag out in second," I said. "The elevator actually goes up to the next floor with a special code."

"Oh." She looked down.

"Eva, I need to know what is going on. Are you okay? What happened?"

"I don't know," Eva sobbed, moving forward to wrap her arms around me. "I'm so broken."

"Come on," I said. "Let's sit you down. Does a cup of tea sound good?"

"Sure," Eva sniffled.

I tucked her into the living room couch and went to make a cuppa for us. All the while, the wheels turned. Was it something I did? What about my mother? Had she said something to Eva? Had her parents thrown her out for staying the night? Did they think it was 1066?

"Milk or sugar?" I called into the living room.

"Honey," she said.

"I don't have honey," I laughed. "I was raised by a Scot!"

"Damn it," Eva said. "Sugar—two."

"Alright," I dumped two cubes in her mug and carried it to her.

"What happened?" I asked as she swirled her tea bag.

"I left my parents' house, and I don't think I can ever return."

"Eva, that's not possible. They love you—"

"Brooke called me a whore. She said there's a reason I don't stay pregnant. She said I couldn't attend the baby sprinkle because I'd be an embarrassment to the family. She said you'd never end up with me. And... she'd probably be right if I wasn't having these babies and..."

Her words fell to the side as she shook her head, fighting tears.

"Eva, I love you. That's not true," I said. "None of that is true. I cannot imagine a world in which you—a high-ranking leader at an international firm with an Oxbridge education would ever be labelled an embarrassment. And as for being a whore... I won't hear it."

"I know I'm not... but she's sure I'm your beard."

I snickered. "That is a new one. If so, I have a beautiful beard."

She shook her head. "Now's not the time, David."

"For what?"

"Don't call me beautiful. I don't feel beautiful. I don't feel loved or protected or—"

I stopped her. "Hey, you are wonderful. And I love you and will protect you. But I think your parents—"

"They refused to say anything to her, David. Ian ripped my nephew out of my hands. He was sobbing. It was traumatic. He went from smiling at me and bopping around on my knee to seeing me as a monster. My parents didn't say anything. They refused to hold her accountable. Davey, I cannot let our children grow up around that. I love my parents fiercely. I know they love me, but if they cannot hold her accountable, I can't do it. You must think I'm being stupid but... I'm not."

I shook my head. "No, baby, I don't. I think you're protecting yourself from someone toxic. Being family isn't an excuse for abuse. She hurt you. She did it in front of her own child. That's totally fucked up."

"But there are no consequences!"

"I'm sorry, but there were. She lost you in that moment. That is awful, but it's what she earned. I would never let someone talk that way to you. I'd have packed us up—same as you."

"Davey, I'm scared." Eva collapsed, curling in my lap.

I tried to calm Eva with back rubs. After a few minutes, she fell asleep. I grabbed a pillow to slide under her neck for support and slid from beneath her. Eva's tired body barely moved. She was emotionally exhausted. All I could do was think about how angry I was. My mother might have been a classist asshole, but she wouldn't have tolerated a rant like that aimed at my sisters. I was sure somehow it could be fixed, but I didn't know how to get there.

26. ROOMMATES

Eva

"Eva, can I bother you?"

I looked up as Claire entered. "Sure. Of course."

I stood, hoping my computer hid the fact that my *work* pants were nothing more than a pair of flared yoga pants. I'd been at Davey's for three days. Ellie brought me a restock of "forgiving" clothes, but even with a hair tie, none of my dress slacks convincingly fit me. The babies officially took over my body.

"So, my daughter is having surgery next week," Claire said. "It's very pressing. She fractured her elbow so badly that they need to put pins in. Damn monkey bars! I'd decided to go in Daphne's place to London, but I don't think I can swing it. And we need someone who both understands our need to get them on our devices and network and can read legalese. That leaves you. I didn't know how you felt about going with David?"

"Uh... I..."

"I didn't even know if you were allowed to travel."

"I am," I said. "I can, for all I know. But I don't know how David feels about it."

"I wanted to ask you before I asked him. Have you seen him this morning?"

"Not particularly," I lied. "Just in passing."

Of *course* I had. He'd woken me up and insisted on eating me out. We still hadn't resolved what we *were*, but we fucked like rabbits. Getting off was the best coping mechanism I had. Thankfully, he was good for that and a back rub afterwards.

"He's in a good mood," Claire said. "I'm sorry. I don't know what the deal is. It's awkward and Daphne being gone... I'm making it weird."

"The whole us getting together before I started here—by accident—bit is what makes it weird," I said. "Sorry. And the babies are fine. It's not like there's anything wrong there. But it's still awkward."

"I am glad all is well there. If you two aren't on good terms—"

"We're fine," I said. "Do you think trying *not* to make it weird is... in-fact... making it weird?"

"A little. I think we're all just holding our breath until we can tell everyone or... not."

"That has to come from David."

"I think he's afraid to say anything without your go-ahead."

I rolled my eyes. "Of *course* he is."

"Maybe talk to him while you're in London? Not to... tell you what to say, but it might be helpful if we could at least tell direct reports."

"What, you don't think they can tell I'm pregnant, right?" I joked. "None of my slacks fit. I'm barely still making it into my tops. It's a hot mess."

"Get the stretchy pants. They are ugly, but you'll thank yourself."

"Thanks," I said. "Do you want me to talk to David?"

"If you don't mind. My morning is—"

"Got it," I said. "I hope the surgery goes well and she's back to monkeying around soon."

"Me, too. Thanks."

Claire dipped. I pulled up my yoga pants and decided to see

what Davey's schedule looked like. His assistant glared. She had it in for me since discovering we were scheduling time off together. I knew she thought we were having an affair. The truth, however, was worse.

I peered into the room through the windows, watching David talk on the phone.

"I just need to get a spot on his schedule about the London trip," I said.

"He's very busy, Miss Pavlak."

"I am aware, but this is coming from Claire," I said, annoyed.

"He's very busy."

"I know that. Can you get me fifteen minutes or not?" I asked.

"He's not some friend you just call up and he jumps to help you, right?"

"No, Meg," I said. "It's far too complicated for that. But this is coming from us in InfoSec. I need to speak with him."

"Maybe Ms. Nguyen should come on her *own* accord?"

I set my jaw. "I asked a yes or no question, Meg."

"I don't like your tone, Miss Pavlak—"

"Excuse me," Davey poked his head out. "Is there an issue?"

I glared at Meg.

Flatly, she answered, "Miss Pavlak is demanding an audience. I've explained you're very busy. She has become aggressive."

"I doubt she's aggressive, Meg," Davey said. "I can speak to her now."

He held the door as I stepped in.

"Is this good or bad?" Davey asked.

"It's bad to the point I want to strangle an old woman," I said.

"Oh, Meg? She's old-fashioned. She was my dad's assistant for at least twenty years, Eva."

"She thinks I'm some silly child who is monopolizing your time. It needs to stop."

Davey sat on his desk and rubbed his temples. "I will speak with her, okay?"

"If it's going to be like this when we have a legitimate incident—"

"I know, if something happens with the twins—"

"I meant a *cyber* incident. A major incident," I said.

"Oh, shit. Yes. Work."

His mind was anywhere *but* work.

"Look, as much as I do *not* want to go to London right now, Claire's kid is injured. She wants to be in Chicago for the surgery. She asked if I could go. The D/CISOs are covering for her as per usual. At least here. They need me on the road covering for Daphne unless you have a better idea."

Davey smiled. "Wait, you don't want to go to London? C'mon, it would be fun, right?"

I winced, "Fun?"

"Sure. We get to take the big plane and stay at Daphne's place. It's beautiful."

"Davey, I left London in a panic. I'm returning there two minor people bigger. I don't really think I'm the one you should take. Is it appropriate? What if someone *says* something? It could kill the deal."

"I am bringing my very capable BISO with me—Daphne's protege—on the road to buy a company. If anyone says anything about *us* all it will be is an assumption that I decided to stick my hand in the cookie jar and hook up with one of my sister's very hot direct reports. And oops! No one will judge me for that. It's a tale as old as time."

"But *me* Davey?" I asked, annoyed.

"Eva, your qualifications speak for themselves. We decided to do this. If you didn't want to be associated with me—and all that goes *with* me, my love—then you're SOL."

He was right. I hated the gossip.

"Then, go out there and announce it," I said.

"What?"

"If you're not afraid of everyone knowing what we did and

what is going on, you need to tell everyone that you're the father of these babies."

"Eva, how would I do that? Send an all-employees email?"

"You're the CEO. Figure it out. We're roommates now, right? We show up at work together. It's on you to do something else and fix it."

"I would like to think we are *more* than roommates, Eva," Davey said.

"Well, prove it," I stormed out.

The ball was in his court. I couldn't do his job. And even if I could, I refused.

* * *

Davey

"Prove it."

Eva rushed out. Due to my plate glass windows and open door, everyone milling on the c-suite floor heard our argument. Meg entered as if trying to protect me or stop the fallout. Yes, if Eva were any other employee, I would have gone to her direct supervisor and told them to handle it. Instead, I couldn't exactly *do* that.

"Sir, are you alright?"

"I'm fine."

"Would you like me to call Ms. Ngyuen?"

"No." I shook my head and massaged my temples.

Prove it. This wasn't about disguising things or trying to divert attention. Eva only grew more pregnant by the day. Meg knew what was happening—I suspected many people thought they did, too—but it was time to be abundantly clear.

"Meg, can you close the door and take a seat?" I asked.

Though concerned, she followed orders.

I cleared my throat, preparing for this uncomfortable conversation. "The situation with Miss Pavlak may be confusing sometimes. For that, I apologize, but... she is a valued employee here. As she and Claire fill in on the operations side for Daphne, I would ask you treat her as you would my sister. I don't know why you argued with her earlier, but that cannot happen."

Meg shook her head. "I worry for you. Mixing home and work like this… while she galivants around… it's not good."

"Galivants?" I snickered. "Eva is least likely to galivant. She's quite calm and laid-back in real life. She doesn't put on airs."

"She is *demanding*. She speaks out of turn and defies authority."

"Only with me. And she has every right to question me right now," I said. "On the personal side, Eva and the twins take priority and always will."

"I don't like how she mixes the two and expects you to drop everything. It's not proper behavior."

"For whom?" I chuckled. "Mum would have marched in here and demanded Dad immediately pack up if she needed him to attend a band concert for Derrick or a play for Lanie. I don't think I've met a more demanding woman than my mother."

"Your parents were married. I do not understand this at all. This is… it's highway robbery!"

I should have called her out, but I decided the best approach was to let Meg vent and redirect.

"You are correct that we are not married, but that makes no difference. Eva will forever be in my life. No one is robbing anyone. We agreed to have children together. That is all. It is also beside the point."

"Oh?"

"Yes. Meg, you prevented Eva from doing her job. She asked me about official business. Claire is sending her to London in her place. She needed to confirm that with me. And now, I need you to confirm that you can get her on the passenger manifest for the jet. Do not do that again. I know your first impulse is to protect me—and the company—but Eva shares in that motivation. We are a team. I need InfoSec to have access to me while Daphne is out. Claire and Eva get priority in the case of an incident. You need to treat them both with respect. Do you understand?"

She nodded. "I don't mean to be rude."

"I know," I said. "Uh, besides adding Miss Pavlak to the manifest, can you organize a meeting with all my VPs and directors for this afternoon? Clear schedules if you must. Exclude Eva and Claire. Neither of them needs to be there. Claire is swamped and Eva won't want to attend."

"Should I include an agenda, sir?"

"Call it contingency planning and leave it broad."

* * *

The afternoon rolled around. I found myself in a conference room with everyone with a rank of director or higher—minus Eva and Claire. Their faces signaled concerns about mass layoffs rather than my poorly-put-together pregnancy announcement. I flew by the seat of my pants as much as ever, trying to channel the What Would Dad Do of it all. I reflected on the number of times people criticized Mum for being "too involved", but also how her vision made the company a retail powerhouse. In our case, Eva needed levity not only for family sake, but because she was key to modernizing our tech strategy.

"Thank you all for being here," I said. "I know it is very busy, so I will not keep you long. Look, this isn't a layoff or anything. We're thriving and about to close the London deal. There is no reason to worry. However, I called you here to discuss some upcoming changes and planning for the future."

People relaxed when they realized this wasn't a layoff.

"So, does anyone want to know what my father said made this company exceptional?"

No one responded.

"Okay... well, maybe you think it's rhetorical, but... it's a family-run company. For awhile, I wanted so badly to IPO, but no. I am reminded that our strength has always been in our ability to rally together as a family and a team. Recently, we've forgotten this —despite the big flashing signs otherwise."

I paced. "Daphne being on leave is complicated, yes. I've heard some rumblings and complaints. The truth is, we should be happy for Daphne. She's transformed our retail sector and saved hundreds of jobs in her past year here. It thrills me to see another generation here filling these halls as all of us kids did and as Dad and his siblings did before us."

Some heads nodded.

"Now, there is an elephant in the room I want to clear up—a lot of talk about whether there has been some sort of foul play or affair involving myself and Ms. Pavlak. Some in this room have felt it acceptable to poke fun at her or act insubordinate or rude. I'd like to remind you that this is unacceptable and will be seen as harassment."

The most reliable of the rumor mill looked down.

"Yes, Ms. Pavlak and I began seeing one another *before* Daphne hired her. Yes, we are expecting twins in the new year. Yes, we remain professional."

Audible gasps filled the room, but I continued.

"No policy has been violated. In the spirit of our past, I will take leave, just as Daphne has. She is aware she will be in charge. You might not like that, those are *your* opinions. However, my father took time off for the birth of every one of his six children at a time that was uncommon. I won't hear criticism of either people giving birth or supporting people through bonding time with their children."

The room fell silent.

"After you leave this meeting, please remind your employees that our family leave policies exist to ensure a balance in their work lives with the thing that matters most—their family. Happy, fulfilled people are the backbone of our company. Let's not lose sight of that. Furthermore, if I hear any of you being unkind to any person at the company about to give birth or support a partner through that process, I will take action with HR. Such behavior is discriminatory. Thank you. That is all."

The room remained quiet as people filed out. I realized Eva had watched the whole thing from the coffee machine, curious. I met her gaze before filing out.

"I just handled it," I said. "Can we go to London and put this all behind us?"

She shrugged. "We can try, but shit is still complicated."

"It always will be," I agreed. "That's life."

27.COMPLICATIONS AND FRUSTRATIONS

Davey

"So, ready to prepare?"

I busted out the hospital folder from or last doctor's appointment.

"What?" Eva looked up from her laptop.

"We're at cruising altitude. You should be sleeping, but I know you won't," I said. "Not yet, anyhow. So, let's look through the stuff we need to do before the multiples class starts."

"We have like a month."

"That will fly by," I said.

Eva closed her laptop, "Davey, this is the most ridiculous thing. We're on the company plane and we're talking about baby stuff. It makes no sense."

"Meh, it's fine," I said. "So, we need to set time aside to buy baby stuff. Do you have preferences about safe sleeping surfaces?"

"Are you serious?" Eva laughed. "What?"

"Well, they recommend an in-room bassinet for each baby. Then two cribs in the nursery."

"And where is the nursery going, David?"

"I assume in the room next to my office."

"Why?"

"Because that doesn't make sense as a guest room."

"You want to hear them crying at night while you're trying to work?"

"Choose a room. We'll put it there. And then night nurse can have the other room."

"Oh, on that," Eva perked up. "I got recommendations from Daphne. She sent them over."

"What? How are *you* getting recs from Daphne, but she won't text me back?" I asked, offended.

"I'll email them," Eva opened her laptop, not answering.

"Okay, let's go shopping maybe Sunday next week?"

She shrugged. "Let's see how I feel."

"Uh… we are working on childcare." I read on. "So, we're ace there. You've told HR you're taking leave?"

She nodded. "As have you… and the entire office."

I snickered. "It was an interesting move, but one I do not regret. Okay, so what about the birth plan?"

"I want alive babies. Next please."

"Eva, I'm serious."

"Davey, I will probably end up with a c-section. You heard the doctor. I'm not going to get wrapped up in worrying about it. All I want are healthy babies."

I let that one go.

"Done!" Eva said. "Sent you the list. Can you be responsible for lining up interviews?"

"For what?"

"Nannies," Eva answered.

"Why is that my responsibility?"

"Why is it *my* responsibility, David?"

Drop the rope, Davey.

"Alright, I will try to fit that in. Would you like to attend the interviews or—"

"Yes, David. Good lord! All I asked was that you have them scheduled, okay? I am managing this trip on top of my current workload *and* covering for Daphne."

I winced. "Gotcha. You're right."

"What now? Are we done?"

"Preschool."

"Preschool?" Eva scoffed. "David, this is nuts. Who the fuck thinks about preschool with fetuses in utero? For fuck's sake!"

"Daphne and Cal have put in for placements at like three schools," I said. "It gets competitive. It is cutthroat."

"They can go to any old preschool when the time is right," Eva said. "I went to fucking Oxford and only went three days a week for three hours to the local parochial school. I'm fine. They will be, too."

"It's about being connected, Eva—"

"David, let's talk about this later."

She was tired and grew short.

"Okay, last one. I thought this was funny. Circumcision. We need to tell the hospital to schedule it."

"Or not," Eva said. "Because we're not."

"No, I think we should," I said.

"And I think we shouldn't, David. You want to do it?"

"Well, yeah."

"Why?" Eva asked, eyebrows tight as she scowled. "It's ridiculous. I cannot with that. You have no religious observance that suggests it."

"So? I think we should do it. And I'm the one with a dick, so—"

"I'm their mother," Eva said. "And you aren't circumcised. Are you *trying* to pick a fight with me over something silly?"

"Eva, this is something—"

"No," Eva said. "Absolutely not. It's not up for debate."

I couldn't understand why she was so callous about this.

"Eva, you have to at least consider where I am coming from."

"Okay, fine. Where are you coming from?" She crossed her arms.

"I was bullied, okay? All through school and sports as a kid."

"What? David, you're hung like a fucking horse. What are you talking about?"

"I was the only kid for miles who wasn't, okay? Mum refused to because they don't do that over there. And... Dad just let her manage it. I dunno. I have strong feelings about this. You do realize it's different?"

"Yeah. And I don't agree with it." Eva said.

"It doesn't bother you?"

"Davey, why the fuck would I have opinions about your foreskin? This is such a weird conversation. For reference, I've only seen one circumcised penis in the flesh—on my high school boyfriend. Every other one was uncut, so... I don't really remember anything negative other than the man couldn't find my clit. His dick was not the problem."

"Women have opinions," I said. "And I don't want them bullied. Can you at least consider that?"

She breathed. "You really are bothered by this?"

"Guys can be sensitive, too. We have our own shit."

"I am so, so sorry anyone said those things, Davey." Her empathy was genuine. "My high school boyfriend told me my lips were too big, and I had hangups for years. It took about four girlfriends before I calmed the fuck down."

It was such an odd statement.

"You have an absolutely wonderful cock that does magical fucking things," Eva said. "And I am sure no matter what, those people would have been absolute dickheads about something else if not that. It's like girls making fun of my big boobs. And that was while I was realizing I *liked* boobs for the first time."

"How was that?"

"How was that for you?" Eva directed it back, as if annoyed. "It was like it was for you except no one called attention to it because you have a dick. Luckily for me, I wasn't dealing with sporadic boners every time I thought about tits."

I laughed. "God, I love you."

"What? Why?"

"Just... you are so dry. It's funny. I love listening to your rants, my love."

She softened. "Let's take a minute. Review some stuff and table it?"

She pushed the table over, moving the seat into a reclining mode. I followed suit, ready to turn in for the night.

"Okay," I agreed as she rested her head on my shoulder.

I kissed her head, breathing in perfume. "Eva?"

"Yes," she murmured.

"I love your brutal honesty," I said. "Even if it's sometimes a lot, I love that you are straightforward with me. Don't stop."

"Don't stop being vulnerable, okay? It encourages me to try harder," Eva admitted. "I am glad we talked about this. Even if you're not right about this subject, at least we could have a productive discussion."

"Is that a good thing?" I asked.

"I think we've officially reached the stage where we can just *talk* without it being an issue, yeah," Eva whispered.

PART IV

FAMILY

28.LONDON

Davey

WE LANDED IN LONDON AND HEADED TO DAPHNE'S POSH HOUSE—
the one she inherited from a rich aunt in spite. She fought hard to
keep it in her contentious divorce. Now, it was all ours. The place
was a palace. Daphne rarely used it, instead either renting or
loaning it to friends and family. When people came over to repre-
sent the company, they stayed here.

"Are we pretending to be chaste and have two rooms or just
one?" I joked.

"Uh, I think we're beyond that point," Eva said.

I deposited our bags as she looked around and onto the street
below.

"The address was impressive, but the house is even more so,"
Eva said.

"Well, Daphne is like my mother—very into grand houses. The
place is beautiful."

"When is our first meeting?"

"We don't have anything until the evening," I said.

"Great. I'm going to hop in the shower."

She kicked off her shoes and started to undress as I pulled the curtains. By the time I turned, she was there, half-naked, taking up all my brain space.

"What?" Eva asked. "You want to join me?"

I stammered. "I… I don't have to."

"I wouldn't complain. Look, I'm horny. If you're in, join me."

I kissed her. She was sexy as hell. I undid her bra and played with her nipple. She moaned and bit my lip. I ran my hand down to her panties, but she stopped me and walked away.

"If you want me, join me…" Her words faded as she bent over before she kicked her panties aside.

I watched in agony as she slowly left the room, her hips swaying painfully.

"God damn it, Eva," I groaned, cursing myself for still being clothed.

I found her in the shower, pressed against the shower wall, holding herself up by one forearm while her still-recovering right hand tried to work its magic. She ran her fingers in her pussy, moaning as she brought herself closer.

"I'm sorry, who said you could start without me?" I joked.

"You took too long," Eva said.

I stood by her, trying to touch her.

She batted my hand away. "No. You get to watch, but you have to wait."

I should have been infuriated, but I was intrigued. She panted, growing closer to her climax. I soaked up the warmth of the shower while pumping my shaft. I enjoyed the visual, but I also loved hearing her cum. She moaned louder, desperate to get off.

"Oh, fuck," Eva said. "Come here."

I obeyed, moving close. She pulled my hand towards her.

"I want you to feel me cum," she moaned. "Please."

She played with her clit as I slid my fingers inside, slowly tickling her G-spot.

She moaned, "Oh, God! Yes, Davey! Fuck!"

She collapsed against the wall briefly, still pulsing around my fingers. As I pulled my hand back, she brought it to her face. With full eye contact, she sucked on the two fingers that had just been inside, then reached down to my cock. The way she freely owned this moment left me reeling.

"You like that?" I asked.

"Uh-huh," Eva moaned. "Yes, Daddy. Now, fuck me."

Oh, fuck.

I took a seat on the shower bench and beckoned. "I'm not going to fuck you against the wall, Eva. That's too dangerous. But you can ride my cock if you want."

Sometimes, I couldn't believe she even responded to me when I got like this. These days, her way of dealing with anything frustrating or boring was to proposition me. Luckily for her, I didn't mind being her plaything and loved watching her use me to get off.

Eva straddled me, slipping onto my cock. She kissed me. Her taste lingered on her lips. She felt so wet and perfect wrapped around me. I slowly guided her as she bobbed. I didn't want her going too fast or I'd cum.

"Will you cum again for me, baby?" I asked.

"Uh… uh-huh," Eva moaned, biting her lip.

I slapped her ass. "It's yes or no, Eva."

"Yes, daddy," Eva said. "I wanna cum."

"You better cum hard then!" I watched her grind against me slowly.

Nostrils flaring and chest flushed, she dug her palms into the base of my neck, trying not to scratch me or squeeze too tight. The truth was, I loved it when she did. She liked to pretend I was in control. It got her off. But she owned every moment. I was completely satisfied, letting her control the dynamic. I gripped her face in both hands as she wound up, close to climax.

"Cum for me, Eva. Cum for me, baby," I said.

"Oh… fuck!" Eva shouted. "Oh, God! Yes! Yes!"

She threw her head back and shuddered, stopping only as she felt me close to climax. It was glorious. I loved cumming with her like that—wrapped up, completely focused on one another, and feeling nothing but obsession with her. Eva was like a drug I couldn't quit. Getting her off was the sweetest fix.

* * *

Eva

I held my phone in my hand, looking at three missed calls—all from Mona. Then a text.

> **MONA**
>
> Please call, Eva. It's about Carter.

My heart dropped.

Davey kissed my shoulder as he passed. He sensed something was up. I called her back.

"What's up?"

"Uh… Mona is trying to reach me," I said. "It's… I gotta take this."

I caught sight of Davey's confused expression in the mirror as I took my robe-clad body into the still-steamy bathroom. Fear set in.

"Hi, Eva," Mona answered, voice sounding low. "I know it's late there. It's… what—"

"I'm in London," I answered. "I just got in."

"Oh, really?"

"Yes," I answered. "I'm here for work. What do you need? What is going on with Carter?"

"She's crashing. We found a mass a couple of months ago—"

"A mass?" My jaw dropped. "Like cancer?"

"She's holding on, but it's not looking like she will make it through winter. She's still doing okay, but I figured… I knew you'd want to remember her this way, not where she's going. I figured I'd drop you a line. I know you're ignoring me for—"

"It's… it's okay. Uh, is she at the house… your house?"

"Yes," Mona said. "I'm here all day working from home. I've

been trying to do that more to spend time with her. She'd love to see you."

I thought about Davey and how he'd react to me saying I'd like to visit my ex before our meeting later.

"I will try to swing by," I said. "I'll text you."

"Great. Okay. Just let me know, darling."

Darling. Normally, that would have warmed my heart. Instead, it made me sweat in a bad way. I wanted to puke. I wasn't sure I could handle seeing Mona right now. I also didn't want to miss saying goodbye. Returning, I stared at Davey as he fumbled through his suitcase for something.

"You alright, Eva?"

"I… my dog is dying," I said. "The one my ex stole from me. She's sick. She has cancer. I want to see her."

"Oh… okay?" He didn't look fussed.

"Can I go? The only issue… it's in Richmond, which is… not super close. By the time I get ready and head over there, I will only have an hour or so before doubling back."

"Why don't we do this," Davey suggested. "You take the car out there, see the dog, and I will get in the car and head back to get you. I'll wait. I'm not going to come and get you. We'll just park and you can find us, Eva."

"That doesn't bother you?"

"Should it?" Davey snickered.

"I dunno."

"Eva, I trust you. I love you. I know this isn't a ruse to sleep with your ex. You look like you've seen a ghost."

"Thanks, Davey," I said.

* * *

I rang the bell at Mona's place in Richmond. Her semi-detached house looked exactly as I remembered. I felt awkward in a cocktail dress during the afternoon. I couldn't miss our meeting, and we were about to have a posh dinner. She appeared, our Corgi, Carter, at her ankles. Before greeting Mona, I bent down to give Carter ear scratches. Tears welled before I knew it. I didn't expect them right away, but I realized how much I'd missed this face or the way she always nosed my ears as I hugged her neck tight.

Still fighting tears, I looked at Mona. "She still looks really good."

"She does. But her last scan a couple of days ago doesn't," Mona sighed.

I tried to stand but couldn't. I was stuck, betrayed by my non-existent core.

"Can you help me up?" I winced, extending my left arm.

My right remained weak.

"Okay," Mona said, confused.

I stood with help, forgetting that she didn't know I was pregnant. Suddenly, I panicked. *Don't cup your stomach, damn it!*

"Come in," Mona said. "I'll make tea."

I followed Mona inside. It smelled different but looked mostly the same. I noticed a pink coat in the corner that was too big for Mona. My stomach sank as I felt replaced the same as I had when I spoke with her two weeks after our breakup to divvy up some of our bills and realized she was already seeing people on a dating app. As her notifications went off, I couldn't help but think she was sending a message to me. It was a big middle finger. I got nothing in the breakup—not even my dog. I'd been too beaten down to fight.

I sat at the window seat in the breakfast nook off the conservatory. Mona put the kettle on, then fetched two mugs. Carter hopped up by me, her tail wagging like a propellor.

"You still want honey?" Mona asked in a judgmental British tone.

"No. I'm used to sugar now."

Her mouth dropped as she sat down the *good* biscuits. Any posh-o reserved such delicate, elegant biscuits for company. This choice signaled I was a guest rather than family.

"I'm living with the child of a Brit," I said. "And honey in tea is verboten. I've adapted."

"Good on her. You have a roommate?" Mona pitied me. "Oh, Eva, that's rough. I'm sorry."

I didn't correct Mona's assumption. Carter attempted to climb into my lap, something that was difficult for a body her size. She made it work but got a reaction out of me I didn't expect. Something fluttered inside me. Given I'd barely eaten, I didn't think it was gas. Those were *baby* flutters. I started to sob uncontrollably as I realized Carter would never meet my babies—my first baby would leave this world never knowing the twins.

Mona brought two mugs back—the same way Davey always did when I had a shitty day.

"It will be okay, Eva," Mona said. "God, I didn't think you'd get this emotional."

"I… I love this dog, Mona. I am sorry, but it is hitting hard. I appreciate you ringing me."

"Of course. I feel like… it's the least I could do, darling."

We sat in awkward silence as the dog slept in my lap. The flutters continued.

"So, are we going to talk about the obvious thing you did behind my back?" Mona sighed.

I furrowed my brow. "What?"

She nodded towards my stomach. "You aren't going to explain that? Was that your last order of business? How did you manage it?"

"I didn't do it behind your back," I said, angry she felt control over my body like that. "I was free-and-clear. You don't own me, sweetheart. You broke it off. I was the one who had to move out. You insisted on keeping Carter, too. Don't rewrite history."

She furrowed her brow. "Did you not use the last straw?"

It took me awhile to figure out what she meant. "You mean the sperm bank straw?"

"The one we said you wouldn't use."

"The one you *accused* me of wanting to use," I clapped back. "No. I would never do that without your consent."

"Good, because it was my money—"

I set my jaw. It was the same argument every time—her money, her time, her place.

"It was our money. I paid for half the treatments, Mona. And I'm not arguing about it. This wasn't the straw."

"How… how are you *so* pregnant? When did this happen?"

"After I moved back. I'm having twins," I answered.

"You found a sperm bank that fast?"

"It's really none of your business," I said. "They aren't your problem."

"That is irresponsible, Eva. You aren't in a place—"

"Mona, save your condescension for someone who gives a fuck," I said, even more hurt. "I didn't come here for your verbal abuse and judgement."

She fell silent. I pet Carter, silently wishing I could steal her away and let her spend the last couple of months of her life in my office at work sleeping on a bed fit for a princess—the way I had when in London on Fridays. Davey would love her, right? We'd have an apartment dog. Mona would never allow it.

"You moved on, too," I was salty and unwilling to give up the argument before winning. "I saw the coat in the hall."

Mona looked down. "Look, I'm seeing someone, yeah. But that is very different—"

"So am I," I said. "This was… unexpected and unplanned, but a blessing for us both, okay? We're doing our best and I don't need your judgement on top of Brooke's blatant slut-shaming and homophobia."

Mona looked up, sympathetic. "Oh, she finally made it there? I'm sorry, Eva. Fuck Ian."

"Indeed. I'm not speaking with her right now. I didn't go to her stupid baby sprinkle. Now, I cannot talk to my parents."

"They love you, Eva."

"They do. They also didn't stop her from calling me a whore and accusing me of being someone's beard."

"So… he's a guy? I shouldn't assume, I suppose—"

"He's a dude, yes," I answered. "Make all the jokes you want to your girlfriend. I don't want to hear about it."

"I'm not going to poke fun, Eva. I'm just surprised you'd trust someone. That's got to be a good sign."

No thanks to you! She saw this as a way to alleviate her own guilt about dumping me in the middle of a miscarriage.

"When are you due?"

"January."

"And your job?"

"They are understanding. You know Daphne will take care of me. She's about to have her baby," I said. "She gets it."

"And her boss?"

"He doesn't have a choice but to accept it."

"Can I ask who he is?"

"Can I ask who she is?" I clapped back. I knew the answer was no.

She looked down. "Well, as long as you are happy and healthy, that's what matters."

I nodded. "Same."

"I'm glad for you. Relieved, even. It's selfish, but I know you wanted so badly to be a mum. Now, you will be. That is good, Eva."

"Do you ever regret not being a mum?" I asked.

"No. But I knew you would. That was the issue, darling. Do you think it will work out with the dad?"

"I hope so," I said. "He's been there for every appointment. He did all this research and even made a labor and birth prep check-list. It's annoying."

"But sweet," Mona giggled. "That's adorable."

I shrugged. "He was a bit of a man-child. I needed him to prove he was going to show up more than once or twice. And ever since what happened with Brooke, he's been there for me."

"So, you're living with him?"

"Are you living with her?"

Mona sighed. "Do you have a comeback to everything, Eva?"

"Are we both attorneys?"

She snickered. "Your spark is back. Good for you. I hope it works out. I'm sorry about Carter. I wish I had better news, but I am glad I got to see you. You're glowing. I hope the babies cook a long time and come out looking just like their mum."

"Oh, we already have side profiles. They have my nose and his chin."

"Is that good or bad?"

"Good," I said. "They're beautiful. And even if they were hideous, I'd be head-over-heels, you know?"

* * *

Davey

"I am looking out the window and I have no idea where the navy Rolls is," Eva sighed. "It's pouring and I'm dressed to the nines. My hair will—"

"I know. I can bring an umbrella, baby, but I don't want to upset you."

I needed to pick Eva up for dinner. She'd been at Mona's place in a very posh part of London. We were parked on her street in a downpour, but Eva didn't want to leave until she spotted the car.

"It's okay," Eva agreed to my surprise. "Just come to the door and I'll meet you."

"Sure."

I hung up, proceeding to the door. We were a block off the last remaining space during the evening rush home. I suspected all these houses were owned by high-ranking professionals. It was an idyllic little street. Even Mum would approve.

At the door, I didn't know what to expect. I rang the bell and Eva answered. A dog rushed up, tail wagging. Out of habit, I bent down.

"Are you Carter? Oh, you're sweet," I cooed, then looked at Eva.

"I knew you liked dogs," Eva said. "This is Carter. She's the sweetest girl."

"She is," I agreed. "I actually love dogs, even if Mum hated them and refused to own one."

As another woman with a trendy haircut approached, I stood. This must have been Eva's ex. She was and wasn't what I expected. She was taller than Eva, but far more feminine than I first assumed. The woman was very pretty, about my age, and sported a serious look.

"Well, Eva, can you introduce me?" She asked.

"Sure," Eva looked nervous. "This is David Delphine. My boss's boss."

Her boss's boss?

"Oh, shit," Mona said. "I thought this was… the guy?"

"He is," Eva said. "But we're here on business and I'm never sure how to answer."

Mona did a double-take. "That is not like you, Eva."

"I mean, you and I met through work," Eva said. "But… David and I weren't together when we met. It was a freak coincidence."

"How did you—"

"As you would say, Mona, I lived under a rock and became a hermit. I never met him. Yes, he's Daphne's brother, but I never put together that her brother David was a man named Davey who sometimes hung out in Wrigleyville saving women from gropey straight dudes."

"They were out for Ellie's hen party," I said. "And she was… flailing. Men threw themselves at her. She was there with her friend's sibling, and it was *not* their scene."

"Straight women drinking beyond their capacity," Eva giggled. "And Davey stuck around."

"Because I was also throwing myself at her," I admitted, unashamed.

That caught Mona off-guard. "And you clearly wasted no time."

I sensed a competitive side to Mona's retort.

"Yeah, well, this wasn't planned. We tried to prevent it... but life is wild." I smiled. "Eva is wonderful, as you well know. And clever, which is why she's along for the ride while Daphne is out."

"Good to know."

"Now, Eva, I think we have a deal to close?"

"Correct," Eva hugged and kissed the dog. "I love you, baby. Be good for Mummy. I am sorry to leave you."

It hit me in the feels. She'd never spoken to anything with such sweetness in my presence. The dog meant so much to her.

Eva left, holding my hand as if for support. I rushed us to the car where the driver stood holding the door. Eva slid in indelicately—we were beyond that point in the pregnancy—and settled in.

"Thanks for coming to get me," she said as the driver headed towards Shoreditch.

"Of course. I'm sorry about your dog, Eva. If I couldn't be there for her...it would be hard."

"It's awful. Mona took everything—she needed to win. It was always *her* money, *her* house, *her* plans, and *her* priorities. Speaking with her today, it rang louder than ever. We were pleasant, but she initially accused me of stealing the straws she believes she paid for."

"Straws?"

"Sperm. We had one last straw left in our arsenal from our donor when I miscarried. The first thing she told me when we met post-breakup to divvy things up was she didn't want me to use that straw. It hurt— a lot. It's gross to think I had such a good five years with her. Was it even the truth or just control?"

I squeezed Eva's hand. "I think she still cares about you, but breakups are messy, Eva. They bring out the worst in us. Even the best people can sink to new lows during a divorce. I watched my sister lose herself while Chandler dug in low enough to leak a sex tape. He was never my favorite person, but I didn't see that coming."

"Sadly, it didn't surprise me," Eva sighed, resting her head on my shoulder.

"I think you can love the good parts as much as you feel the pain of being blindsided," I admitted. "When Dad died, I struggled to deal with any of the good memories. I was so broken over the loss and taking over the responsibilities of the family that I reacted erratically and with anger. People saw me as the villain—especially Daphne. I don't blame her, but that wasn't the goal."

"What do you mean?"

"I hid all the pictures in my office of the family because I couldn't see Dad smiling and us all happy without crying. I hate to admit that, but it's the truth."

"Davey, that's heartbreaking, but understandable."

I loved the sweetness in her face now.

"Grieving something... it's not linear. I wanted to hurt everyone around me to feel anything," I said. "And I regret it now. I even tried to kick Cal's ass."

"What?" Eva laughed.

"Daphne ended up injured after falling off his sister's horse. Cal brought her home, and I found out not only were they fucking but that Dad wanted him to take over the company instead of me. I was a third choice—Daphne, then Cal, and finally me. I saw red. In the end, we worked it out. I'm still a little salty. We've always been competitors, you know? There's no way around it."

"I hate my brother-in-law, so I have no place to talk. Now, fill me in. I've been so distracted. I apologize. What is going on with this company?"

"In my attempts to expand our sustainable development empire," I explained, "we're courting a company developing a unique insulation solution. I want it so we can control its use in the U.S. Market. It's a nice feather in the cap, but the owner is a fucking narcissist."

"So, what, I'm here to be a buffer?"

"You'll be a lovely help. He's a techie. You'll do great, baby."

"You really think that?"

"I know that," I said. "Eva, you're my partner in crime if you want to be."

29.TRAINSPOTTING

Davey

Eva excelled when she could talk authoritatively about tech solutions. The meeting with Pimm, our acquisition contact, was her time to shine. After some coaching, the asshole agreed to the redlines, scheduling a time to sign in the morning. *Success!* Papers sorted, we went back to Daphne's, and I tucked her in bed. She'd given so much emotionally and intellectually, I couldn't expect anything more out of her for the rest of the trip.

We woke the next morning, heading to a highly recommended breakfast spot. Eva was quiet, still held in jet lag's chokehold. Despite this, she offered to join me on a voyage to a platform at Gatwick. I never expected her to come, but she took a coffee to go and sat waiting for a train.

"You really must be bored," I looked down the line.

"The weather isn't bad, and I need to be awake," Eva said. "Now what is this train and why the fuck are we here just to see it?"

"It's a 73/9. It's super rare. They're using it on the rear of a train to move new cars. I heard it would be here in approximately ten minutes."

"What is a 73/9?"

"A locomotive."

"But like… what type?"

"A 73/9." I couldn't understand what she wasn't getting.

She set her jaw. "But like does it carry people or—"

"Oh, layman's terms! It carries freight—or rather pushes freight in this case."

"Ah."

She sat quietly, scrolling on her phone until I heard the train down the line.

"It's coming!" I announced, pulling out my phone.

Eva pulled herself from the bench and joined me. "Do we pull our arms down to see if it will honk at us?"

"It's a horn or a whistle and no. That would be amateur hour."

She rolled her eyes. "But isn't that the fun part?"

"When he's closer to the platform he will blow the horn." I waved as he approached

Seconds later, he proved me right. Eva adorably jumped and latched onto my arm. I waited for her to complain, but instead, she laughed. I recorded the passing train, amazed by the sight.

"That's really cool," Eva said, to my surprise.

"You don't have to lie."

"No, it was. I'm glad I got out. Honestly, I miss the tube. I miss good rail service. The South Shore would never."

"The double-track is pretty spectacular I hear."

"And yet, you'd never ride it."

"Fine. Someday."

"Not that you need to. Not that it matters since I don't go there—"

"Hey," I cut her off, feeling the spiral. "It's not forever. Someday, we will take those kids on an adventure. And if nothing else, we can ride the Wolverine up to Buffalo Shores."

"What the fuck is a Wolverine?"

"An amazing train. It's so fun."

She smiled. "If only you could see the way your face lights up! I want to poke fun, but it's honestly adorable."

She gave me a sappy kiss. I lived for these. Eva took my hand as we went to catch our train back to central London. I couldn't help but tell her what this meant.

"I'm glad we got to do this," I said.

She smiled. "Me, too."

"But it's not just you humoring me like this. I wanted to let you know how much I appreciate your work last night, Eva."

"Davey, you don't have to blow smoke. You needed a warm body with a pair of tits," Eva sighed.

I shook my head. "No, Eva. That was... I never thought that about you—ever."

"Uh-huh."

"Eva, I wanted you because I knew you'd be an asset."

"You didn't want me at first. I was the best you could do—"

"I didn't want to put you in a bad situation."

"Well, we got away with it."

"I don't think about getting away with anything. I told everyone what was going on. I copped to it. I told them I was excited and to stop attacking your credibility. I threatened to sack people over it, Eva. This isn't about you being pretty or me protecting you because you're having the twins. It was an earnest compliment."

Eva softened. "I'm sorry. I'm in a bad place this morning over Carter. It's stupid—"

I squeezed her hand. "Don't say that. And if you don't want to talk, we don't have to."

"It's okay," Eva agreed. "I'm sorry. My experience with male bosses has been that they think I'm a pretty whiz-kid. Well, they always did until they realized I was with a woman and pulled back. Now, you aren't like that, but... I expected that was why you thanked me."

"You have great tits," I said. "We both do. It had nothing to do with my gratitude. You're an excellent partner, Eva. That was why I said what I did. You add value to the company and *care* about the company. That is the big thing."

"I want to do a good job. I want to prove myself. This was a huge promotion, Davey."

"You fooled me. You do your job with authority. I trust you."

Loving Eva meant it was more than that, though. It went beyond my appreciation for her professional accomplishments or affability. Now, I knew it was more. It hit me. We were such a good team.

"I love you, Eva. And it's not just because I crave you. It's not just because you leave me tripping over myself intellectually. No. I can trust you with this stuff. Being a Delphine—and being in the company—goes beyond all of that. It's an obligation. Somehow, I know you can handle the heat in the kitchen. Our boys will come to appreciate that history. You'll not complain about it."

She cocked her head. "I never thought about that, Davey. Sometimes… I really worry about fitting in. I'm not one of you. I'm not old money. I didn't go to finishing school in Switzerland."

"That's a thing?"

"Mona did. Her mother always joked about wanting her to marry a prince. Oops!"

I chuckled. "Don't they all?"

"For real. Do you ever think I could even fit in?"

"Mum inexplicably adores you," I admitted. "That doesn't happen. I don't know why or how, but she prefers you to me. And no matter where this goes, Eva, I know you'll be valued. You're the mother of my children, but you're also one of the family's greatest assets right now. I don't want it to sound transactional, but I want you to know, I'm not about to throw you under the bus and own your accomplishments. Dad was excellent at giving out credit where it was due. Daphne says I'm shitty at that."

"You aren't good," Eva admitted. "She is."

"Daphne is dynamite at managing people. I hate that shit," I admitted. "Markets? Cashflow? I like that aspect. That's why I made a terrible president, I guess. I'm better as CEO, but I'm flagging."

"Have you ever thought about doing your own thing?" Eva asked.

I stammered. "Like… leaving the company?"

She shrugged. "Or starting your own business. You'll always own shares. You'll always be invested, but if you don't love it, is it not worth doing something else? Or, maybe you could step down to be president of another business unit? I am not here to tell you want to do, but you mention this a lot, Davey."

"It feels like admitting defeat. Dad would—"

"Your Dad never wanted you miserable. He left you millions, right? He wanted to see the company thrive, but you deserve that, too, Davey."

I never considered anything *but* CEO. Being president was a temporary thing to get to the big job. But I'd reached the peak, and it was a lonely one. Only Eva would have been brave enough to suggest it.

"I should think about it, Eva. Thanks."

"I hope I didn't offend you, but you said we were equals. Your work life—and mine—affects the boys. We gotta think about it like a family, as you said. I don't plan to quit my job or pull back—"

"I'd never ask you for that," I said. "I wouldn't dare ask you to give up. You're too young not to do bold, brave shit. Never change, baby."

30.MADE OF DISHONOR

Eva

"They're out there," Davey confirmed, meeting me in the hall outside the bride's suite. "But you got this. And you look gorgeous."

I gave him a quick kiss and tried to worry about my parents. Ellie wanted to uninvite them to spare me, but I'd not taken up her offer.

"Thanks. It's going to be awkward as hell, but it was unfair to tell them not to come."

"Sure, but… I don't think your parents are the type to raise a dramatic fuss. I simply gave them a little hello. They responded in kind and left it there."

"It probably knocked them over dead that you were here, David."

"Yeah, well, I love you. So, I'm here. Do you need anything? Water? Anything?"

"I'm good," I agreed, touching my stomach. The flutters strengthened. I stopped to appreciate them.

"What? Is something wrong?" Davey panicked.

"No," I laughed. "The babies are kicking. I've been feeling it more, but… it's not a bad thing."

Davey put a hand on my stomach.

"You're not gonna feel them, Davey. Someday soon. I promise."

"Eva, come on. We've got to take pictures," Callie called.

"Coming," I said.

Davey gave me a longer kiss. "You'll be great. Have fun."

I followed Jace, who waited down the hall.

"They want bridal party pictures before we go down."

"The groom is secured?" I asked.

"His people have been notified," Jace confirmed. "I just texted his brother."

"Great."

"So, you and the billionaire?" Jace snickered. "You never talk about him."

"It's awkward."

"Doesn't look awkward. Girl, he was *drooling*."

I snickered. "I don't get it. I am sweating like a pig. I hope the photographer can edit out pit stains."

"Relax. You look like some glowy pregnant lady. It's kind of amazing. You're growing motherfucking humans in there," they said. "It's wild."

"It's weird," I admitted. "I hate how much I love it when they kick me."

"Aww, you should. It's special. I won't fault you. Now, if I was pregnant, I'd be freaking the fuck out, but it suits you. And homeboy laps it up. Don't complain. It doesn't look like it's slowed you all down."

"It's for the best. The thing about this stage of pregnancy is I am constantly horny. I swear to God."

We stopped in front of the garden in the courtyard. Ellie tried to straighten Jane's dress.

"I got it," I said.

"No, stop!" Jace called me out. "I got it."

"Folks, I'm not broken. I can fix a dress!"

"Babes, if you squat right now, you're not coming back up," Ellie giggled. "Calm down. It's fine."

"I have been useless all day!" I whined as she beckoned me closer.

"You're not. You are the best moral support available." Ellie gave me a hug and a kiss. "How could I do this without you?"

"How could I not be here?" I sniffled, fighting tears.

"Tissue!" Callie called.

"Got it," Jace pulled one out of their jacket.

"Ladies, let's get together," the photographer insisted.

"Folks or y'all. We're not all ladies. I'm a Maid of Dishonor," I corrected him with some self-deprecation.

Jace shot me a look of solidarity.

"Come here and shut up," Ellie said. "You're adorable. Show it off. You're beautiful."

She was right. I was happy and safe. Brooke couldn't call me whore. I didn't have to fear my mother's judgement or the press's eagle-eyed awareness that I was carrying David's child. His mother insisted we do some sort of formal announcement via the publicist. I was wary but the *Tribune* already knew everything our workforce did. Why they withheld the news I didn't know. Maybe it was out of respect for David Sr's widow? No one knew. I was done being mortified. I couldn't exactly hide it any longer. Davey didn't want to. What more could we lose? The world hadn't ended.

* * *

Davey

"Can you tell Eva we didn't mean to miss her?" Bert asked.

He rushed over after the ceremony. I worried this was about to be a fight at the worst time. The newlyweds took pictures while we drank in celebration of their nuptials. The wedding was sweet and relaxed. It was perfect. The weather was a little warm, but nothing too bad for Labor Day. I didn't want Bert and Mary to ruin everything.

"Excuse me?" I asked, confused.

"We meant to tell her we loved her—and not say anything about Brooke. We don't want trouble. We are trying to figure it out, okay? I cannot see my baby up there looking so pretty and not say anything. But Brooke is in labor."

"Oh," I said. "So, you just want me to tell her that?"

"Yeah. We need to pick Miles up, so we're rushing to the hospital right now. You don't have to tell her all that. We're not trying to play favorites here. Just... we need to figure out a way to protect Eva and I don't think Mary is ready to admit all of this is futile yet."

I nodded. "Okay. I will do my best. I hope it all goes well."

He patted my arm. "Thanks, son."

Son. I couldn't help but feel bad. Eva was still rightfully angry with her parents. Discussions ended in tears—as did everything these days. They had no idea Carter was dying and that she cried anytime Mona sent an update. Eva was simultaneously happy about the babies thriving and grieving the loss of her beloved dog.

Eva appeared forty minutes later, looking exhausted. Cocktail hour was all about standing, but I knew she needed a break. We escaped outside to the ceremony space to sit. I grabbed her a pop.

"Thanks," Eva said. "God, I'm so tired."

"I hope you're not too tired for a dance later," I said. "I plan to take you out."

"Oh, really?"

"Yeah. It might surprise you to know I actually *like* to dance."

"Really?"

"I was in show choir in high school."

She snickered.

"What?"

"That is the nerdiest thing ever."

"Uh, join show choir and touch a boob. That was our motto."

She giggled. "Good to know you like to dance. I don't. I will because Ellie does."

"It's a wedding. Dance with me," I said.

"I will. Promise. That is if my parents don't ruin it all."

"They left," I said. "And wanted you to know they loved you and were working on it all. You should probably let the bride know, too."

"She'll understand."

"I think they meant well, but Brooke is in labor, and they had to pick up Miles. They didn't want to hurt you or play favorites."

Eva looked at her hands.

"I love you, Eva. I know they do, too. We don't have to talk about it right now. You don't have to feel any one way. I just—"

"You're the messenger. I will tell Ellie they send their best. She'll like to hear that," Eva interrupted.

"How has it been so far?" I changed the subject.

"Honestly, fun. I am trying to sit as much as I can. My back is killing me. My feet are swollen."

"I'll give you tons of back and foot rubs. Promise," I said.

"I will accept your offer. A dance for rubs? I can manage it." Eva grinned.

"Eva, they're doing the grand entrance," Jace approached. "You okay?"

"I'm good. Just taking a break," she held her hand out. "Help."

Jace pulled Eva back to her feet and led her into the hall to receive the new couple. They paraded in with Jane. The kid was over-the-moon happy to have a stepdad.

"She's elated," I said as we settled into our dinner seats.

"She's so excited. She loves Mike."

Jane flitted back between her mother's seat and that of another man across the room.

"That's her dad," Eva read my mind. "They coparent well. It wasn't always so chill, but it's good. He and Mike even talk. It's not bad."

"There's hope," I said. "Coparenting can work."

It was a deflection—one for her benefit.

She squeezed my knee. "I really want it to work, okay? You gotta give me time, but I want to raise these babies together, alright? Like really, really together."

It hit me in the feels. "Really?"

"Yeah. I think we should plan to live together—for good. I don't see my feelings changing. We're a good team, okay? I hope we can be a family—even if we're a little unconventional."

"I can manage that," I agreed.

31. THE INCIDENT

Davey

CYBER INCIDENT. THE WORDS CAME FROM EVA'S MOUTH AND MY heart stopped. Thankfully, I missed all the context, and it was better than I suspected. I'd been focused on her tits so much in this work dress—since I got in the shower this morning and she left early under suspicious circumstances—that I missed this was a *vendor* issue. Apparently, a conglomerate pushed a patch, tanking one of our key services. While this meant online retail was down, it wasn't a data breach.

Around eleven, Eva rang.

She asked, "Can you call the OB and reschedule our fucking appointment? I have no time."

"Eva, it's our big scan," I protested. "You have time if I say you have time."

"David, don't fuck with me. Can you just do it?"

"Don't fuck with me. Is that how we're talking now?" I chuckled.

"Punish me for my mouth later."

"Okay naughty girl. Can't Claire manage—"

"I know how Salesbot works better than she does. I have dealt with similar incidents—their cloud provider likes to fuck with them and their change management team could be better. I do not have time to argue.

"Okay," I agreed. "I can call them. But only if—"

"I signed the damn release. You have access. Congrats, Daddy, you're able to do this."

"Eva, I still think—"

"Do you want me to lose you millions of dollars?"

"No," I answered.

She hung up.

I never saw Eva like this. She didn't *get* frantic. My worlds collided in the worst way. Despite disappointment, I rescheduled for next week. I'd counted the days until we got to see our boys in vivid 3-D detail—maybe for the first time in full. This was the one that would tell us if they were fine—or not. I expected good things but remained nervous. Eva was, too. So, this had to be something else.

Around one, after zero response to my text confirming that I'd rescheduled it and Meg had her assistant add it to the calendar, I stopped by her office. Two explained something with some guy from the SOC. I didn't really *know* what an SOC was beyond it handled incidents and did cool cyber things. Everyone stared. The younger people scattered.

"I come in peace," I joked.

The SOC director made some sort of hand gesture I did not return.

Eva facepalmed, "Star Trek, David. It's a reference."

"Oh, no clue," I said. "Does anyone need anything?"

Eva shook her head, annoyed at the distraction.

"Eva, when was the last time you ate anything?"

"I literally don't know," she murmured. "I don't have time, David."

"Does anyone here want anything—food, coffee, snacks? Anything?" I asked.

One of the kids piped up. "I'd do almost anything for a burger."

"Cool," I said. "Anything on it?"

"Whatever they've got," he answered.

Everyone else added their support for burgers.

"Eva?" I asked.

"I want three scoops of ice cream. That is about all I can manage right now. The hazelnut they have over there at the cafe. But who is running for this order? Meg is out for lunch."

So, she *did* get the message with the calendar invite. I found Eva so infuriating sometimes. How long did it take to send a thumbs up emoji? Three seconds!

"I'll do it," I said. "Does Claire need anything?"

"Get her a burger anyhow," Eva said. "She will not turn it down."

I rang my sister's kitchen to put the order in. When Dahlia came back to revitalize the company's flagship restaurant, things took off. Evening was high-class, but lunch was the busiest meal. It was a little less white tablecloth, and the Wagyu burger was to die for.

"Davey, we're in lunch rush," Dahlia rang back, groaning. "You're asking for a lot. Twenty hamburgers?"

"We have an ongoing issue. Eva's team needs fuel. I just bought enough for the key players."

And then some.

"I thought you had the scan—"

"Cancelled. She insisted and was over it. Eva just wants that hazelnut ice cream but add a large order of fries on there and a coke because she'll eat them. It's one of the only foods I can reliably get her to eat."

"Okay," Dahlia sighed. "I'm not going to starve our nephews. I'll have a runner bring it to the desk."

"I will come down to meet them. Text me when the order is up," I wanted an excuse to walk.

Thirty minutes later, by some miracle, Dahlia texted a three-minute warning and I ran downstairs with an intern to bring the bags of food upstairs—past Eva's office. Her eyes followed, so I *knew* she was flagging. About to play hero, we sat the bags down in the conference room.

I popped my head into her office. "Food is here. Everyone help yourselves. And if you want to use the big conference room instead of crowding here, please do."

The guys filed out. Eva followed and called to one of the analysts, "Hey, Jim, can you go run down to the floor and tell the others to come up, so we don't have to keep doing this over the phone? We've got space. And tell Claire there is food. Tell red team to come up."

"Will do," he agreed.

I pulled the tiny bag with Eva's order aside. "I got you a Coke because I knew you'd want it along with ice cream and some fries. There is ketchup in the exec kitchen."

"Why the fuck are you doing this?" She whispered.

"Because I love you and you weren't going to listen to reason unless I took matters into my own hands."

She shook her head. "Well, I'm somewhat grateful."

"Somewhat?" I scoffed.

"Okay, it's honestly good for the team to see you like this. They were frightened at first, but they've come around."

"Frightened?"

"You are imposing, David. They are... softening. You seem human. Keep it up."

* * *

Eva

"You alright?" Davey popped his head into my office.

"I am trying to test stuff," I said. "Or, rather, break shit."

"Why?"

"That is how we find if it *can* be broken. Claire went home. I'm going to be awhile."

"It's already six on a Friday."

"And you're free to leave," I said.

"I'm not leaving without you."

"Nah, go," I said. "If you stay, I'll be distracted and… that won't help anyone."

"You don't need anything?"

I needed a million things. I was exhausted, frustrated, and simultaneously willing to jump his bones—not here, but somewhere.

"I don't need food. I will grab something on my way home."

"Eva, come on. You can do this—"

"If my team is still here, I am," I said. "You can grasp that, David."

He backed off. "Okay. But, you get to take a break. Have dinner with me at least?"

He sat on my desk, puppy dog eyes begging for guidance. He wanted me to call him a good boy and give him a chore.

I shook my head. "No. That's not it. And people—"

"The whole floor is gone, Eva. I can grab food. What do you want? What does your heart desire after the longest day?"

"You want me to go home," I sighed. "I want that, too, but I doubt it will happen before midnight. There are days like this, David. I'll call the car."

"I want you home—in bed, in compromising positions," Davey growled, voice low.

I bit my lip.

"You want the same. Come home. Can't we—"

"Any amount of downtime on a Saturday costs us revenue. The linen sale is upcoming. We do not want to crash because we cannot support the traffic. What we've given everyone is a work-around that *should* stabilize things—in theory. I need to ensure the testers, and I can confirm it works."

He groaned, standing and throwing hands up. "Eva, throw me a damn bone!"

"Davey, you're killing me. The only way you're going to get

what you want is to order delivery and take me in the supply clos-et," I laughed. "That isn't happening."

"No one would care."

"David!"

"No one is here, Eva."

"Okay, I want food from that Persian hole in the wall on Randolph," I said. "Order it. You get fifteen minutes, and we need to make it look somewhat credible. So, close your windows and let's just do it on your couch."

He did a double-take. "Are you fucking serious?"

"Sure, why not. I'm desperate. I missed what *would* have been a good time this morning. Why not. If you're willing to do the order and go down on me, I'll fuck you."

"You're adding more to this list, Eva."

"You love when I'm demanding," I said.

He raced to his office like a kid on Christmas hearing Santa arrived. I tried to break the system as best I could and told the team Davey needed something. They were began wrapping their current project up. Red team wasn't finding instability, so I sent them home. That was the time my phone lit up.

"I did it. Why are you not here?" Davey asked.

"Give me a sec."

I hung up, rose to my feet slowly—something that grew more challenging by the day—and walked to his office. He'd turned the window masking on. It worked like a charm. When I entered, I found him pacing. The look on his face was one of pure disbelief as I locked the door.

"We're really doing this?"

"Yes. I said we were. I'm too frustrated and lonely. If you want me, you'll have me."

"Then get on the couch and take off your panties," Davey demanded.

We didn't waste time. I kicked my shoes off, tossed my tights, and sent my panties flying. I tried to ignore the fact that by this point, I was rocking unfortunate pregnancy undies. To my surprise, he never minded. I reclined on the couch as he knelt before me, pulling my legs apart and diving between them.

I threw my head back, looking at the office ceiling. He was *so* good at this and got better with time. We may not have always agreed, but we were doing our absolute best today. I gripped his hair with one hand and clasped another over my mouth. I needed to be quiet and that would be hard. His tongue brought me to the edge. And as his fingers dug into my thigh, I found myself fading deeper into oblivion. I loved how I could lose myself.

We shouldn't do it, but we did. I moaned, trying to keep my noise level at a minimum, and bit my own fingers. The release required something to ground it. Legs twitching, I lay there, panting in recovery.

Satisfied, Davey's head finally popped into view. "Happy?"

"So fucking happy," I said as I rose once more to a sitting position. "Take your pants off."

He obeyed, finally ending up on his couch with me straddling him. It was about the only position that would work on this furniture. I would have suggested him taking me from behind, but his stupid couch had no arms. It made everything a little awkward, but possible.

As I ground against him, I saw his nostrils flare.

"You're fighting it, huh?" I asked, torturing him.

"This is… undeniably hot."

"So, you don't take girls here and fuck them all the time?"

"Absolutely not. You're the first."

I smiled and bit my lip. "Oh, so we're christening the space."

"Yes," he groaned.

I didn't think I'd cum again. He'd left me spent. And, anyway, it was sort of thrilling to try to get him off fast. Davey could usually run a marathon to the point of *my* exhaustion. Tonight, though, I wanted him to cum fast.

"Your tits are everything."

"Yeah?" I asked.

"So good. I've been trying not to stare at them all day. God, they're perfect."

"Uh-huh." I took the compliment.

Yesterday, I started leaking while waiting at the cafe downstairs for a cinnamon bun. A baby cried and my body responded in ways I couldn't predict. However, right now, I didn't feel like a vessel. He made me feel like a fucking sex goddess.

I kissed him, bringing him closer. I knew he didn't *want* to cum so soon, but it would thrill him if I could get him there like this.

"You want me?" I whispered.

"So bad. So fucking bad."

He was close. I gripped his neck gently by his collar bone, knowing it drove him mad. It was over. Davey grabbed my hips, pressing me into him. He grunted, then sat, breathless, staring at me like I'd made the universe.

"Good?" I asked.

Davey spanked my ass. "That was absolutely inappropriate behavior, Miss Pavlak."

"Are you going to write me up?"

"You're getting a pass this time."

32. BROTHERLY LOVE

Davey

THE DOORMAN RANG AROUND TEN. I WONDERED IF EVA NEEDED help, but I had an unexpected guest.

"Sir, your brother is here."

"What?" I asked.

"He is here, and he has a couple of friends with him."

Derrick was training in California last I heard. He'd been deployed, then back for a hot minute, but returned for test pilot school. I didn't ever know where the little asshole was. He was in his early thirties and never quite sure of his next assignment. The best part? He didn't have to care. The Air Force told him where to go and when. Why the hell was he here? And why didn't Mum say something? Why were there stragglers? It didn't surprise me he showed up unannounced, but I didn't expect a crowd.

"Hey man!" Derrick shouted. "Can we come up?"

"Let them up," I sighed.

A few minutes later, Derrick arrived with two of his buddies known only as Scram and Bark. Everyone went by call signs. Derrick's was Flipper.

"There you are, old man!" Derrick announced.

"Why the hell are you here?" I hugged him.

"It's Scram's bachelor weekend and we flew in. I didn't tell anyone because Daphne would want us to come entertain her and Mum is Mum."

He had a good point. Daphne was overdue by almost a week and pulling her hair out. I knew for a fact she corresponded with Eva all day. I half expected her to show up today trying to save the world. Mum would have insisted Derrick behave, something I didn't expect he wanted to do this weekend.

"Where's the little lady?" Derrick asked.

"Uh… she's still at work. Please don't call her that, man."

Eva would *hate* that.

"You make your girlfriend work when you don't?"

"No. I told her to come home. She elected to stay and clean some stuff up. We had an incident of sorts. She's got it handled."

"He got his secretary pregnant," Derrick announced. "Or something like that."

My eyes widened. "No, Der. Eva is an exec. She's in the C-Suite and is *not* my assistant. Please, please, please never refer to her that way."

"Is she *hot* though?"

"How much have you boys already had to drink?" I sighed.

"Not enough!" Scram declared. "We're about to go out some more. Come with us."

"Come on! It's been ages. Come bar hop," Derrick demanded.

I sighed. "I need to run that by Eva."

"Ugh. You're whipped, man," Derrick groaned.

"I'm a responsible adult and you randomly showed up at my house. Eva lives here, too," I protested.

"Fine."

I stepped into the butler's pantry off the kitchen to call Eva. My goal was to have her *deny* my request so I could give Derrick an honest no. It wasn't that I didn't want to spend time with my baby brother. It was just that I was about to be forty and running around to bars with him seemed like a lot. After all, that's how Eva and I ended up in this mess.

"Yes?" Eva answered.

"So, my little brother randomly showed up. It's apparently an ambush bachelor party. They want me to go out with them—"

"Go," Eva said. "We have an issue. Can I sleep on your couch?"

"Baby, come home and sleep," I sighed. "Don't sleep on my couch."

"I can't," she said. "Go spend time with him. You can take care of me tomorrow."

"Oh… okay," I stammered. "Are you sure?"

"Yes."

"Okay. Well, I love you."

"See you on the flipside," she sighed.

I hung up and approached the guys again.

"Well, I suppose I'm off the leash."

"Fuck yeah!" Derrick declared. "Let's get fucked up!"

* * *

I did *not* plan to get "fucked up". I intended to be an adult and babysit—as Eva and I had that fateful night. However, after two drinks, I realized I was completely out horsed by my brother's squadron. These guys drank like Brits on a university Fresher's Week—but with much better stamina. That is how we ended up in a bit of a predicament.

"Next place! Next place!" Derrick announced like an excited caveman. "Bus! Now!"

"Where?" I groaned, already winded.

It was midnight and I had been up since six.

Somehow, we ended up renting a party bus. Derrick made a big show of putting it on his credit card—as if that was something special. My brother was odd. I suspected he just wanted to show off for his friends. The lights disoriented me until I realized where we were. Somehow, the bus was on the Skyway.

"Where the fuck are we going?" I asked.

"The titty bar!" One of the guys loudly announced. "In Indiana."

Indiana's strip clubs had fewer rules than ours. If you wanted to enjoy yourself, you drove across the border. I was in no mood to go to a strip club and suspected it would anger Eva. But, what she didn't know wouldn't hurt her, right?

"I didn't sign up for this," I protested. "You said *clubs*."

"It is a strip *club*," Bark said. "It has *club* in the name."

"Not what I was thinking, but sure," I groaned.

"He *is* whipped!" Derrick cackled. "Boy, you are fucking broken. Where is the Davey I know?"

"He grew up in the past two years since we last did this," I sighed.

"What? Do tits offend her? Women just put up with this shit, man. You'll be in the doghouse for awhile. Flipper, tell him it's going to be okay."

I suspected Eva wouldn't have a problem with boobs—she never had issues with boobs—but would complain about exploitation and me trying to pull one over on her.

"Jesus fucking Christ," I sighed. "No, tits don't offend her, but I'm afraid she's going to be upset I didn't clear it with her."

"Clear it? Are you married now?" Bark laughed.

"I mean, I'm having kids with her, so yes," I answered. "Pretty much."

"Live a little, man!" Derrick smacked my back. "And drink up!"

I went in, resolved to hang out in back and touch *nothing*. Derrick, however, took this as a challenge. I got several uncomfortable lap-dances out of the deal and ended up spending more at the ATM than I wanted. The fees were *madness*, but these kids had no clue. They didn't care. They had nothing but hazard pay to burn, I assumed.

When we finally headed back to my place to crash on every available surface, I climbed into bed next to Eva. Things must have resolved at the office. She stirred, rolling over to stare at me. I was drunk as a skunk, not remotely articulate, and had lived a little too large.

"Did you fix it?" I asked.

"Yeah," she murmured. "The linen sale will hopefully succeed despite the best efforts of our shitty vendor. I think we need to look at other options before our notice period is up next month. I'm done."

"Oh… okay."

"David, you smell like a fucking bar. And…" She stopped. "Cheap perfume. What the fuck?"

"I… I didn't ask… I didn't want to."

"What?" Eva demanded. "Did you fuck someone?"

"God, no!"

"Then what did you do?" Eva looked near tears, sitting up and glaring with the angriest expression I'd ever seen.

"We went to the strip club. I was already almost in Indiana before Derrick told me what was going on. I behaved. I promise. I—"

"Why would you do that? Why didn't you tell me? God! You're the fucking worst!"

As predicted, the move went over like I expected. I was in the doghouse.

* * *

Eva

"Why would you lie?" I demanded. "Am I so disappointing that you had to do that?"

I saw red. I did something I shouldn't have in the heat of the moment with Davey—something that put *my* reputation at risk, not his. And he paid it back by going to a fucking *strip club* for lap dances!? Who did that!?

"What do you mean, Eva?"

"I gave you the best I could, and *this* is how you respond. You don't even remember!"

He rubbed his temples. "Baby, my head hurts. I'm so hungover and—"

"I just slept on your couch until Sec Arch woke me up and told me they'd figured it out about 90 minutes ago. I am miserable. Your babies are kicking me so fucking hard that I cannot sleep. My hips are fucking on fire. And you go out and let a bunch of strange women grind on you?" I flailed, climbing from bed. "No!"

"No what? Eva, I love you. I didn't do anything bad. I swear. Derrick is the issue. I thought of all people, you'd be down with boobs—"

"Down with boobs and hearing that you went to a fucking strip club after I let you take me in your office are two different things. Was that enough for you? Do I just disgust you or something?"

Tears rolled as I stood there.

"Eva, you're perfect. What are you talking about?"

"You degraded me!" I shouted. "And I'm going to go sleep downstairs!"

"There are servicemen on literally every fucking surface, Eva. My brother's stupid friends—"

I sobbed. "You must hate me—"

"I really, really don't. I love you. I don't want to fight. You can yell at me after you've rested but please go to sleep. I'll sleep in my office."

Davey scuttled off. I sobbed until falling asleep, waking to the smell of coffee. My eyes opened. It was nearly one and I had to pee like a racehorse. I wandered into the bathroom, finding Davey in the shower. He'd turned on the steam, casually whistling away like nothing was wrong. Men were dumb. How could he think everything was fine? Ignoring him and needing to go, I peed, and because I was saintly, didn't flush.

I was washing my hands when I heard the shower turn off. I was ready to launch into a rant until a naked man—not the one I was presently with—appeared. This was Davey's little brother.

"Oh, fuck. You really *are* pregnant!" Derrick declared.

I stood there in nothing but panties and one of Davey's shirts while he was there buck naked and otherwise unfazed. *What an asshole!* Why would he think this was fine and not rush to at least pull on a towel? Also, how was *everyone* in this family so fucking attractive? It made it worse. I turned away, facing the mirror, but couldn't avoid him there. I rushed to the linen closet and threw two towels at him—as if more was better.

"Calm down!" He laughed.

"I'm standing here in panties and you're naked. What the actual fuck?"

"Ah, it's nothing. I didn't see anything. Stop freaking out."

"This is my room! You're in MY room! Get out!"

"I still gotta shave! And it's Davey's room."

"Get out! Fuck your shaving! Why couldn't you—"

"What is with all the shouting?" Davey appeared, looking miserable.

I almost felt bad for yelling at him.

"Your girlfriend is giving me the third degree!"

"He's here *naked* and I'm here in panties," I finally pulled on my robe. "I *peed* in there thinking it was you in the shower. He comes walking out completely naked!"

"How was I supposed to know you were in here?"

"It's my fucking room!"

"No, it's Davey's."

"Hey! It's her room, too. Not yours," Davey said. "Jesus Christ, Derrick! What a great first impression you've made! Eva, this is my baby brother Derrick. Derrick the Fuckwit, this is my girlfriend, Eva."

"Charmed," I growled, annoyed.

"She's pretty—even pregnant," Derrick said. "But *damn* she has a temper. They *do* say you marry your mother, though."

"Oh god!" Davey said. "Fuck off! Why are you in here?"

"Bark puked in my shower and Scram was in the other shower."

"Next time, fucking ask. Now, get dressed," Davey insisted. "Go put on some clothes and get to work scrubbing the showers your friends destroyed."

"Davey," Derrick groaned. "Be cool, man."

"Given that I just slept on the floor of my office due to your stupid plans, I have no more cool left. I am *not* getting sick because you all trashed the place."

Derrick left.

"I'll go," I said.

"No," Davey held me by my arms. "Baby, I'm sorry. I will grovel for an eternity if I must, but please don't go. I am sorry this whole thing exploded. I thought I could control it but damn those guys can drink and I'm an old fuck. I am sorry my idiot brother thought this was okay. It wasn't."

Davey's face showed kindness and regret, not superiority.

"I will make sure you don't have to deal with shower puke and that the boys leave you alone, my love," Davey said. "Go back to bed. I'll bring you coffee and eggs."

"Since when can you cook eggs?" I asked, surprised.

"Since Derrick's friend gave me directions."

"The one who puked?"

"Nah, different one. The one who was on the living room couch."

"Ah."

He kissed my forehead. "I'm sorry. So sorry. I should have been here when you got home. I shouldn't have gone to the strip club—"

"I… I'm sorry for reacting in anger," I said. "I genuinely missed you when I got home, yes. I also just… I gave a part of myself I never thought I would to you. And… you stomped all over it."

Davey cupped my face in his hands. "No. That was special. It was hot and impulsive and special as fuck, Eva. The women Derrick paid to grind on me after I explicitly said no lap dances? They didn't mean anything. Their tits cannot compete with yours, either."

"Don't lie, David."

"I'm not."

"Are you sure you weren't just scratching an itch while my soggy ass languishes here?"

Davey smacked my ass. "That? Your totally grabbable little ass?"

"I have a big ass."

"One I lose my mind over, Eva. Fuck, I love you. I don't need anyone else. You're gorgeous."

"Even if I'm pregnant," I joked.

"You're sexy as hell. I just want all of you."

I swooned at the way he said it.

"Okay," I agreed.

"Go, get in bed. I will spoil you all day but just stay away from the boys. They are fucking feral and I'm sorry. They arrived out of nowhere."

"I will take you up on your offer. I'm also taking all of Monday off after the scan," I said.

He swatted my ass. "Good girl."

33.NAMESAKE

Davey

I watched as the ultrasound tech swirled around Eva's stomach, displaying one set of perfect features and then another. I couldn't tell the two apart other than when the tech pointed out situational geography. I fell head-over-heels for noses and faces of people I didn't know but had contributed to. Eva sobbed openly for forty minutes, swearing repeatedly that these were happy tears.

We left with two sets of pictures of babies who remained perfect, healthy, and measuring well. Eva cried the entire way back to my place. Or was it *our* place now? She'd certainly been angry at Derrick for infringing on her space this weekend. *Her* space.

"We really need to buy some baby things," Eva sniffled, adjusting her shirt to cover her stomach.

It was the first time she attempted actual clothes in three days and—seemingly overnight—nothing fit.

"Eva, we need to buy you some clothes as *well* as baby things," I said.

She glared, knowing I was right.

"This weekend, we can go," I said.

"I'm fine."

"Eva, you cannot live in my t-shirts and yoga pants rolled

down. Cute as you are—and you are *very* cute—it would flagrantly thwart dress code."

"I don't get a pass?" Eva sighed.

"Nope. You get lots of passes, but this one... even your cute little ass isn't getting away with it."

"Fine this weekend. But not right now. Right now, I want to nap for three straight hours."

"I won't stop you. I am glad you took a day off, my love."

"What do you have today?" Eva asked.

"Uh, I have a meeting with GC and then I'm going out to lunch with Carlos and Joe," I said.

"You didn't bro out enough this weekend?" Eva giggled.

"Nope."

The car lurched to a stop and the photos flew from Eva's hands.

"Sorry," the driver called. "Standstill."

"It's okay." I picked them up.

"Oh my God! She had it?"

"Who had what?" I asked, finding Eva engrossed in her phone.

"Daphne had the baby," Eva said. "A good labor Cal says. Seven pounds, two ounces. Look at this face."

I stared at the face of my new niece and held up the ultrasound photos. There was a stark resemblance.

"She's one of us," I chuckled. "Sweet. Does she have a name?"

"Cordelia Alma Delphine-Markham. I love that they're hyphenating it. Then she has both sides."

I tried not to roll my eyes. "People won't even bother to remember the Delphine part. Mum is Carlisle-Delphine. She's still just Lady Danna Delphine."

"Well, that's a shame. I didn't know that."

"I mean, our kids will be Delphines."

"Says who?" Eva chuckled. "Davey, they will come out of *my* body. We aren't married."

My jaw dropped.

"Oh, I am sorry straight man, but you aren't guaranteed naming rights. You cannot even buy them. The twins aren't a stadium. They are people."

"Eva, you must be joking. They are *Delphines*. They will be known that way."

"They *will* be?" Eva set her jaw and ripped her phone away. "David, you don't *own* them."

"No one *owns* them, but I do *claim* them," I protested. "Baby, they're my children."

"They're *my* children, too. And I have no guarantees."

"No one has. I could marry you tomorrow and something awful—God forbid—could befall us, Eva!"

"But you wouldn't anyhow."

"Eva, you won't even say 'I love you', so what am I supposed to think?"

"That's not fair!"

"Neither is wanting me to say 'sure, Eva, let's get hitched even though you can't bring yourself to say three little words to me'." As the words left my mouth, I knew I was wrong.

Eva pulled back, voice defiant and masking hurt. "It was a point I was making. I know you have no desire to marry me. It's fine."

"At this moment? No. I think we're both smart enough to put the immediate issues of pregnancy and the business up front and worry about silly things like wedding on the way back burner. But I never said I'd not consider it."

"Uh-huh!" she sounded near tears and stared outside for the final three blocks.

Painful silence overcame me. Why couldn't I make it a day without saying something wrong? It was one step forward, two steps back with us. I was hurt and desperate to hear her say it. I needed to be patient but wanted it so badly. It would be permanent —final. Hearing she wasn't even convinced the babies would have my last name made it hurt worse.

We reached our building. Eva got out without another word. There was no goodbye kiss or pleasantry. She was hurt. Even the driver knew to say nothing. I filed back into work, texted my sister to see if I could send a birth announcement, and sat through a mind-numbingly boring meeting with legal.

I took lunch at the tennis club with my buddies. It had been weeks since we'd all been together in the same space. Things got harder with children, but it was good to be back together.

"You started the beard again?" I asked Carlos.

"Yeah. It's that time of year," Carlos said.

"I tried. Eva shut me down. Apparently every type of beard oil known to man makes her want to vomit right now."

"Pregnancy is fucked," Joe said. "How is she?"

"Good, I guess. The babies are coming along."

"I still cannot fucking believe you, man," Carlos snickered. "How the fuck did you end up in this bind?"

"I don't know," I said. "But it doesn't seem to get easier."

"Oh, yes, newborns are *notoriously* easy. Who would have thought otherwise?" Joe teased.

"No, I mean, everything is a fucking social minefield. Everything from circumcision down to what night nurse we use is an argument. Then, there's their names. She refuses to discuss first names because we just fight. Okay, fine. Well, Daphne had her baby girl this morning. Eva argued with me over the last name—like it wasn't a fucking given that the boys would have *mine*."

"Oh, Daph had the baby?" Joe asked. "Good for her and Cal."

"Sure," I agreed. "Good, but they hyphenated the damn name."

"Well, I mean, given your sister *is* a Delphine, they fucking would."

"Joe, c'mon," I groaned. "We aren't *that* different."

"You are," Carlos laughed. "And this girl has you over a barrel."

"I know," Joe said. "She's pretty, but what the fuck, man? She's living in your house, spending your money, and she's not willing to let you have the last name? That's some shit, man."

"My advice?" Carlos said. "Wait her out. If you fight about it now, she will just dig in. These things work out, but fighting with a woman—especially a pregnant lady—is a losing game."

"Wait until she gives birth. She'll be too tired to argue."

"You do not know Eva, Joe. Eva could fight me over whether the sky is blue any given day."

"Then why stay with her? You don't have to," Joe said.

"Because I love her."

"Love her?" Carlos slapped his knee.

"Fuck, man! You barely *know* her," Joe added. "Who *are* you?"

"I dunno. She drives me crazy, but when I finally get her number and think I have her all to myself, it's glorious. Then, she pulls away. Why the fuck won't she just say it back? It's got to be some sort of sick power move, right?"

"Nah," Carlos sighed. "You're just too fresh in it and it sounds like your girl is a little scared. She's fine. She will come around. When I worry about my wife fighting me on something for an eternity, I know it's best to drop the rope—especially with the kids."

"That must take a lot of self-control—something I lack," I sighed. "I panic and fly off the handle. She's not like any other woman I've been with. I cannot outsmart or outargue her. I cannot buy her off, either. She wants an all-out grovel and even my best doesn't seem like enough most days."

"I don't understand this woman. Doesn't she *want* to have an easy life?" Joe asked.

"She doesn't want to sit around eating bon-bons. She slept on my office couch part of Friday night so she could manage a tech thing with her team—and so our CISO could go home to her young children. She is the most motivated person I know—like Daphne. You know what is BS? Eva got the birth announcement from Cal and not me."

"You haven't laid hands on him lately?" Joe teased.

I glared. "Of course not!"

Joe shook his head. "I don't get her. She should realize how lucky she is that you even want to try to make it work. I know I wouldn't."

Carlos butted in. "That would make you look like a dick. Look man, I see two people who were thrown into a situation Joe and I had time to adjust to. I don't see an ungrateful person not getting how *lucky* she is. I got told that shit all the time when I went to college, you know? Oh, aren't you so *lucky* to have made it? Yeah, well, I still don't know what the fuck I'm doing, but I do know those people only see me as an outsider and don't value me. Davey, she's not like you. She's adjusting to all of this. And you? You're barely out of your fuck up era."

"My fuck up era? You mean like the one where I had a random hookup with a beautiful girl at a bar and got her pregnant?" I sighed. "With twins, no less? Or the one where I accidentally fucked my sister's direct report and knocked her up with twins?"

"Both. But you're trying," Carlos said. "It will work out. Those kids are yours. If she didn't love you, she wouldn't even bother sticking around. Like you said, she doesn't want or need your money. She's with you, for *you*."

34.BABY ON THE BRAIN

Eva

"He's very busy," a saleswoman remarked.

I observed Davey as he paced on the phone outside an incredibly posh shop in a Naperville strip mall. It was almost cartoonish watching a man in a $15,000 Italian suit and $10,000 British-made overcoat pacing on the side of a strip mall in a suburban hellscape. More ridiculous were the women in yoga pants passing, doing a double take, and having him *not* respond in the least. The only bit of this that made sense was that his G-Wagon was sandwiched in a line of Range Rovers.

"Yeah. It's just business. He's not being rude," I said. "This was *his* idea."

It had to do with a real estate deal in New York.

"Dads are always too busy, you know?" She said, chipper.

I handed her a line of clothes that fit god-awful and exchanged them for a handful that could accommodate my massive boobs and wouldn't give me awful camel toe. Everything was stretchy and pulled in places it shouldn't.

"These are good. These aren't," I gestured.

She took the failures and hung them on a garment rack. "Well, should we pull some more clothes?"

"I need something more work professional," I said. "I often dress a little down, but there are days I meet with the board or entire c-suite where I need something smart."

"Most women use pregnancy as a time to slow down and lean into comfort. You're one of those high-profile women?" Her tone suggested that was *not* a compliment.

"I don't know about that." I glanced at Davey outside. "But my CEO is a pain in the ass. Thankfully, I don't think he gives a shit about my wardrobe. Still, I'd like to feel more me, ya know?"

"We have some work dresses that are a little more formal," she agreed.

I followed her to the rows of clothes, picking out a few simple black dresses that I could pair with one of the fifty colorful cardigans I owned. I found two that worked by time Davey finally graced us with his presence.

"I'm so sorry," he apologized earnestly. "Disaster. Chaos. But I'm back. Did you make any progress?"

"I found a few things," I said as the perky saleswoman toted my clothes.

"Good. I'm glad. Did you get something to wear to dinner tomorrow?"

"What?" I asked.

"We're having dinner with the family to celebrate the baby."

"I know. Is it an induction? Do I need robes? Sacred underpants?"

He snickered. "Mum keeps it relatively formal. A dress or jacket sort of thing."

I controlled the urge to roll my eyes. I'd hoped to get away with a sweater, leggings, and boots. Instead, I had to put on a work dress and heels. Just the thought made me want to revolt and say I didn't want to come.

"That's just... how it is. I'm sorry I didn't tell you." Davey realized I was now even *less* enthusiastic.

"So, are we adding those to the registry or... buying them today?" The saleswoman returned.

"Registry?" Davey asked. "No. She needs the clothes. Why would we have a registry?"

"Most people... register for gifts," the woman said, confused. "For their showers."

"Oh, we won't be doing that," Davey said. "Whatever we need, we'll either order or get today."

My face fell. I hadn't expected to care. After years of planning baby showers, I realized I'd never have one.

"You will have people who want to buy you some sweet gifts," the saleswoman said. "And if you don't register, you will have to explain what you do and don't want. Trust me, you will thank me later."

I shot Davey a look, telling him to shut up. I wasn't about to argue, and he got himself in so much trouble over the last week that he knew better than to poke the bear. I wanted to trust him again. I wanted to fall in love with him—just like he wanted me to—but I couldn't get there. Here was a man willing to *do* anything and buy me anything I needed or even wanted. He'd wait on me hand and foot. He did and said stupid things, but only because he wore his heart on his sleeve and I flustered him. He *loved* me. Why couldn't I love him back?

"Sure," I said.

She left. "I will go grab the iPad!"

Davey said, "Eva, it's gauche."

"Davey, I have normal friends who would like to see a registry."

"We don't need people to buy us things."

"And yet, we are here trying to also buy a present for Cordelia, yeah? Wouldn't a registry help?"

"It cannot be that hard."

"So, you do it. Find things for your sister and the baby." I turned the request for emotional labor on him.

"Uh... sure." Davey disappeared to where all the baby clothes lived.

I prepared to be unimpressed with his choices.

To my surprise—and relief—the woman brought *Davey* the

iPad so he could input our details while I continued shopping. There was some justice in the world! I grinned at her as she passed, continuing to file through lines of strollers, cribs, and car seats.

"Are you finding everything alright?" An older woman approached.

"We're browsing, thanks. The other woman is trying to walk my boyfriend through the registry he insists we don't need."

"Well, you will want to order a crib. Are you what… thirty weeks along?"

Twenty," I answered. "Twins. Two boys. Two big, healthy boys that are measuring ahead for twins."

"Oh, I am so sorry. No wonder you all are so busy. Twins are wonderful, but also a hit to the pocketbook right out of the gate. We have a variety of price points—"

She stopped, her demeanor changed as Davey returned holding a dress fit for a toddler and a sack of fancy organic cotton burp cloths. She went from assuming I sought bargain bin options to realizing we had money. Davey got a completely different reception than his average-looking girlfriend. I hated it.

"No to the dress. She's a newborn—and a tiny one at that," I said. "Get her practical things. Your sister isn't fussy. The cloths are a good choice."

"She's a girl. Aren't you supposed to want to dress them up?"

I snickered. "Davey, she's a girl, not a princess. Babies are basically all the same. You don't know what Daphne plans. She may want to lean into gender neutral. I know I do. I want absolutely nothing to do with superheroes or sports shit."

"Not even the Cubs?" Davey asked, wounded. "Or football?"

"You don't even care about the Bears!"

"No. Premier League and our team, babe."

"Our team?"

"We own a minors team," Davey said. "You didn't get this in the presentation?"

"What presentation?"

"Onboarding."

"To the family?"

"To the company! Jesus. I paid a fucking fortune to have that video made. The last president called it 'essential', and they aren't even doing it!? Damn."

The old woman awkwardly stared in confusion.

"Well, the more you know," I sighed. "This is not a today discussion. Today, we need a crib, car seats, and a stroller. That's it."

"A crib for sure. They can take a bit to arrive—they come custom, you know? The good news is a travel crib or bassinet will do for the first few months just fine."

"Months? You don't have anything just… in the back?" I asked.

"Eva, we don't want some stock crib. We want something nice," Davey insisted.

I rolled my eyes. "It's a crib, not an heirloom hutch."

"You can pass them on to future children when they are well made."

"See," Davey said.

Was he really implying I should do this all over? Was he insane?

I shook my head. "I don't even know where to begin there. Let's look at what they have."

Davey and I quickly agreed on minimalist cribs to match the aesthetic of the house—all in a beautiful barely-there blue that the woman tried to talk us out of since we might someday have a girl. I assured her a blue crib would *also* work for a girl. When it came to strollers and car seats, Davey immediately glommed onto a gigantic SUV-size stroller with two car seats priced the same as an economy car. I was too tired to debate him and figured if I hated it, I could buy something else in a few months. We needed car seats that could handle sub-six pounders more than anything, so we bit the bullet.

Davey didn't bat an eye at the more than ten grand we dropped even if I about fell over at the cost. It was hard to consider how little we'd gotten for so much and how he worried even less about it. I still didn't understand these people, their habits, and what even drove them. Worrying I'd never fit in—or that he'd never accept the real me, we put everything in the back of his SUV and drove back to the city. I fought tears the entire way. At the time, I couldn't explain it, but I felt like with every tie binding me and every purchase made, I left a life behind—the one I thought I'd have.

* * *

Davey

Precious Cordelia Alma delighted everyone. Mum had never looked happier than when holding a baby in her arms. Eva came out of her shell—smiling for the first time in seemingly ages—as she held Daphne and Cal's daughter. Everyone perked up, but I struggled. It wasn't the baby. She was wonderful. It was so much more, and I lacked words.

As we left for the evening, Eva faded into her cloud, and I fell silent. After things felt right, they'd fallen apart. For the last week, I'd tried everything in my arsenal to fix things, but they didn't improve. I tried groveling, feeding her, sex, and even buying her clothes. Literally nothing worked. I was out of ideas and beginning to resent Eva's mood.

Returning home, Eva said, "I'm going to bed. I am going to meet Ellie in the morning and I'm tired."

I couldn't hide my feelings. She read my face.

"You know, Davey, I am sick of whatever this is. I don't owe you anything. And if you want to fuck me, you can do it, leave, and then go back to whatever video game you're playing with your friends."

"Way to go," I said. "Way to ruin the evening!"

"Me? You were all happy until we met the baby. Then, we did, and you went all quiet. Are you going to be like this with our babies?"

I resisted the urge to slam the kitchen island but balled my fists.

Eva, tearful, demanded, "Are you finally getting cold feet? After all of this, you're finally going to leave, aren't you? Or, rather, you're about to kick me out."

Realizing how much I'd hurt her, I pled. "No, Eva, calm down."

"No, you hold all the power, and this is yet one more move—"

"Oh, really! Because you deny you love me to torture me, and you are holding everything with these babies over my head! *You* are the one pulling one over me!"

"I don't do that. And it's not... I cannot do this!" Eva turned, striding towards the stairs.

She raced up so fast that she tripped, barely catching herself. I approached in a panic, and she pushed me away.

"No, Davey! No!" She continued to the bedroom where she attempted to rummage under the bed for her suitcase.

I pulled her back. "Eva, I love you. I am only trying to help. I am not getting cold feet. I... I need support, too. All I want is for you to be there for me for once."

"Why? So you can throw all of it in my face about where I am failing?"

"Not everything is about you, Eva! Jesus fucking Christ! I'm human, too. I need love and support. I give you everything, but I cannot help but feel *you* aren't invested."

She stopped, tears streaming. She sat on the bed, rubbing her stomach. I realized it was now or never. She was finally listening.

"Dad died before there were any grandkids. I know you didn't meet him. And the more things we do—the closer we become—I struggle because I know he would have loved you. He would have been the first one to rush in excited about our happy accidents. I know he would have never put Cordelia down. To know that Cal was in the family and they had a baby would have made him cry tears of joy, Eva. Sometimes, all of this feels so hollow. It's got nothing to do with you. It's loss. It's grief. And it's much more than whatever crawled up your ass this week."

Eva cried more. "You can be upset without always taking it out on me."

"Eva, stop. I don't—"

"I miss my family," she interrupted. "I am sorry about your dad. I know what that feels like because it seems fucking pointless. They will never know our boys. They will never give a flying fuck about them."

"Eva, that's not true."

"It is. Everything I knew I wanted when I had kids is dead."

I sat in bed next to her, realizing we felt the same. *Fuck.*

"I'm sorry, babe. I get it," I said. "I wish we'd just talked."

"I thought you were just happy-go-lucky while I was starting to die inside."

I wrapped my arm around her. "No. I'm just better at masking it, I guess."

"You're better at compartmentalizing."

"Hard disagree, Eva. I can never get the full story from you, baby. Let me in. If you do, I think we'll communicate better."

"I tried. I tried at the doctor's. I tried at the baby store. I keep trying and it just doesn't work. Maybe *we* don't work? We just don't live in the same world. We don't speak the same language, Davey."

"I refuse to believe that. Tell me what is bothering you. I'm listening." I rubbed her back, giving her time to breathe.

"I want my mom. I wanted to go shopping with her and pick out clothes and plan the nursery with her. I wanted my dad to help build something. I wanted to do the things my sister got to do with them. And I wanted *so* badly to have a shower. You can say it's gauche or stupid, but where I come from, it's a big fucking deal. It's a huge thing. And... I won't get that. You made it so clear. It doesn't fit into *your* world. It doesn't meet *your* family's expecta-tions. So, we cannot do it. Our children need to sit completely in your little world—a domain I don't understand. It makes me what to scream. I feel like an accessory whose wants and desires don't matter. That's why when you brought up names, I had a meltdown."

"Shit. Eva... I didn't think you'd care about any of that. I want you to fit in—and you do. Mum loves you. My sisters adore you. Derrick likes to joke with you, so that's as good as it gets."

"I mold myself to fit in. I know how to talk and act as well as I can, but it's not the same thing when you're having babies—when you're trying to raise them. I want them to have drive and to appreciate hard work. And I want them to love and respect their grandparents—both sets—regardless of what their bank accounts say. I won't get any of that, Davey."

My heart broke.

I pulled her closer. "Your parents love you, Eva. They will come around."

"I have heard nothing. They will stick by Brooke and want me to play nice. And even if they threw me a stupid shower, you'd fight me, and she'd show up and fucking ruin it."

"I want to believe—and truly do—that they will fix things. It will never be perfect, but they love you. Why don't you call them—"

"I'm not in a place I can emotionally do that." Eva shook her head. "And you deserve better than this. You're right. I should—"

I cupped her face. "No, Eva. I am sorry. I should have just told you how I felt—confided in you. We should have communicated better. But there is no one else and there's nothing more I want than for us to just be happy—all four of us, okay? Stop going there. Stop doubting your feelings."

"I am trying, okay."

"Don't leave. I'd never forgive myself if you did." I kissed her forehead. "I love you—And these babies. Just let me love you."

35. SHOWING UP

Davey

AT TWENTY-FOUR WEEKS, I NEEDED TO DO SOMETHING TO BLOW EVA away. We'd hit the illustrious viability day. Things were better than before, but nowhere near perfect. Eva continued trying. We talked about things not just after a good roll in the hay, but over meals with our clothes on. She no longer resisted eating a lunch with me for fear of what people might say. Slowly, her walls came down.

But no matter what I did, I couldn't fix the underlying problem. So, on viability day, I held my entire afternoon—saying nothing to Eva. I made a trip south, all while ensuring she had a cake waiting for her with "Happy Viability Day" written in bubbly letters. I sent her flowers and looked for no big response. These weren't grand gestures, and I wasn't there for her to coo over it, so she'd feel more comfortable accepting.

What I did in the wake of those things was take a ridiculous journey south to Eva's homeland. I posted up at her parents' house unexpected, finding only her dad's truck near the barn with Eva's beloved childhood horse in the crossties. Neither of her parents were in sight. I patted the horse.

"Hey, Poco. Anyone around?"

The horse bobbed his head to say yes, but I heard nothing.

I called out over the radio playing classic rock, "Hello! Bert? Mary?"

Nothing. I filed down the barn aisle, past another horse in a stall, and into the pasture behind the barn. I spotted Bert trying to tack a third board on the fence.

"Shit," I trotted over. "Bert!"

He dropped the board and turned, not expecting anyone.

"Can I help?" I offered.

"Dressed like that?" Bert wiped his brow. "I don't think so."

"I can help," I said.

"Poco went wild and decided to kick down the fence. He ended up down the road eating grass on the golf course," Bert said. "Mary went to town. I figured she'd be back by now, but no. I've been lugging this thing around trying to nail with one hand and hold it with the other. But I forgot my glasses and I cannot even see."

"Can you hold the board?" I asked.

"Sure," Bert said.

I grabbed the hammer and nails, placing them on the fence post. As Bert held the board steady, I nailed three in before moving opposite.

"You're a lefty," Bert observed.

"Yes, I am," I agreed. "To my mother's dismay and that of the nuns in my preschool who tried *so* hard to stop me from writing left-handed."

I wondered to myself if our boys would be stuck with that regrettable trait.

"Lefties are supposed to be world leaders, aren't they?"

"No clue," I laughed, setting the hammer in his toolbox after the final nail.

Bert and I stood back and looked at our progress.

"It should do. That little bastard better watch himself," Bert groaned. "He's an old man. I told him he should know better."

We returned to the barn, Bert lugging his toolbox. I put Poco in the pasture and found Bert filling the water trough.

"Why are you here? Without Eva?" He asked.

"Eva doesn't know I'm here. She didn't send me. I'm trying to help her fix things. She wants you in her life but cannot deal with Brooke. She thinks you will never love her and accept our kids like you do Miles. I know that isn't true, but she needs to hear it."

A car pulled up. Eva's mother approached, probably confused to see my driver.

"Is Eva here?" She called.

"No, Mary. It's David. He wanted to talk about Eva."

Mary approached, purse over her shoulder, face angry, and arms crossed.

Bert turned off the spigot and shook his head. "Like I said before, we love Eva and want to be in her life, but we struggle with the Brooke part."

My stomach lurched. "Which part? You can honestly say you want nothing to do with our children? That doesn't seem right. Brooke is your child, but she's also been a homophobic, shitty person to Eva. She's shamed her and accused her of everything under the sun. I understand your desire to make it all work, but neither Eva nor I will tolerate that behavior around our children."

"It's not that we want that. It's that I think we can put aside differences. With Eva, everything is black and white," Mary curtly said. "There is no compromise with her. And you being here on her behalf is living proof she's unwilling to talk about any of this."

"In many ways, I agree," I said. "Eva is especially stubborn, but she does what is right to protect the people she loves—that includes you. She didn't send me. She doesn't know I'm here. I do this because I love her and I know you do, too. There must be a way."

"Not if she cannot compromise—"

"Mary, listen to him a second," Bert groaned.

I explained, "To Eva, it is something she is. It is who *we* are as a family, too. I'd agree with you that we could agree to disagree over putting ketchup on a hotdog, but this isn't like that."

Bert said, "That's it! This isn't a political disagreement or a spat.

This is who Eva is. When Brooke says these things, she knows it hurts."

"I never see it that way. What does it matter? Eva is with David. They aren't a gay couple. Their kids don't even need to know."

I rubbed my temples, trying not to fly off the handle. I heard my sister Dahlia's voice in my head—her annoyed retort and Mum's insistence that dating a man "cured" her. She'd shouted, "Good dick doesn't change this! I'm me!" Mum regretted those words for months after she returned to culinary school and didn't come home for a year. Daphne and I tried to protect Dahlia and do the legwork, but it took years to rebuild things between them.

"Eva would tell them. We would tell them," I said. "Besides, they have an aunt who has mostly dated women. This is a topic we cannot avoid—wouldn't avoid. I haven't changed Eva. I didn't rewrite her past. I didn't want to."

"Doesn't talking about it bother you?"

"No. Why?"

"I cannot imagine having to compete with the idea of women *and* men," Mary cringed.

"I'm not in competition with anyone," I said. "I don't worry she's going to run off with a woman any more than I worry about her running off with a man. Regardless, we have kids together— kids that Eva wants you to know. I'm not asking you to consider loving your other daughter less or to never speak to her again. Eva would never want that either. It's why when Ellie suggested she uninvite you to spare Eva the awkwardness at the wedding, Eva told her to not do that."

Mary and Bert stared dumbfounded at one another.

"It wasn't out of cruelty," I said. "It was just… out of Ellie's concern for Eva."

"So, what do we need to do?" Mary asked.

"I think she needs you to tell her that you love her, that you love our babies and want to be in their lives, and that you would protect them."

"But they will see Brooke—"

"No," Bert shook his head. "What Eva wants is to not be around Brooke unless Brooke is willing to apologize."

"But Miles and Hannah would never be with their cousins. And we couldn't possibly have two Christmases, two Easters, and everything else!" Mary declared.

"Everyone has two by the time they have kids and are married," Bert said. "Why not us?"

"I also don't know that Eva wants to exclude Miles. She loves him. If Brooke was willing to drop him at yours when all the kids were a little older and we could drop ours... I think Eva might come around to that idea. But right now, she's very, very pregnant and her emotions always run high. I know normal Eva rolls with the punches and never cries, but pregnant Eva needs a lot of support and cries all the time. Trust me."

"Are you done yet?" Mary asked, annoyed.

"Not in the slightest," I answered. "Not with this or Eva. I come from stupid, stubborn stock and never want to admit defeat."

"We need to talk to her, sweetheart," Bert said.

"You're right. I just... where do we begin?" Mary asked.

I smiled. "I think I have an idea."

36.SHOWERED

Eva

"DON'T WORRY. THERE IS PLENTY OF SPARKLING JUICE," DAHLIA laughed, handing me a wine glass.

I turned my nose. "Too sweet. I'm good with water."

We looked over the lake from the Delphine family's beautiful house near Holland. The air was crisp, leaves vibrant, and everything felt cozy with a warm fire in the deck's fireplace. It was my first time coming this far north with David's family and it almost made up for my homesickness. It was harvest season. And, as always, the farm put together a fall market and tapped the prior year's favorite wines for an early tasting.

Of course, nothing the family did was *simple*. Everyone wore jeans—ones made by Dior, Balmain, or someone. The boots were Hermes or Stella McCartney. The glasses were all English-cut crystal. Nothing about this was *average*. Still, I preferred my maternity jeans to all else.

Daphne sat by me, Cordelia looking sweet in a sling.

"How is it going? Are you surviving? I swear we haven't talked."

"We finished the god-awful birth class and received a stupid certificate which Davey put on the fridge. It was so annoying. He couldn't *wait* for that gold star."

She snickered. "He's finally a nerd."

Cordelia yawned loudly. It melted my heart.

"I love her," I giggled. "She's so emotive."

"I love her, but I need her to sleep. Thank God for the night nurse, but I am not sure what we will do up here. It's a shame Dad isn't alive. He would have gladly taken the night shift."

"Make Davey do it," I laughed. "Tell him it's good experience."

"He'd only want you to help. I am *not* doing that to you."

My belly lurched.

"Oh, kicks!" Daphne laughed, guessing what was happening. "Has Davey *finally* felt one?"

He had—at the most inopportune time. I didn't mention how. I wasn't about to say that he got kicked in the face while going down on me. The worst part was that he remarked on it, continued to kiss down my stomach, went down on me, and I didn't stop him. Instead, I let the earth-shattering orgasm go. I was mortified but unwilling to ignore how badly I needed to get off.

"A couple weeks ago. It's spotty, though. They're shy for him."

"Aww, but they are sweet."

"They are," I agreed, looking at my moving stomach.

We were only a couple months away from holding our babies. Each week showed how much I loved and couldn't wait to greet them.

"Any names?"

"Don't ask. All we do is fight about it," I said.

"Oh, that's normal. Cal and I fought tooth and nail about Cordelia's middle name. He liked Elise."

"Oh, that's nice."

"It's his mother's name," Daphne said.

Enough said. Thankfully, I didn't mind Lady Danna, and she seemed to like me enough. However, I wasn't about to call one of the children Don, either.

"Cordelia is a sweet name," I said.

"It was my aunt's name—the one who used to own my house in London."

"Your house is so lovely. I can understand why you didn't want to lose it."

"It is so important to me. We lived there when I was a baby. I don't remember that bit, just always staying there when we visited."

"You lived in London?"

"Davey didn't tell you?" Daphne asked.

Cordelia pushed an arm from the wrap. Daphne looked lovingly at the baby.

"No."

"Davey and I were born in the UK. We each have two passports because of it. Dad was stationed in Wales, then deployed a couple of times."

"I thought he retired?" I asked.

"Nah. He took time off to go to Oxford on scholarship, then had to go back for about five years. Finally, he retired and took over for grandpa. The Air Force kept him there training with the RAF. Mum obviously didn't mind. She also didn't long to live in Wales. So, when he wasn't there, we lived in London."

"That is… wild. I had no clue."

"Come with me! I want to show you something!" Daphne stood and helped me up.

I followed her downstairs to a big family room. She handed me the baby and disappeared into a closet for a box.

"We used to be here a lot. Dad always kept his collection here. I haven't gotten any of these out. Mum doesn't like it—I think it's painful for her. Anyhow, just trust me."

I held Cordelia on what was more shelf than midsection as the boys battered her.

A video with a man's voice in the background played before the camera focused.

"Daphne! Look here!"

The voice sounded *so* much like Davey's. As a chubby, smiling baby came into view, I realized it was his father. Daphne, sat up proudly in the comfort of a tiny living room, smiling.

"Davey! No!" I heard Danna's voice sharply call.

A child rushed over, dragging a laundry basket filled with stuffed animals. Daphne fell over, but didn't cry, and stared at the toddler, confused.

"Davey, don't run in the house," the voice said. "You knocked Daphne over."

"Daddy, I wasn't *running*," a pint-sized, argumentative Davey replied. "I was stalking. We're on a hunt."

"What is that accent?" I laughed.

"Right?" Daphne giggled. "Oh, all of these old videos, it's very lost-in-the-Atlantic."

"He was so adorable," I said. "Oh my God."

"Well, let's calm down," David, Sr. said.

"Can I put the baby in here?"

"If you won't run," his father answered. "You have to be calm and if she tries to stand up, we will take her out."

"David!" Danna said.

"Hold this."

He handed his wife the camera and stepped into view. Davey's build was a spitting image of his father's. He ducked, picking Daphne up and plopping her into the basket.

"There," he declared. "Calmly. And no stairs."

"That is the difference between your first and second kid," a voice spoke behind us.

I turned. Davey, tears in his eyes, watched. Danna stood to his right, looking overcome. Davey locked eyes with me, hovered over the couch, and kneaded my shoulders.

I looked up. "Your accent was adorable."

"Maybe we should move back?" Davey joked, wiping away tears.

"Oh God, you two were too much for that house," Danna said. "We had the tiniest cottage I'd ever seen when Daphne was a baby. Your father must have deployed about a month after this—I swear —and I went back to London a day later."

"He missed a lot, then," Daphne said.

"He did," Danna agreed. "He hated it. With David, he was around more. With you, the timing didn't work out so well. It's probably why he always spoiled you so much—he had to make up for it."

Tears hit. I started sobbing. I didn't know why or how, but I cried.

"Hey, are you okay?" Davey rushed to sit by me.

"I just... I miss my parents. I cannot help but worry about how much they will miss if—"

"Shh... Davey interrupted. "They will come back around."

"I need to see them," I said.

"Someday soon. We'll make plans," Davey said.

And by some miracle, I believed him.

* * *

Davey

"David!"

Mum's voice rang, its tone judgmental. I walked on eggshells as I checked my watch and wondered if this would happen. I tried so hard to bring it all together and keep it low-key. I was *not* a party planner. Thankfully, there were enough women in the family assisting.

"Yes, Mum?" I winced.

"A couple in a *Prius* just arrived. Could they be Eva's parents? Don't they drive a Honda?"

The way she noted the vehicle's model made me snort.

"Mum, you've been here five times asking about people's cars. These are Eva's friends and family. I do not know their cars. Can we stop judging people by daring to choose reliable Japanese cars. Also, a Prius is a Toyota."

She rolled her eyes. "How would I know? No, I am not trying to judge them. I want to ensure I greet Eva's parents warmly and try to make them feel at home. I am *trying* not to run them off."

I made eye contact with Lanie across the room, as if pleading with her to save me. She rushed over to talk, followed closely by Chloe.

"Lanie, can you help Mum figure out when Eva's parents arrive. She really wants to give them a warm greeting but cannot spot a CR-V."

"Oh, wow," Chloe said. "Lady Danna, we can hook you up."

Lanie knew the drill. *Keep her on a leash.*

I watched them depart, turning my attention to Daphne and Dahlia as they ensured all the food ordered was on hand.

"It looks great. So much cheesecake," Daphne clapped her hands. "I love it."

"I think it is incredibly sweet that you decided to just make this a cravings buffet," Dahlia said.

"For real. I wish I'd had something like this."

"Mum hates it," I said.

"No. She doesn't care. She hates the idea of showers but wants Eva to feel loved. And, believe it or not, she is *very* excited to meet Eva's folks," Dahlia noted. "The caterer did a beautiful job with all of this. No notes."

"Also, we got your girl some alcohol-free wine because she was *not* about the fake bubbles last night," Daphne said.

"There is an alcohol-free liquor store in GR," Dahlia added.

"It's a faux-liquor store," I said.

"Well, I bought her a case of options after doing their tasting. They have an alcohol-free Somme guide. I liked it."

Only a chef would feel the need to go to that trouble, but Dahlia hadn't failed me yet. Her eyes moved from my face to beyond me.

"What?" I asked.

"It's the arrival of a gay icon," Dahlia gasped.

"You invited Leah Roughy?" Daphne asked.

"Well, Eva knew her through her ex beyond that, no comment other than Lanie knows her through work. I'm guessing Leah was visiting her dads. I have no clue."

"She also has twins," Daphne pointed out.

I did a double-take. "That woman has twins?"

"She's basically a princess and she's a genetic freak," Dahlia said. "Eva is *beloved*. And I'm so jealous."

"Why?" I laughed. "I barely know her. We've met, but only briefly. She's Lanie's boss. I am sure that is why she came."

"Doubt it. No. Your girl got Prince George's daughter in the divorce. Her ex is gonna be *so* pissed when she finds out."

I snickered. "Are lesbians that petty?"

"Anyone is capable, but I get the feeling attorneys are the *most* petty and they are both attorneys," Dahlia said.

"We are *definitely* the most petty," Daphne agreed.

"There is… a star here," Ellie stepped up. "A bonafide princess movie star."

"I hope Leah doesn't take all the attention, so Eva feels shorted. If so, I will kill Lanie," I said.

"She won't. Eva is the one having the babies. She's just got mad street cred now," Ellie said. "Everyone from fucking Krakow is going to shit a brick and Brooke will kick herself for being such a cunt."

I did a double take at sweet-seeming Ellie dropping the c-word.

"Who are you?" Dahlia said. "My God, I love you. Who is this woman?"

"I'm the bestie," Ellie said. "I worked with Lanie a lot on this."

"You're amazing," Dahlia giggled. "And she's *definitely* acting like a cunt."

"Where are her parents?" I panicked. "What if they don't show?"

"They will be here. They love her," Ellie agreed. "And the boys. Wait, has she finally broken down about the names?"

"Nope," I said.

"What are your choices?" Daphne asked.

"I don't want to get into it."

Any opinions shared would filter to Eva and make her even more vulnerable. Names were hard, and I sensed the general uncertainty wasn't helping.

Mum reappeared, talking rather gleefully with Eva's parents. I watched carefully to read their reactions. It was good. Bert chuckled. His wife nodded with a smile. We were in business. Maybe it wasn't everything Eva wanted, and it would never match the plan in her mind, but I thought this was as good an attempt as any straight man made at a baby shower. I did my best. Now, I waited.

* * *

Eva

"Let me grab it," Dora rushed to grab the shopping bag before I reached into my trunk.

"I'm fine," I said. "Promise."

"I know," the youngest Delphine daughter said. "But I wanted to do something nice for *you* so having you carry all those clothes into the house doesn't make sense."

"Dora, it's a tiny bag of adorable baby clothes," I laughed. "And I had a great time. I am glad we finally got to chat."

Dora was sweet. She was young, motivated, and would do about anything to help the world. She was idealistic in a way I never was. Her altruism reminded me of Ellie in her early twenties —sweet, capable, optimistic.

Dora opened the door, beckoning me into the quiet house. Davey had taken his mother to do an errand and everyone else was busy. Dora took me for coffee and to entertain for a few hours, so I agreed. It was day three of my adventures in Bruges, Michigan— the sleepy suburb of Holland.

As I stepped in, I heard the eruption of a "Surprise!"

I saw dozens of people looking at me. Ellie ran to hug me. Through tears, I looked at her.

"What is this?"

"Your baby shower," Ellie laughed. "Come on in!"

I looked past her to see Daphne and Danna standing with my parents. My Dad was straight up crying, which made me sob more.

I gave him a hug and kiss. He hugged me tight. It was so wonderful to smell his aftershave and feel his safe hold around me. Twin A kicked him hard, prompting him to pull back.

"They're getting strong," Dad said.

"Uh-huh," I agreed, wiping tears before Mom hugged me.

"I missed you so much, Evangeline."

"I missed you, too, Mom. Both of you."

"There will be plenty of time to talk about all of this," Dad said, "but just know we will make it work. We were glad Davey thought this out. You should go tell him thank you."

I turned left, finally meeting his gaze. I walked over.

"Hi," Davey said, nervous about my tears.

"You did all this?"

"I had a lot of help, but it was my idea," Davey agreed. "You wanted this. And your parents wanted to be here."

"You got them here?" My tears rolled harder.

"Well, it involved me helping your dad fix a fence, but yes."

I cocked my head.

"That's a story for another day, Eva. You aren't mad? Or sad?"

I shook my head and took his face in my hands. "I am so incredibly surprised, but I love it. I love this. And I love you."

I leaned in, kissed him, and decided that would do. If I had to awkwardly drop an "I love you" it better be over something like this.

I pulled away. "You get me. You really, really get me."

"I *so* don't," Davey chuckled, wiping my tears, "but I love that you think that. It means everything just to see you happy. And, clearly, if you're dropping an l-bomb, I must not have fucked it all up."

I shook my head and gave him another quick kiss, then realized I was amid people expecting me to say something.

"Oh, shit," I laughed. "Um… thank you for coming. I appreciate it a lot. I love you all so much for being willing to come up here and celebrate our boys. I never thought this would happen somehow, but I'm so glad it has. Also, are those cheesecakes?"

Dahlia nodded, "The menu is all foods you were craving—my brother's idea."

I turned to Davey. "Who *are* you?"

"A sap who waited *months* to hear I love you."

"Was it worth the wait?"

Davey kissed my forehead. "It was worth every moment. I love you, too."

37.SPARRING

Davey

EVA AND I HIT OUR STRIDE IN NOVEMBER. I LIVED FOR THE occasional 'I love you' that came. Eva didn't dole them out as freely as I, but when she lavished me with one, I knew it meant everything. The boys grew bigger, stronger, and more exhausting to deal with. I'd never seen Eva as tired as she was between year-end regulatory bullshit and not being able to sleep for more than two or three hours. I encouraged her to quit, but she refused.

I wanted to quit. Daphne returned from leave part-time and had magically straightened everything. She never turned it off. We had Thanksgiving at my mother's house—Eva not ready to put the pressure of a big holiday and separating time out with her parents—and even there, talking shop reigned supreme.

I couldn't stop it. For the next two weeks, I wanted to talk about the babies and finish the nursery with Bert's help. Even as we hung shelves and painted walls, Eva sat in the very expensive glider custom made with her choice of upholstery while working on network integrations and change management plans.

Out of nowhere two days before Christmas, things fell apart. We planned a date to travel to her parents for Boxing Day for gifts and a simple dinner. Some of my family went north to the farm in

Michigan, but we'd stayed in the city. We already had two car seats in each car, a go-bag that I kept constantly updated, and the paperwork I thought we might need. Eva felt it was too soon to worry, but that was *my* job. I was the support person.

"Eva, where are you going?" I asked, exasperated.

She stood in our closet in a pair of maternity leggings and one of my shirts—the thing barely covering her stomach.

"The office," she answered. "We have a London incident and Claire and I—"

"You are officially on leave as of yesterday."

"I am on work-from-home only."

I groaned, "Does this integration need to happen before Christmas?"

"Look, it needs to happen. Buy-in is fleeting. And if we don't integrate, we cannot meet GDPR and everything else. It's a hot mess. It's bad enough I cannot be there. If I was in London—"

I groaned. "If I was in London. Again, and again."

"Davey, ninety percent of my job is unfucking things across the Atlantic. You *know* this. Don't act like I'm doing this for fun. It's not, but I feel guilt daily for not being there. If... if only I'd been there, everything would be different."

I didn't understand. She was so flustered, but I received no notification about a major incident. Why was she in such a damn hurry to leave? And why in the past few weeks did she never stop worrying about London. Things weren't always puppies and rainbows with our acquisition, but it didn't seem that bad.

"I am fighting the urge to get on a plane."

"Eva, no one in their right mind would permit it." I snickered.

My laugh further angered her.

"This isn't a fucking joke, David."

"Don't you think I know that? Whose head is on the line, Eva? Not yours. Mine."

"You should be more worried about London."

"I have knowledge of financials you do not, my love. I have insight you don't. Let London go."

She set her jaw, annoyed. I rubbed her shoulders.

"This is really important, and I need to go, David."

"To London?" I joked.

Voice sharp, she said, "Out. To the office. I'm not running to London!"

I chuckled. "Well, let's hope. Can you just explain—"

"I'm already running late," Eva insisted.

"Call in," I urged, worried. Nothing about this made sense, but Eva was a hormonal ball of nerves.

"I cannot work on an active incident like this. I know it sounds stupid, but I cannot—"

"You can." I needed to talk her down.

"God, do you want to *track* me?" Tears welled. "God damn it David! I am trying to fix things. I have a life. I had one before you. I have a career. I will hopefully have one after all of this."

She thew her arms around.

"All of this?" I asked.

"The baby shit, your constant obsession with organizing the nursery. Your fussing. Your policing my movements. Your worry about the babies more than the company. Good lord!"

"You are about to give birth. This is what happens."

"Not to me! Not right now. I'm not... it doesn't matter. You won't fucking care."

"You know that isn't true."

"I am a walking incubator. So, what if I went to London? You'd only be sad because you couldn't talk to my stomach and reorganize the hospital bag. I am useful. I can be, anyhow. I know that place. I know the players and the regulators. And..."

Tears rolled, but she couldn't finish.

"Eva, I respect you. I see you as a human. Yes, you had a life, but *this* is your life now."

"Yes. I'm just the little mother I'm—"

"You *are* a mother, though. Is that so bad?"

"It is not all of me. Damn it, David! That is what I am telling you. You just want me to ignore everything before—the stress, the move, the new job, and all of this—and move on. I cannot talk to you about anything without it coming back to the babies."

"Can I not be excited? Can't we just focus on them? Do you really thing work is more important than our babies?"

Eva glared. "David, I never said that. Stop putting words in my mouth!"

She slipped into a pair of fluffy boots and strode to the door. "I don't have to choose."

"I know," I relented. "But there is so much to do. Can you not just give it a rest, stay home, and focus on—"

"No," Eva shook her head. "That's not me. And you should want this. This company is your baby. It is what you worked tirelessly to acquire. I am doing this for both of us."

"I don't need you to—"

"I am motivated. Sorry if you're not!" Eva said, annoyed. "If I wasn't tied down right now and stuck, I'd already be in the air. Just let me do this!"

She pulled her maternity coat on, but it didn't button. It was a waste. She was so cute, but I knew everything got to her these days. I didn't want to point out how much I loved soaking up these moments where she was so different than the woman I'd met. I wanted to do anything but fight, but her words got under my skin.

How had she been so docile an hour early—putty in my hands as I took her from behind. Could we not go back to cuddling and joking about the most recent flubs made by our governor? No. That would be too simple. That wasn't Eva. What I didn't understand was why she was so whipped up out of nowhere. Why was she in such a hurry?

"I love you," I called as she boarded the elevator.

She glared. I wondered if she knew how much it hurt me for her to go to this place and ignore me. Wounded, I turned back to sorting the nursery's mountain of clothes. I got a text from Daphne an hour later asking if I wanted help. I knew she'd spoken with Eva but didn't want to be alone. I gave in.

Daphne arrived, noting Cal was home with the baby. She dug in, sorting clothes on the floor by me.

"I went in. Eva is a mess. I hope this brings her closure," Daphne said.

"What?" I asked.

"Well, her dog died, you know? And her ex is in town handing over half of the ashes."

Confusion struck.

"Oh, sorry. You didn't know," Daphne said. "She didn't tell you?"

We'd discussed this to death. If you need something, tell me. And if you meet with an ex, you *have* to say something, right? That was never explicitly said, but it was the kindness she extended previously. Had she given up?

"Not about the dog. Not about Mona, no," I said. "I need to call—"

"Davey, she has reasons, I am sure."

"She lied and said she had to deal with the situation in London. She wants to be boots on the ground but cannot be there!" I pulled out my phone, worried I knew what went on. "She lied."

"She was at the office," Daphne said. "She didn't lie. Her ex was just going to meet her quick. She was here on business and wanted to hand the ashes over since Eva can't very well go to London. Lord knows she'd try with all this technology bullshit—"

London. I couldn't listen past that word. *Certainly, she wasn't serious about getting on a plane, right?* No. I knew better. Still, the fact that she'd lied about where she was going and who she was meeting upset me. *Why had she lied? What more was she hiding?*

"Davey, calm down, okay? You're driving her off. This isn't about a lie. No doubt she didn't want to bother you."

"Bother me?" I gasped. "She *lied.*"

"Davey, she loves you. This isn't about holding a candle for Mona. I promise you—"

But I'd already lost my mind. Phone in my hand, I was about to play warrior—like it or not. I wasn't about to lose the best thing I ever had. Eva *would* talk to me. We *would* resolve this. It wasn't about Mona. That was a symptom, not the problem.

* * *

Eva

I spotted Mona across the room of a cafe near work. Palms sweaty, I gave a nervous wave. She responded, a grand smile on her face. Inside, I hurt. I loved Carter and hadn't been given a final goodbye. I wasn't there for last kisses and ear scratches. Full of emotions and terrified about pushing two humans from my body, I'd had no quiet space to grieve. It was all baby clothes and how next Christmas would be all about the boys. If I told him, he'd either be a dark cloud or tell me to let it go because it was Christmas, after all. I wanted to get the ashes, grieve alone for thirty minutes in my office, and go back to him in a better mood.

Mona gave a quick hug. "You look so cute."

"I'm miserable and look ridiculous."

"No, you don't. You're so close. I'm happy for you."

"I cannot stay long," I apologized. "It's been a wild day. I wish this was under better circumstances."

"She had a good last day, Eva," Mona said. "I promise you it was peaceful, and I did right by her."

"I know you did," I said.

Mona passed a small box of ashes across the table. "Your half. Do what you want with them. I know how much she meant to you."

I teared. *I'm not going to cry here, damn it!*

"Thanks."

"How are you? How is David?"

"He's fine," I answered.

"And how are *you*?" She repeated.

"I'm…" I glanced at my phone. It was Davey.

"Oh, he's calling you," Mona said. "It could be important."

"He's upset with me," I said. "I didn't tell him about any of this. I sort of lost it, and… he's angry."

"Take it. Apologize."

I took the call against my better judgement, feeling bad for how things ended.

"Davey, hi," I said.

"Are you with Mona right now? And don't lie again. Daphne told me!"

My heart sank.

"I… I met her to get Carter's ashes."

"Why the fuck would you hide that from me? Why would you lie, Eva?"

"I didn't do it on purpose. You've been so happy about the babies that I didn't want to bring the mood down. Emotionally, I'm so worn down and panicked about being on leave. We're at a cafe. Nothing is happening."

Mona's mouth dropped, as if she knew what this argument was about.

"Your lying makes me think otherwise."

"Davey, I am allowed to—"

"We talk about things like this. When you hide things, I don't trust you. I don't care about you talking to Mona. I *do* care about you lying."

"I'm not up to anything."

"Eva, when you lie about one thing, I assume you're lying about much more! Prove me wrong!"

I fought tears as his voice rattled in anger. He thought I was *cheating*? Why would I do that? I'd confessed my love for him and fought for us. I'd chosen to stay even when shit got hard. I'd given so much of myself—including my body.

"What more could I leave out? It was a white lie—"

"It was *still* a lie. And that coupled with all this discussion of running off to London understandably concerns me."

"I want to go to fix the business shit. I want to go because it feels like home. I want to get far away from my own fears about all of this."

"Us? You are suddenly worried about us?"

"David, don't do this! Don't speak for me. Motherhood scares me. And you? You don't get like this. Why are we here? Why are you putting all this doubt on me? It's scaring me!"

"You don't lie. Because this is so out of character for you, I have a reason to give into this idiotic fear that you're going to run off to London—"

I laughed nervously. "Oh my God, I would never—"

"Don't act like I'm being ridiculous! We aren't married. You could run off with the boys wherever! What is to keep you from running off with my babies to anywhere?"

I debated just telling him this was the only little white lie. I was sorry he was just in a pre-baby tailspin over this. It wasn't my intent. I wanted to apologize, but when he said that they were *his* babies, I lost it.

"*Your* babies?" I gasped. "Davey, last I checked, they were *ours*. And you don't get to accuse me of that!"

"Why not? If you are going to lie about one thing, why not just lie about everything?"

A pain hit deep in my stomach—one felt a couple of times in my office. I knew it was a contraction, but I ignored it. They were mostly silly, and I could work through them. This time, I gripped the table with my spare hand, barely breathing as it rolled through me.

I sobbed, "You don't get to make assumptions. I've given you no indication I would ever do that. I've been loyal. I've put up with a lot—"

"So have I! Being happy is just impossible for you! I cannot do this anymore!"

He hung up as I fell apart.

"What is happening? Is he cross with me?" Mona asked. "Eva, didn't you *tell* him? You've walked into a straight man minefield—"

"I didn't think he would care," I gasped. "I'm... I'm sorry, but... I didn't tell him. I thought I'd just drop in, get this done, and not bother him."

"What is going on? How can I help? I feel awful, Eva."

"I'm… he just broke up with me. I have absolutely no idea—"

"Why would he do that? I doubt that is true."

"No, I am pretty sure that was the implication."

"You should go right home and talk to him. He seems to love you. The stakes are high and… well, I loved many parts of you, Eva, but you are not easy to decipher. You hold it all in. You cannot do that with him."

I cocked my head. "What do you mean?"

"Things fell apart when I felt like you never told me anything. I said this to you. Clearly, you haven't learned from it, though!"

I didn't need her derision now. Another pain struck. I panicked.

"Eva, are you okay? I didn't mean to upset you—only help."

I groaned, "No. I'm… I'm having contractions."

"Oh, bloody hell! Contractions? Do we need to get you to hospital? We do, don't we?"

"Calm down, please," I begged. "I need to go in. I'm fine, but I do need to go."

"Well, I'm taking you."

"Please, Mona—"

"No. I am taking you." She stood. "C'mon."

38.SURPRISE ARRIVAL

Davey

"What did you fucking do?" Daphne roared. "What did you do?"

I stared at my phone, terrified. What *did* I do?

"I dunno," I stammered. "I... I guess I said something I regretted."

"You broke up with Eva right when she's about to give birth."

"We have three more weeks—"

"Davey, she's in such a bad place right now. Things are messy. I know things feel better and that she loves you to bits. I've never seen her like this with anyone—not even Mona, okay? But she thinks she needs to move this acquisition to make you happy."

I knew my sister was right.

"Yeah, you fucked up *big* time," Daphne said.

"Don't sound so satisfied, Daph!" I paced. "Fuck!"

"I'm not satisfied. I'm worried about both of you."

"Worry about her! She's being erratic. I just responded with the same energy—"

"Davey, she's having twins with her boss while coping with a technology meltdown. Like any Type-A career woman, she fears losing her identity. Your constant daddy doting isn't helping."

"Daddy doting?"

"You have given her *no* space to talk about anything else. You don't give *anyone* space. Good God! Do you wonder *why* she fibbed? She did it to protect you. I bet she worried it would harsh your vibe. I know Eva. She's terribly loyal and honest in a way that bothers people sometimes. She struggles to find that balance. But you? She babies you. She *cares* about you, and you just broke her heart. I'm going to help you put it back together again even if I'm too tired and shouldn't."

"I didn't actually break up with her."

"You said you were done and hung up after interrogating her. What would you call that?"

I turned back to Daphne, stopping still. She was right. "Fuck! Do you know where she is? I need to speak to her right now. I need to call her."

"Her assistant would know," Daphne said.

"But what if she doesn't accept me? What if I've fucked it up? What if she moves to London?"

"Apologize for accusing her of running off with *your* babies as if you assumed she was out to get you. She's been broken up with and thrown out after losing a pregnancy. She's a mess. You are, too. Just apologize and realize that you hit a sensitive nerve. David, she's going to stick around and marry the fuck out of you someday if the two of you can get your heads out of your asses."

"You really think that?"

"Yes. I think once the babies are here and the two of you have a lot of time to yourselves—and she's not miserably pregnant and insecure about it—you will come to that place and naturally approach things. I love you, brother, but this is not your strong suit. It's also not Eva's. If she didn't love you, she wouldn't be here. And she always tries to make it work. She doesn't trust men but knows you will respect her. Somehow, you built trust with her."

"Well, after this, who knows?" I panicked. "She thinks I'm trying to control her, right?"

"Before the call? I think she just wanted to avoid hurting your feelings with this talk of the dog dying. She didn't want to ruin Christmas or this time for you—for all of us. But after the call? Yeah. You were acting like an ass. It's totally out of character for you."

It was. I didn't know what set me off. I paced, then dialed, unsure of what else to do. If I didn't apologize, there was no hope for us. While I waited on the assistant, a call from Eva came in. I answered it, hanging up the first call.

"Baby, I'm so sorry. I didn't mean it. I am so, so sorry. Please come home. Let's talk. All I want to do is make it up to you—"

"Hello. Uh, this isn't Eva," an unfamiliar voice cut me off. "So, apologies, but I am taking Eva to hospital. She's in labor, I think. I am so sorry, but we are racing there."

Was Mona taking Eva to the hospital?

I raced to the foyer, "I... I will be right there. Thank you, Mona."

I hung up, gaping at Daphne who had chased me all the way. "She's in labor. I need to get everything to the hospital."

Daphne helped me load the car, hugged me for encouragement, and I departed with a flash. I had no idea what to expect. The babies were too early. Everything was a hot mess. I couldn't express the fear and turmoil inside except through tears. So, I drove, crying, and finally stopped after being stuck in terrible traffic for forty minutes.

Taking a moment at the valet to breathe, wipe my tears, and compose myself, I dropped the car and proceeded in.

"I'm... I'm looking for my girlfriend," I said. "She's in labor."

"What is her name?" The receptionist asked.

"Pavlak. Spelled P-A-V-L-A-K."

"Got it," the woman scribbled. "Here is her room number. You can go up those elevators."

I followed where she pointed, racing to the maternity ward. After being buzzed in, I had to answer a barrage of questions.

"Look, I need to get to my girlfriend. I am her support system.

Someone brought her in—a friend—but she's not the other parent. I am."

I was back near tears again, feeling so helpless.

"Okay, give me a second." The nurse tried to calm me with a sweet tone.

I watched her go down the hall, suffering as I worried Eva wouldn't let me in. What if she was so angry I'd never see my babies? What if I couldn't be there to hear their first cries? What if I missed out on everything under the sun? Why did I fuck it all up so badly out of anger and jealousy?

The nurse returned, smiling. "We just are required to check. Sorry. You can go back."

A weight lifted. I approached the door—now slightly open— and entered. Mona sat on Eva's bedside. Eva spoke with a nurse, not yet acknowledging me. There were half a dozen people around, poking and prodding. I saw the instruction board and burst into tears. Without a single word from Eva, I knew we were okay.

Everything was there—her pregnancy details, her weeks and days pregnant, and the names of our babies.

Robbie and Max Delphine. Somehow, seeing those names, I realized she wasn't going anywhere. I sobbed tears of joy at this news —not because they carried my name or had won, but because we were okay.

"Davey," Eva said. "Are you okay?"

I couldn't say more than, "I love you so much, Eva. I am so sorry. I have no idea what got into me."

* * *

Eva

Davey approached my hospital bed, brushing by Mona, who moved aside.

"I'm going to give you all space," Mona said. "I want to hear when they are here, okay?"

"I will send you a text," Davey agreed. "If that is cool?"

"That's perfect," Mona smiled. "Good luck, Eva. You'll do great."

Mona patted Davey's back, and he dropped to the chair where she sat. He pulled it closer, holding my hand so tight. I'd never seen him cry like this. It occurred to me we'd never broken up, but he worried the same. Why was he so emotional? He wasn't angry or cold.

"I never wanted to say such awful things, Eva."

"I get why you were upset," I sighed, brushing his cheek. "I *did* lie. I *did* meet Mona."

"Let me be clear that it really wasn't Mona. It was you keeping things from me, but I understand I wasn't exactly sensitive of what you needed. You could have told me about Carter."

"It's okay. We were both raw and I worried you'd hassle me about working too much or being too invested with the dog, but I should have known better. I should have trusted you would support me."

"I never would have said that. I did want you to stop working on leave, but also… I didn't know you were working so hard to make me happy or how much it mattered to you. Eva, *you* make me happy. This…"

He put his hand on my stomach. "This makes me happy. These babies mean everything to us both. I don't need anything else."

I grunted through a contraction. "But you have the company—"

"Fuck it," Davey said. "It is meaningless if I do not have the three of you. Set that aside. All I want to do is focus on getting these babies here safely, okay? No more work talk. We'll have months to discuss what is next."

"Okay," I agreed.

"You… you named them?"

"I hate that Robbie will be David Robert the Third or whatever. It's annoying, but we can agree to call him Robbie. I thought about it a lot. He has my dad's name as his middle name—same as you.

And your dad meant the world to you. I gave in. Max was perfect, as you well knew. So, I made the choice. You don't hate it?"

"I love it." Davey leaned to kiss my forehead. "With one important change."

He hopped up, grabbed the dry erase marker and added something.

Pavlak-Delphine.

"They deserve both our names, Eva," Davey said. "You made them, and it is *your* determination that will make them strong. They're Pavlaks as much as Delphines."

Now, *I* fought tears as our doctor appeared.

"So, it looks like they might give us a *bit* of an unwelcome surprise," he said. "But we're in good shape. I think the best way to proceed here is to see if the labor stops. If it gets more consistent or your water breaks, I will suggest we decide by five tonight Twin A is in a good position, so we can attempt a vaginal delivery, but I'll give you some time to think about that. More than likely, I think you will be parents soon."

That was final. We were having these babies.

39. THE BOYS

Davey

HOW WOMEN MANAGED TO EVICT CHILDREN FROM THEIR BODIES I
didn't understand, but Eva was a warrior. She gave birth in an
operating room—a precaution for the twins—and didn't bat an eye
at the two-dozen people present. Our goal was to deliver two
premature babies into the world. We all silently prayed for strong
lungs and a healthy mom. Eva's normal argumentative, demanding
side didn't come out. I worried her quiet demeanor signaled something was wrong.

By instinct, Eva preserved the energy her body needed to expel
two humans, aware it was a marathon, not a sprint. I focused on
her cues and beat down my squeamishness. There were *so* many
germs and things that could go wrong, but I couldn't worry about
those problems. They didn't matter. I dabbed her forehead with a
cold washcloth. I held her legs as she pushed, and I quietly encouraged her. Sensing too much hubbub would annoy Eva, I kept my
voice quiet and calm.

"Just a few more pushes," the doctor said. "You can do this!"

"You've got it, baby," I said. "Just a couple more."

Eva dug deeper, giving over to her competitive side. What
might take a mortal three pushes, took her only one. The silence in

the room faded as two neonatologists took over, shepherding the baby to an incubator. I expected a cry but got nothing. I saw only a flash of him—no face, no adorable feet. They worked tirelessly to stabilize him. Thankfully, the nurse at Eva's head had words of wisdom.

"He's doing well. They are getting him ready to transfer. Not every baby cries."

Eva nodded. "But he's okay?"

A doctor called, "I promise he's doing well. We'll let you get a good look at him soon enough."

Eva nodded bravely.

"We need to flip this baby. It may be uncomfortable with lots of pressure," another doctor said. "But it will be quick."

Eva had been so brave to this point, but the feeling of them rolling the baby around in a belly that just pushed *one* baby out seemed brutish. She gripped my hand for dear life. I watched the doctor grimace as an alarm sounded.

"What is happening?" I asked, nervously.

"We need to do an emergency c-section," the doctor said, as if it were simple.

"What? Why?" I panicked.

"Baby's heart rate is dipping. We will get him out," a nurse said.

Eva shut down. I waited for them to open her up right there. I was rushed into the hall while they put her under. I left the three people I cared most about in a room. Feeling like a coward, I paced, unable to come down.

"Sir," the nurse said. "It's okay. These things rarely occur—but they happen. Some babies don't handle the version well. The doctors are going to get him out quickly."

"I'm going to miss his cries. What if he cries?" I found myself in tears for the second time this day.

"There will be millions of cries in your future," she assured. "As soon as they settle the babies in the NICU, I will come get you. The doctor will be out as soon as he can. Is there anyone nearby who can help Eva when she is in recovery?"

I knew I'd have to go with the babies. Eva and I discussed this to death, but we assumed it would be because she'd be having a big dinner weaning off an epidural if the babies needed NICU care and would be along soon after. We'd made rational choices about rational things, but nothing about this felt rational.

I looked at my phone. "It's midnight. Her parents live in Indiana and won't make it."

"Any friends? Family that would work for now?"

I groaned. "My mother. She's leaving for Michigan in the morning, but she's still around."

* * *

Eva

Everything happened so fast. Before I knew it, I'd gone from worried to pleasantly asleep. When I woke, I heard chatter—but no one I expected. I opened my eyes slowly and found myself in a new room—a smaller than where I'd labored. I turned towards the voices and saw a nurse and Lady Danna.

"Oh, there she is," Davey's mother said sweetly. "You're back with us, Eva."

"Lady Danna... what are you doing here?" I asked.

"Danna, darling. Please. Davey rang me when they swooped you off to surgery. He's with the boys. They are doing beautifully," Danna said, proudly.

I smiled. "Good. Both of them?"

"Both of them. Big, strong, healthy thirty-four weekers," the nurse said. "Both of them are on oxygen, but neither needed a vent. Since they are both over four pounds, their prognosis is as good as can be."

That was good news. "I feel so dizzy."

"That is the magnesium," the nurse said. "It will be okay."

"I feel so out of sorts."

"You will—even if the birth was textbook," Danna said. "I did this six times. It is always challenging and different every time."

"I'm good for now," I said. "Considering I failed to do things the way they 'should' be the first time."

"No, darling. You brought two lives into the world. Against all odds, they are *thriving*. And Davey is there with them. He sent photos. Do you want to see them?"

"Yes, please!"

Danna leaned over, scrolling through the impressive number of photos he sent in the hour he'd been there.

Their faces were obscured some by the cannulas in their noses, but they were beautiful to me. I couldn't help but cry.

"God damn it," I sniffled. "They're perfect. But why the hell do they look like him and him alone?"

"They always do at first," the nurse said. "It will even out. They're perfect."

"God, they are! I did it. I survived and got them here."

"Let's give it a little more time and then I will bring you down," the nurse said. "You can meet them. They have quite the birth story."

"I'd like to forget the eventful parts," I sighed.

"I was talking about their birthdays. Robbie was born last night. Technically, Max was born this morning. They have separate birthdays."

"Really?" I asked. "Oh my God!"

"That's going to be a nightmare as they get older," Danna chuckled. "But you've got time to worry about that."

"This is what my body gets for going into labor early and then kicking into full gear."

"It did a great job. They were just ready to meet you," Danna said. "Babies come when they want to—not a minute sooner or later."

* * *

Davey

The boys—*our* boys—were actual perfection. They'd done nothing so far other than breathe and fuss a little, but they needed to do nothing more to impress us. I loved them and felt guilty for getting all the quality time with them, but before breakfast, Eva arrived in a wheelchair. She looked better than expected—if not a bit exhausted.

"There they are," Eva said, tears in her eyes as a nurse wheeled her over to the incubators. "Our boys."

"They are doing so well," I said.

"Who is who?" Eva asked.

"Robbie is on the left. Max is on the right."

"How can you tell?" Eva snickered. "Is that terrible?"

"They have labels. That's all. At home, we're fucked."

"You will figure it out," the nurse said. "Nail polish on toes. It will help. Give it a few days. You'll know. Promise."

"I hope so," Eva said. "Damn. They really are carbon copies of one another."

"From what I can tell, Robbie is the quiet grouch. Max is the loud one. He's going to be a party animal," I said.

"So, Robbie is me and Max is you," she giggled.

"You said it, not me," I insisted.

"You can hold them if you want," the nurse said.

"Yes, please!" Eva grinned.

We settled into two rockers, Eva oh-so-gently easing. I didn't know how a person could have their stomach torn up completely and still be moving within a six-hour period. I was certain I couldn't do the same. Eva rocked Robbie while I held Max.

"How long do they have to stay?" Eva asked. "I want to bring them home. I'm also terrified to take them home. Is that bad?"

"Totally normal," the nurse said. "It really depends. Some born at this point stay two weeks and some that stay past their due date. It just depends on the baby. The good news is your boys are big, and their lungs are doing well. We will need them to breathe room air, to regulate their body temps, and eat on their own before we send them home. In about a week, we'll really want to get them feeding. If they respond well, we can send them on their merry way."

Eva looked down, adoringly. "Can you all give it a good try? I'd like to have you home soon."

"Hopefully, you have your mother's iron will," I noted. "If so, you'll be home in no time.

Eva gave a sweet smile. It was enough to urge me on. The road would wind. The days would be long, but we'd make it. Stronger than ever before, I knew this was my little family.

40. AS IT SHOULD BE

Eva

"THEY REALLY TRUST US WITH THEM?" I ASKED.

Two sleeping babies sat in the foyer in car seats. It was our first day home as a family of four. I half-expected them to never let the babies out of the NICU. After three weeks of monitoring and countless sleepless nights worrying, we returned home *with* them.

"It will be fine, baby." Davey hung my coat in the hall closet. "They will do great."

I hoped he was right.

"Let's get them settled in, Eva." He picked up the car seats.

We had a baby nurse, but she was in the burbs. She'd asked to start Monday since the boys were released on Friday afternoon as a massive snowstorm barreled into the city. Out of compassion, we didn't want to call her in to get stranded for four days.

"Go downstairs, then. Settle in. I will change the boys and bring them down. Get whatever you want. And get loads of snacks. You're right. We're going to need them."

"How will you bring them both—"

"Don't worry about it." Davey kissed me. "I've got this."

Somehow, I didn't doubt him. It hadn't occurred to me that running across the house with two babies would be complicated, but I never had twins living in my house, either. I plopped on the couch, putting in a delivery request for pizza. I ordered a delivery from the fancy grocery two blocks away—prepared meals, good cheese, and sweets galore. I added a beer delivery, too.

By the time I was curled under a comfy blanket, Davey approached carrying a laundry basket full of babies. It made me giggle as he sat them down before me like two little dolls. They still wore their going-home outfits. I'd argued these onesies with trains were aggressively masculine, but he insisted girls could like trains, too. I wouldn't debate Davey on the matter. Since knowing him, I'd realized how much he loved the Class C 999. His brother, Derrick, had them made custom as a nod to their father's love of the Science and Industry Museum's locomotive. There was nothing I wanted more than to include Davey's dad. I knew it meant a lot.

"Davey, what the hell? What is this?"

"I saw our nanny do this once with Dora. I figured it could work. I took the elevator."

"I forgot we had that. I suppose I should use that more," I admitted.

"We paid for it."

"You paid for it."

"It's ours," Davey said. "I will get bottles if you just watch them."

I leaned over, observing our babies in the laundry basket—awake but quiet.

"What did he do to you?" I cooed. "How did you end up there?"

They stared back. Robbie gave me a face as if this were a personal offense. Max tried to understand what the light fixture was by the looks of his head tilt. I didn't wonder anymore who they were. We knew who each was almost all the time. And I knew their cries by heart. Max's cry was more of a dull roar. Robbie's was a slow wind-up.

Davey returned, setting the bottles down before handing me Max. I plopped a bottle in the younger twin's mouth. After a little coaxing, he caught on.

"I don't regret that bottle maker," Davey said.

"I still feel guilty."

"Don't. You're perfect, Eva. You did a great job. It didn't work."

Breastfeeding was a bust. My milk never came in and they never learned to latch. I cried endlessly until both his mother and mine told me to stop. I'd lie if I didn't feel a pang of jealousy that things came so easily for Daphne and Brooke.

"They're healthy. That's what matters," I said.

"What did you get for dinner?"

"Pizza."

"Nice. A good choice."

Robbie loudly sharted.

"How many diapers are we planning on going through? Do we have enough?" I asked.

"We have dozens. A ton. It's fine. It's okay. And Walgreens is gonna be open." He chuckled. "Although, that's how this whole thing started."

"They didn't make the Plan B, Davey."

"No, but they were out of condoms—except the shitty generics I bought."

"Generics can work, too. We just got unlucky," I said.

"Not if they are truly too small. But I wanted you so much, I didn't think twice. I was *desperate* for you, Eva. And now look at the result of my impulsive move."

I looked over at sleepy Robbie, rubbing his head. "It was a wild ride. Not how you thought you'd spend your fortieth birthday, huh?"

"We'll have the party. I let Mum throw it. I relented."

It was Davey's birthday, but he didn't want a fuss. We planned something for next week to celebrate. While he fought at first, he gave in.

"Having them home is the best gift." Davey played with Robbie's little Cubs sock-clad foot. "I never wanted anything more."

"They're special. It's terrifying, but I'm relieved, Davey."

"Me, too, baby."

I looked out on the falling snow. "It's beautiful, you know?"

"It is. A menace tomorrow, but tonight we've got peace and quiet and hopefully pizza."

I rested my head on Davey's shoulder. I forgot about the world outside. I didn't worry about how the next eighteen years would go or panic about diapers and how we'd get them to sleep tonight. I focused on how I felt like I was home—here with my whole little world.

EPILOGUE

Davey

"Okay, that's unfair," I chuckled.

"What?" Eva asked.

"You look so comfy there. And here I am about to leave the house to kick my own ass."

Eva lay in bed bathing in early morning light. She was altogether too inviting, despite messy hair.

"Fuck the club, come back to bed then. But I warn you that the minute you get comfortable, they will wake."

"I'll take my chances!" I tossed my shirt and hopped in bed.

I'd ignore everything if it meant I got rare time alone with her. These moments felt more fleeting than ever. We'd find a rhythm only to have everything change. It was one thing after another—if it wasn't a sleep regression, it was a cold. Right now, all I had to consider was Eva.

I pressed her into bed, pinning her arms. Eva's defiant gaze met mine.

"And why should I let you do that?" Eva asked.

I pulled the blanket aside, playing with her nipples. Eva arched her back, let out a pleasant shudder, and gave me a cheeky grin.

"Fuck me," she plead.

"Why don't you fuck me?" I asked. "Why should *I* do all the work?"

"You're right," Eva said. "Why should I?"

I kicked off my shorts and boxers. Eva, slid onto my cock, groaning low as she did.

"Yeah?" I asked.

"Yes. Oh, God, it's been too long."

It had only been three days. That was a long time for Eva. Anything more than two days made her rage. I tried to keep up.

She leaned forward, kissing me, hungrily growling, "God, I love you."

I craved her love. I loved how she loved us—me, the boys, everyone—but right now, all I wanted was to have her. Feeling her breasts pressed against my chest and her ass in my hands, life couldn't have been better. Eva was the best I'd ever had but also the most precious thing I almost lost. It made it all sweeter.

Eva ramped up, taking me in deeper. The heat rose up her neck, revealing just how bad she wanted to cum. I loved this vision of her—pleasure and desperation for release overcoming her delicate features.

"Yes, baby, cum for me," I said.

She gripped my chest for dear life, digging her fingernails in. Still, I couldn't even think about any momentary discomfort.

"Oh, fuck, Davey! Yes!"

I smiled, content to satisfy her. Eva came, pussy pulsing around my cock hard. She again bent down, kissing me again before pulling back.

"You're so beautiful," I said. "Fuck. I have no idea what I did to deserve you."

"I love you so much. So… fucking… much."

She was trying to cum again.

"Cum for me, Eva. Don't hold back. Take what you need, baby."

She pressed her fingers into my collarbone now. I shivered, loving how that felt.

"I want…"

"Yeah, you want it all?"

"Another…"

"Another orgasm?"

She came once more, screaming, "Baby!"

"Good girl," I swatted her ass, unable to hold back much longer.

We'd been three days without sex. Three days without backup because of our nanny's scheduled vacation. I was desperate.

"Oh, fuck, Eva. Fuck!" I drove into her, holding her hips for dear life.

I waited to catch my breath, still pleasantly inside her.

"So, what do you think?" Eva asked, hands on her hips.

"Of what?" I panted. "It was… good."

"No. Having another baby."

I attempted to not panic, but my face gave me away.

"Davey, I… we… I'm sorry. I want another baby."

She fell to my left. Knowing she would shut down in approximately three seconds, assuming I was rejecting her, I flipped on my side.

"I do, too. At some point."

"But not now?"

"Eva, they're five months old."

"I know… but… I want to have a career. I want three. I'll be happy with three."

I brushed her cheek. "You have a career. A brilliant one."

"I want more. I'm not done, Davey."

I kissed her slowly. "I think we can make it all work. Somehow, someway we will."

"So, you don't mind?"

"It's now or never," I said. "We're insane, but… when haven't we been, my love?"

WANT A FREE BOOK?

Do you want a free book? Want a Danna and David Prequel?

Don't worry! If you join Maude's newsletter, you will be one of the first to grab it once it goes live.

Scan here or click to reserve your copy!

ACKNOWLEDGMENTS

To the Sisterhood of the Traveling Cocks/Grandma's Pizza Basement, you're the best. Without you, where would I be?

And as always, to my beta, alpha, and ARC readers, thank you for your support.

Thank you Becky for believing in these two!

ABOUT THE AUTHOR

Maude Winters is an author of open-door contemporary romance. She's a horse girl through and through. Though raised in Chicagoland, she lives in Michigan with her husband, a horse-obsessed child, and three dogs.

Maude loves to write strong female characters who challenge institutions and heroes who aren't afraid to let their ladies take the lead. Her readers expect the drama of a prime-time show with all the stakes and swoon they can handle.

ALSO BY MAUDE WINTERS

- Executive Decision - Book 1 *Lakeshore Empire*
- Matrimonial Merger - Book 2 *Lakeshore Empire*
- Other Books by Maude

* 9 7 8 1 9 6 9 2 4 7 0 0 2 *